Enthusiastic reviews for Lior Samson's novels –

Always Me

" [A] captivating puzzle that pulled me into the mind and heart of a woman who doesn't dare be who she is. ... I didn't dare put it down."
— *M. Thornberg, author*

Distant Sons

" [A] book that will stay with me, probably for the rest of my life, and that I know I'll read again. ... It enlarged my experience of being human."
— *M. Thornberg, author*

The Rosen Singularity (The Immortality Quartet)

" The plotting is ingenious and the characters come through strongly."
— *Rebecca Goldstein, MacArthur Fellow, author*

The Millicent Factor (The Immortality Quartet)

" A solid page turner. The author keeps the pace just right with action and chases ... and backroom dealings."
— *RJ Beam, author*

The Intaglio Imprint (The Immortality Quartet)

" Super-realism and compelling rationale, ... an intricate and incisive creation."
— *George Church, geneticist*

The Drucker Proxy (The Immortality Quartet)

" An edge-of-the-seat, emotionally gripping, intimate, arousing, techno-legal tour-de-force."
— *Phillip M. Samson, attorney*

Bashert (The Homeland Connection)

" Samson writes with a crisp elegance, like John Le Carré, and weaves his plot magically."
— *James A. Anderson, author*

The Dome (The Homeland Connection)

"An excellent read, and very highly recommended."

— *Midwest Book Review*

Web Games (The Homeland Connection)

"This extraordinary author has the ability to anticipate events. ...
You will not put it down." — *Alan Caruba, critic, BookViews*

Chipset (The Homeland Connection)

"[A] multi-dimensional thriller ... populated by flesh-and-blood
characters." — *Avraham Azrieli, author*

Gasline (The Homeland Connection)

"[A] great novel . . . high concept, flesh-and-blood protagonist,
and realistic action. ... [It] will raise your blood pressure and
make you think." — *Columbia Review of Books and Film*

Flight Track (The Homeland Connection)

"Stunning, compelling, thought-provoking. To the book's broad
scope and expert pacing, add three-dimensional, engaging characters." — *M. Thornburg, author*

Exit Plans (The Homeland Connection)

"The author handles this tapestry of tensions with his usual as-
surance and dexterity, which means that I was on the edge of my
seat from page one on." — *M. Thornburg, author*

The Four-Color Puzzle

"[A]n authentic thinking person's ideal mystery; an eloquent feast
of words and an excellent story." — *Jeanie B. Clemmons, author*

ALWAYS
BEGINNING

ALWAYS
BEGINNING

a novel by Lior Samson

GESHER PRESS

Gesher Press
Rowley, Massachusetts

Gesher Press and the bridge logo are trademarks of Gesher Press.

5 4 3 2 1

ISBN 978-1-7326091-9-8

Cover and book design: Larry Constantine
Set in Alegreya

For Donald Norman, designer of everyday things, colleague and friend

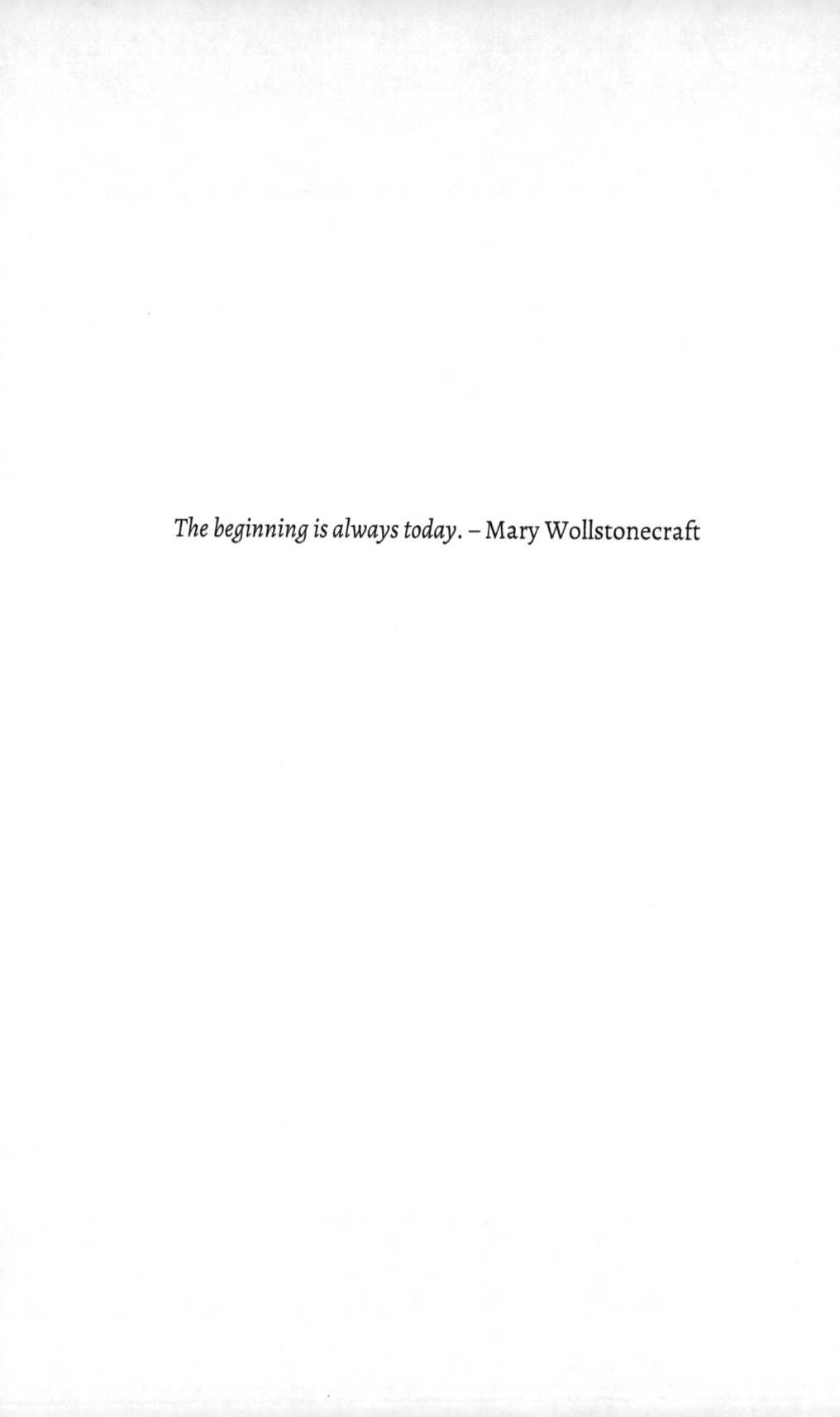

The beginning is always today. – Mary Wollstonecraft

✌ Prologue

SHANNA FROZE. It had been a mindless moment, her guard lowered in an innocent reach for a tissue from the glove compartment, but it was Rand's car. His handgun lay atop the cracked blue vinyl folder that held the owner's manual and registration. Even without picking it up, she could feel the compact semi-automatic in her hand, the sensation at once both alien and familiar.

And then, suddenly, there was Guy standing in front of her, rock-hard handsome, looking down at her and laughing as she raised the gun in an unpracticed two-handed grip learned from watching television. He was still and always Guy, just a guy, because even now she stopped herself from saying his real name out loud—or in her mind. Names can conjure, and she did not want to risk conjuring up ancient demons from distant worlds, even a world only decades ancient and hundreds of miles distant.

Over the years and miles, she was never sure how much of any of these intruding images was real. But she remembered details: the smell of her own sweat, the cool handgrip of the gun slowly warming in her palm, the way Guy shrugged in a wordless act of dismissal. You are nobody, his gesture said, not even who you are, not even a real person, and certainly not worth my doing anything about the gun in my face. All of that had been said in that single shrug, and both of them knew it, had parsed the silent sentence in the same way, all except for the final punctuation at the end, which would surprise them both.

You didn't know me, she thought, and you certainly didn't know what I was capable of. Hell, you didn't even know my name. You called me Louise because you didn't know better. And now? What would you call me?

Shanna Grace Newsom sat in the scruffy green Honda Civic and closed the glove compartment. There were no tissues, only triggers, only images and objects from another life, a life that sometimes flashed into existence without invitation. They were reminders that vigilance was the substance of her survival, the rent paid on her settled life teaching at Holcomb University after running away from the past and starting over. Twice.

She sat in the car, suppressing a shiver and looking around to see if anyone had noticed, but the students streaming past in the between-classes shuffle were too intent on each other or on the playlists sounding in their earbuds or on rehearsing an excuse for not having completed an assignment for the next class. She recognized some of them, and they certainly would have recognized her. She was a campus icon, the charismatic history professor who usually rode a bicycle to school and daily ran the hill trails and had recently won notoriety for her prize-winning book on the slave-built foundations of Southern higher education. Many would have recognized her had they not been immersed in their own separate worlds and had the windows of the Civic not been so conveniently coated in dust.

Shanna let out a shaky sigh, ran fingers through her

shoulder-length hair with its gray highlights, and brought herself fully back to the present and the campus and the teaching load that was a real bitch but also a blessing that gave her little time for unplanned excursions into dark pasts or for obsession over an uncertain future. It was the only future she had ever known in a lifetime of uncertainty—more than one lifetime's worth.

She looked carefully around before pulling out from the parking spot, checking, in a ritual of situational awareness, the position and color and model and make of every car in her immediate vicinity, verifying that none were occupied, noting the ones with Holcomb stickers and the few with logos declaring divided loyalties or touting old connections. There was Gene Vallencourt's black VW with its Georgia Tech bumper sticker, a nostalgic badge from a lost dream of aerospace engineering, and the Wollenders' Ford with decals from four Canadian universities, banners that still oriented them, an ever northward-turning compass that might someday be followed. Or might not.

And there was Afsa Tingerly's BMW in the spot marked "Reserved for Dean – SHHS," its bumper adorned with a singular string of decals—the flags of Pakistan, Texas, the United Kingdom, and the U.S.—a graphic precis of a multinational, multi-ethnic story. Dean Tingerly was head of the School of History and Human Sciences and Shanna's ever-indulgent mentor.

Details, attention to detail—these were the tools of her trade as a quantitative historian, an unearther of numbers. These were, as well, the personal armor she wore to protect herself from surprises and from triggers that could send her spinning into other worlds, other lives, other times before she had reinvented herself. Don't forget to swing by Righteous Hall, she told herself, and drop off the boxes promised for Dean Tingerly.

Promises. These, too, were a source of security, like beads on a rosary, beats in a walking bass line, repeating tokens, reminders of the rhythm of the life she had invented for herself—was still inventing. The boxes on the back seat were the whole reason she had Rand's car. Filled with books borrowed from Dean Tingerly's personal library for a project on the economic impact of South Asian immigrants in the American South, they were too heavy for the rack on the back of her bicycle, and she didn't have time for multiple trips to and from the house on Racine Circle. It was less than a mile by the footpath through the trees, but sometimes it was a world away.

As she backed out of the parking spot and touched the brakes, the door to the glove compartment dropped open, and the weighty handgun slid out and flopped onto the passenger seat. Rand had mentioned the faulty latch and announced his intention to fix it. She had promises and commitments, Rand had intentions—usually good, mostly sincere, but something short of a promise. Theirs was an odd pairing, except in their shared need to distance themselves from disowned pasts and in their common commitment to their reinvented selves.

Checking first to make sure that no one was watching, Shanna picked up the gun, held it for a long second, and returned it to the glove box. She remembered to bang the door shut with her fist and tried to forget the cold, comforting feel of the pistol in her hand.

❧ Chapter 1

WITH EACH TURN of her spade, the deep cecil soil, rich with loam from gardens past, wafted its musty perfume into the humid air. In the rising heat of a late-spring southern afternoon, Shanna worked to reclaim the long-abandoned plot in the backyard of the new house. A runner's white terry-cloth headband kept her hair in place and the sweat out of her dark eyes. Working in her shorts and under-tied tee shirt, she could almost pass for one of her grad students at the university.

Her spade struck something with a dull crunch, neither the sharp ding of a rock nor the woody thump of a tree root. It was hardly the first time in the small plot. The low wall edging the garden held a growing temporary exhibit of found objects: potshards, a corroded fork, the blue-green sheared-off bottom of a vintage Coke bottle, a rusted and battered Tonka Toy bulldozer. She could still remember Professor Belknap with his hearty laugh as he once told her that buried history was so common in Taggerts County one could hardly turn a spade without uncovering old bones or bullets. So far, her efforts had yielded neither bullets nor bones and little in the way of history. Ah well, she thought, all work and no play makes the historian a drudge. And too much play in the garden makes the historian thirsty.

She took the interruption to the rhythm of turning over the soil as an excuse to pause. Thirst and her relaxed rhythm overrode curiosity. She was in no hurry. Taking a sip of iced tea from the insulated water bottle resting on the rail of the back deck, she surveyed her handiwork. A garden. Again, she thought. She had not had a garden since the window box in her Manhattan apartment when she was a girl, the one she had tried to keep hidden from her father. How many years ago? How many lifetimes? She was Shanna Newsom now, and had been for many years, but she had once been someone else, and before that yet another. What was real, she wondered. Was she also these other abandoned selves? The window box had been real. Yes, she was certain of that. And she could still see the quiet rage on her father's face after he discovered her plantings. Or had he screamed at her?

This was the problem of reinventing yourself. Which were the things that had happened and which the inventions rehearsed and retold so many times as to take on the trappings of truth and dimension? Shanna had slowly accepted that the only reality to be trusted was the one in front of her, the one she could hold and touch. Her doctorate in American History from Kennilwirth University in Vermont might be real, but she could not be certain. Her book on the slaveholding history of Southern colleges and universities was real because she could lift the last of her author's copies from a bookshelf in her office and riffle through its nine hundred plus pages. The years of research that led up to publication were now a memory, and memories could never be fully trusted to have been real.

Methodically working the soil was proving to be therapeutic, manual medicine for the mind to take it off the perpetual threats in her life, real and invented, along with the end-of-term pressures at Holcomb, where recent losses of faculty left her teaching four sections of two courses in the spring term, leaving no time for research and not even much for preparation. That Shanna had finally made tenure as a Professor of History and Economics did not exempt her from pulling her weight and taking up slack in lean times. Even so, she counted herself lucky. Her partner, Rand McMurphy, an adjunct instructor teaching under renewable contract, was juggling four different courses, including a first-year sociology course with nearly two-hundred students. It was his own doing. She had advised against agreeing to the load, but he was paid by the course and was ever mindful of the fact that she outranked and out-earned him.

Why, she wondered, were men, even strong, capable men—or maybe especially such men—so vulnerable? Why was the male ego so easily threatened by things that ultimately did not matter? It was a perpetual puzzle to her.

Despite now living in the same house, it seemed as if she and Rand could hardly find time to see each other since the start of the semester. She was looking forward to the summer term, when each of them would be teaching only one elective and the two of them could get reacquainted. If Rand was up for it.

They had been riding a relational rollercoaster ever since she bought the new house nearly a year earlier. She had some idea what the house meant for him because she knew what it meant for her. It was about commitment, settling down, taking the long view, maybe with an eye toward starting a family before that option was closed out. She hated the metaphor of the ticking biological clock, but she could hear hers chiming the hours, measuring the years.

What was it with men and commitment? What made it so hard for so many of them to sign on the dotted line, to make a choice and stick with it? She, of all people, knew what it meant to turn a sharp corner in one decisive moment and then see the journey through, wherever it led. Rand should know, too. He was an ex-cop, now teaching criminal justice and sociology, a New Englander making a new life, a smaller life, at a small Southern university. Like her. Except her life story was even more complicated than his.

Digging up the old bed and planting a garden at the new house had been Rand's idea. He thought it would give her an outlet for pent-up energy; she thought she needed the energy more than the outlet. Of course, his agenda also included hoping to have a ready source of fresh herbs for his culinary digressions. In one corner, a parcel of basil and parsley were already yielding cuttings, but the rest of the planted portion was stubbornly barren.

The new house on Racine Circle had once been identical to the old one down the street. Both had been small bungalows built in the late forties as low-cost housing for returned veterans attending college on the G.I. Bill, but this one had been extensively remodeled over the decades, with an attached garage and a two-bedroom addition and the living room now fronted by a bay window. A deck off the expanded kitchen overlooked a spacious backyard that once had sported a small garden and a swing set, both now represented by mere traces in the weedy landscape.

Shanna had been skeptical at first about gardening, but was beginning to admit that there was something satisfying and centering about churning up dirt, uprooting weeds, and pushing seeds into mounded rows. The reclamation was slow going, which made it pleasantly different from life at the university, a relaxed stroll instead of the pressured jog of the end-of-term madness.

Returning to where she had left off, Shanna pressed her foot to the top of the shovel blade, and plunged it into the earth. Once again it struck something with that same distinctive crunch. She lowered the handle and turned the dirt from the widening pit. Scraping away dirt slowly revealed the rust-peppered top of a rectangular box. With the tip of the shovel under the edge, she prised the box up enough to slip her fingers underneath and free it from the ground.

She brushed off clinging soil, exposing a hinged metal box the size of a hefty hardcover book, its cover art a painting in warm subdued colors. Despite corrosion from being buried in the ground and fresh scrapes from the tip of her shovel, the painted image of a cherubic child with a fishbowl was recognizable. A scratched but readable banner across the top declared *"Cakes-Fabrik H. Bahlsen"* in ornate art nouveau lettering. Someone might have long ago buried personal treasures and then forgotten about them. Or perhaps it had been fancied as a sort of time capsule intended to be opened at a future date.

The box in the ground was hardly her customary beat in history. As a quantitative historian, Shanna was more practiced in digging through file drawers, scanning images of historical documents, and scrolling through old records to uncover unexpected sums or surprising associations. Still, the rush of excitement that went with discovery was the same, and it called up the same struggle that continued to define her life: her struggle for constraint and control, the means to manage her innate impulsiveness and to fend off the chaos and danger of the rest of life. Her obsession with order was learned behavior, not innate temperament.

Shanna examined the heavy box with its vintage artwork. The underside was more severely corroded, but she could just make out an embossed logo and the word "Hannover" at the end of what might have been an address. Eager to discover the contents and its message from the past, she tugged at the lid, but it refused to budge. She felt a pang of guilt as she impulsively and nervously looked around the empty backyard. Her professional self knew she should stop until she had the proper tools, but, beneath her dedication to order and procedure was still buried an impulsive and rebellious child, one whose own childhood was now being conjured by the forbidden appeal of buried treasure. You're a historian, she told herself, and this is a found artifact. You should be taking it intact to a lab to be opened with care and examined properly. But. She kept hearing that word in her head. But. It's just an old box in my backyard.

"Okay," she said as she stood. "I can do this. I'm a pro. I'll just see what I have to work with." She set the box down gently on the deck, went into the kitchen through the back slider, and started to prepare. Ten minutes later, she had her jury-rigged lab in place. Arrayed atop newspapers spread on the kitchen table were disposable gloves, a scrub brush and a paint brush, paper towels, rubbing alcohol, an open tool box, and her half-frame Nikon digital SLR fitted with a macro close-up lens.

After retrieving the box and placing it on the newspapers, she took pictures from every angle, then carefully brushed away the last of the clinging dirt before taking another set of pictures. Running a toothpick under the edge of the lid failed to free it. What to do? She needed something very thin to try to slip between the lid and the body. A screwdriver? Too thick. A knife? Thinner still would be better, something like a razor blade. She pawed through the small tool box that Rand had given her as a housewarming gift. How romantic, she had thought at the time but had left her sarcasm unspoken. At least he meant well. Ah, there, just the thing, a box cutter. She figured out how to remove the blade from the too-fat handle and started working it beneath the edge of the lid.

It took three slow sawing passes around the perimeter with the blade, each reaching a little deeper under the lip, before the lid started to loosen. On the last pass, the blade suddenly slipped out and sliced into Shanna's other hand. She looked down at the cut welling with blood. Tetanus, a soil bacteria, she thought, better get my shots up-to-date. And I better put a bandage on that before I bleed all over my treasure box.

It took several minutes for her to retrieve the bandages and a tube of triple-antibiotic ointment, then to clean and bandage the cut. In the kitchen, she fetched a table knife and used the blunt tip to help pry open the lid, hoping to keep from damaging it too much. Patiently working the blade under the edge along each side and testing as she went, she gradually freed the top. The rusted hinge complained as she twisted the lid back, like opening a book. Jammed inside was a roughly triangular packet wrapped in what looked to be grease-stained butcher paper tied with twine. She gently slipped the heavy packet from the tin. When she tugged at the twine, it nearly disintegrated and fell away. As she stared at the oddly shaped packet, her curiosity intensified. In for a penny, in for a pound, she thought. Besides, the damage is already done. What's a few more broken rules?

Heart pounding in anticipation, she methodically unwrapped the paper. With the last layers, she began to make out the shape of the contents. Unfolding the final sheet, she realized it was no child's secret treasure. It was a piece of history, both distant and likely nearer. Lying on the paper was a pistol, one so iconic that even she recognized it: a German Luger.

She fought against dark swirls of free association as she carefully refolded the paper around the handgun. Rand will be interested, she thought, and he'll know what to do.

❧ Chapter 2

As SHANNA FINISHED stowing her garden tools in the garage, two cars approached. An unfamiliar black-and-yellow Mustang with an out-of-state plate crept along as if the baby-faced driver in a beat up bomber jacket and a backwards baseball cap were looking for an address. Behind it, Rand, in his well-traveled green Honda Civic, made an impatient bid to pass on the narrow street. Swinging wide, Rand slipped the car straight into the driveway, cutting off the Mustang and earning a middle-finger salute from the driver before the sports car sped off.

Shanna didn't own a car, which was fortunate, because the small attached garage was piled wall-to-wall with boxes, old furniture, and redundant appliances—the remnants of ongoing attempts by her and Rand to merge households. The cluttered garage was a messy museum, a reminder of unfinished business and unresolved issues. The neat and orderly interior of the house they nominally shared was the smooth surface purchased at the price of the disorder still stowed in the garage. Shanna reached up for the pull handle and lowered the overhead door.

"I found something today," she said, turning toward the Civic.

"So did I," said Rand, slipping out of the car. "I was down

at Lewis's Market in Taggertsville and spotted a bottle of that sauvignon blanc we liked so much. They also had farmed catfish, so I thought I'd whip up some Cajun-style blackened fish. What do you think?" Rand was now the self-appointed cook in the household. Having rejected her frozen-pizza-and-takeout approach to the kitchen, he had drawn on an informal apprenticeship with his friend Darlene Shirley to up his game. Darlene, another ex-cop with a history, was the chef-owner of Dahlia's, arguably the best restaurant in the county.

"That sounds good," Shanna said, "but wait until you see what I found." Was it always like this? She wondered. They so often seemed in some kind of verbal road race, matching stride, looking for the means or the moment to pull ahead. What had happened to the easy collaboration of their early days? Or was that a glossy palimpsest she had brushed over a messier past? There I go again, she thought, losing track of what really happened and what is only the stories I tell.

"Great," he said, opening the trunk of the Civic. "Let me get started on dinner, and once I have that under control, you can show me. Or you can tell me about it while I'm seasoning the fish." He juggled a grocery bag in each arm, closed the trunk with his elbow, and strode toward the front door.

Shanna put her hands on her hips. Was this the problem? Were they two people whose only coping mode was self-sufficiency? Had they spent too many years going it alone, watching over their shoulders? Could they ever learn how to make room for each other?

"Are you coming?" he said, holding the front door open.

"Yeah, just thinking."

"That's my Shanna, always thinking. And, knowing you, it's mostly questions, which is why I pushed for starting the garden—mindless, earthy—a change of pace for my numbers-and-dot-plots darling who is perpetually trying to sort out the past." As she slipped by him after his teasing lecture, he tried to sneak in a quick kiss, but she turned at the last second and he got only a dirty cheek. "Okay, I see how it is. What did I do wrong now?"

Shanna kept walking. "Nothing. I'm all dirty and sweaty, and you're all keen to get on with doing your chef-y thing. I'll head for the shower while you head for the kitchen, and we'll meet on the deck in a bit for drinks. Okay?"

"Okay." He watched her go.

❧

Shanna finished twisting a towel around her hair as she stepped through the slider onto the back deck. An advantage of the lone house at the top of Racine Circle was that the backyard abutted woodland belonging to the university and was completely private. Rand stood, smiling, holding two water glasses filled with ice and a bright pink liquid. "And what is this?" she asked.

"A Floradora. Well, Faux Floradora. Couldn't find any gin, so I made it with white wine and upped the lime."

Shanna took a sip. "Mmm, really good. When did you add mixology to your résumé?"

"After hanging around with Darlene last weekend at the restaurant. You can't help but pick up a tip or two from her bartender. When he's not behind the bar, Bennet will just not stop talking. He says it comes with the job of spending so many hours just listening and nodding as customers tell their alcohol-fueled stories."

"Well, I approve"—she took another sip—"of the drink, that is." She was thinking back to last weekend, when Rand had said that Darlene needed to talk business with him. Darlene Shirley was a part of his past, but a past that was stubbornly still present. "So, did you see what I dug up today?"

"No, I was focused on getting the catfish ready. And being bartender. Is your discovery that pile under the newspapers on the kitchen table?"

"Yeah, that pile. I'm curious to hear what my resident forensics expert makes of it."

"Okay, now you're talking my language." He slid open the slider and looked toward the dirty mess on the table. "Where'd you say this came from?"

"The garden."

"Ah, so that explains it. Must be fresh herbs." He gave her his silly lopsided grin. "Let's take a look."

The kitchen of the new house was larger than the old one, but was still a tight fit for the trestle table they had picked up at a yard sale. Under an opened copy of the *Taggerts County Chronicle*, the battered metal box and the partially refolded packet lay atop more newspapers spread on the end of the table. Rand walked over and leaned down to examine them from every angle without touching. "Pretty cookie tin, oddball artwork, looks like maybe turn-of-the-century— twentieth, that is—but I know zip about art." He turned to the refolded packet and sniffed. "Smells a little like machine oil, fine grade, chemicals of some kind, too. The paper is stained, but somebody took some care preparing this before burying whatever it is. You unwrapped it?"

"Yeah, obviously, but I didn't touch it. Take a look."

Rand fetched a fork from the tableware drawer and started using it to work open the partially rewrapped layers.

"I already handled that, so you might as well just open it up."

"Old crime-scene habits," he said. "Besides, we don't really know what's on the paper." He pushed aside the last layer. "Well, what have we here? You taking up a new hobby?" He leaned in close and studied the pistol carefully. "Okay, looks like a Luger, standard officer issue, this one from the Second World War, I think. A little corrosion and wear, not too bad, bluing still mostly intact. And oh oh, look at that. It's loaded."

"What, you can tell all that just by looking at it? How do you know all this stuff?"

"Took a course on historical firearms when I was working on my master's. See, that's the year of manufacture, 1942. This was referred to as a P08, for the year the model was first issued, 1908. Short barrel, so not a navy issue or the so-called ordinance model that had longer barrels for more accuracy at greater range. And see that little metal edge with an engraved word poking up just visible there? That's the extractor. *Geladen*, German. It means loaded. And back there, *gesichert*, secure. The safety's on, but somebody expected to use this again or buried it maybe without realizing there was a round in the chamber. Where did you say you found it? How deep?"

"Right in the corner of the garden, at the edge, about a foot down, in that box, that cookie tin."

"Okay, so, the burier probably intended to retrieve it easily, perhaps in a short time. And now we're faced with a loaded Luger with a round of unknown vintage and reliability still in the chamber. Okay, here's what we're going to do." He reached into his back pocket and extracted a pair of blue nitrile exam gloves. When Shanna raised her eyebrows, he said, "More old habits. Remember, I also still always carry a pair of cuffs with me. Besides, I was demoing crime scene practice to criminal justice students earlier today."

He pulled on the exam gloves and picked up the Luger from its wrappings. "Stay behind me. We're going to go back out on the deck." Outside, he gently set the pistol down on the little wrought iron table, carefully positioning it with the muzzle pointed away from the house. "Probably no latent prints, but one never knows. Okay, first we release the magazine and let it slide out. All right, half full." He twisted the magazine to get a better look at the backend of the top cartridge. "Nine-millimeter parabellum, but not antique, these look like modern training rounds. Now, I seem to remember there's something obscure about disarming this thing. What was it? Oh, right. Okay, to check if there really is a round in the chamber and eject it, we have to actually take the safety off in order to pull back the toggle and open the chamber. I think that was it." He tightened his right hand on the grip and pulled back on the two knurled pads with his left to get a peek into the chamber. His fingers slipped.

Bang! The gun kicked, almost flying from his hand as the spent shell casing shot straight up. Splinters sprayed from the deck railing where the bullet struck.

"What the hell are you doing?" Shanna snapped.

"Oily fingers. Oh, right, and now I remember. To lock the toggle back, you have to have an empty magazine inserted. At least be glad I had the brains to have it pointed away." He set the gun back down. "Well, that ought to get the neighbors' attention, maybe a visit from our friend Officer Arnez of the local constabulary."

"My ears are still ringing," she said.

"Mine, too, but at least now it's safe. And we know it's in working order. And I don't hear any sirens yet."

"We should turn this in, right?"

"Eventually. Maybe." He smiled at her, and she shook her head. Rand McMurphy was a cold-case fanatic who had already dragged her along on more than one amateur investigation into a buried past. "I think we should do some more digging first," he said, "and I don't mean in the garden. I mean, how did a loaded German pistol end up buried in a cookie tin in our backyard? What's the story? How long has it been there? Aren't you curious?"

"Of course, I'm curious."

"Great. And this is a great find." His voice turned excited. "Do you realize I can even use this in my classes: get students looking for latent prints, see whether they're smart enough to check the cartridges, too. And isn't one of your classes that 'World at War' survey course?"

"Well, yeah, but it's pretty much all PowerPoint and palaver. I'm teaching from old Doc Freedman's syllabus and cursing him daily for dying just before the start of the term."

"But this"—he cradled the gun—"is history written in blued steel."

"Not my kind of history."

"Pretty interesting, though. You realize, this is one of the earliest and most successful semi-automatic handguns in military history. Even though it predated the First World War, it was still in wide service throughout the Second."

"Is it still made?"

"Don't think so. If I recall, it continued being manufactured by Mauser, or maybe the Spanish, up until the 1990s. This a piece of elegant engineering. Absolutely beautiful. I fired one once on the police range—Sargent Figlio was a collector—and it's a very intuitive handgun. Like pointing your finger. Lots of fun."

Shanna made a face. "I think that's a guy thing, to call a weapon beautiful or say that shooting bullets is fun. What I remember about guns was neither. It was . . ." Her voice trailed off as she tried not to recall what had once been part of her life. "Well, okay, we can use it as exhibit A in our classes and, as you say, do a little more digging. In the meantime, I'm famished from all the digging I already did. What did you say was on the menu tonight?"

"Cajun blackened catfish, Bahamian-style pigeon peas and rice, and baby okra finished with aioli."

"My, sounds very classy. My live-in cook is stretching his wings."

"Chef, live-in chef. The cook is that fat guy working at the diner down the road." He bent to kiss her, and this time she didn't turn her cheek.

৪১

The kiss turned into an interlude in the bedroom, a swift and sweaty reconnection that Shanna realized was way overdue. After riding him to a galloping climax, she slowed down to an easy cantor that allowed her to watch his face closely and adjust her pace, stretching their lovemaking into a second orgasm that left her mellowed and, for the moment, not on high alert.

She was just drifting off when Rand started to wriggle out from under her. "Gotta go," he said. "Left the fish out on the counter. You shower while I finish making a romantic dinner."

The dinner started well enough, but the romantic ambiance began to fade once Rand started kvetching about his teaching load. "I'm behind a whole lecture in my Field Methods course," he said. "I may have to cut some material. And I have no time for students outside of class. Everybody's clamoring to see me about . . . well, you know the drill. And there's this one student in SocRel. She will not give up, keeps on, er, pestering me for an office meeting, private."

"Can't you make time for her, fifteen minutes or something between classes?"

"If I make time for her, I'll have them twenty-six deep down the corridor. Besides, I just have a funny feeling about this one, like she has an agenda that isn't entirely academic."

"Really? What's her name?"

"Olee. That's what she goes by. Short for Oleander, Oleander Walston."

"Oh, yeah. I have her in my World at War class. Pretty girl."

"Mmm, maybe. Not my type."

"What is your type?"

"Long legs, athletic, brilliant, beautiful, interested in history and numbers and with some life experience under her belt. Like you."

"Some experience under her belt? Are you talking middle aged, waistline spreading?"

"No, I mean young—like you."

"Well, I'd say it might be a good thing this student is not your type—Title IX reports notwithstanding—what with a name like that."

"What about her name?"

"Oleander may be a pretty flower but it's deadly poisonous."

"Really? Well, then definitely I should listen to my instincts about her. I just have to keep her at arm's length until the end of the semester. Do women professors have this sort of problem, I mean, students coming on to them?"

"I suppose it happens. I do remember one of my students . . ."

"Really?" He suddenly looked very interested.

"Yeah, ex-cop, Boston escapee, Irish name, a little younger than me, likes to cook. Very persistent. You know the type?"

He laughed. "I think I do. How'd that work out? Were you able to handle it?"

"No, I failed completely." She leaned across the table to kiss him.

✌ Chapter 3

WITH THE ARRIVAL of the weekend, Rand started flexing his atrophied detective muscles by stepping in to take charge of their investigation of the handgun. "We'll divide up the work. You take the cookie tin, see what you can learn about it, and I'll take the Luger."

"Hmm, kinda stuck on stereotypes, aren't we?" she said. "Guns or cookies, who gets which?" Her teasing had an edge.

"Well, I mean, what do you know about handguns?"

"More than some. But then, what do I know about cookies? You're the cook . . . I mean chef."

"Well, okay. It wouldn't make much sense, but we can switch if you insist."

"No, I just wanted to point out how you just jumped in, automatically, to hand out assignments with that particular division of labor."

"I didn't jump to anything automatically. I just—"

"It's all right. You can't help it. The gene for it is on the Y-chromosome. So, you'll focus on the Luger, and I'll focus on Cakes-Fabrik H. Bahlsen. What else? What comes next?"

"Well, we start with the simpler and more obvious possibilities. I'll look for old reports for stolen pistols fitting this description, check the serial number against online databases, that sort of thing. Meanwhile, I'll get some students doing analytics."

She gave him her chin-down look like a clerk peering over the top of half-frame glasses. "Do I need to say it again? Shouldn't we be turning the pistol over to the police or something? Like you say, it could be stolen property."

"Could be, and we'll look into that, but the basic legal question is"—he put on his serious courtroom face—"whether it's considered lost, mislaid, or abandoned. Those are legal distinctions. In light of the condition of the property, it would most likely be considered abandoned under state law—after one to five years here, if I recall. Since you now own the property on which it was discovered, yours is the superior claim, meaning it belongs to you." He took a little bow and shrugged. "But I'm no lawyer, just an ex-cop. Maybe we can consult Darlene's lawyer friend, Terrell Blackstone, if the need arises. He's been helpful before."

"Yes, Darlene's friend. Darlene seems to have a friend for every need: bartenders, lawyers, you name it." Shanna could feel her muscles tensing.

"Well, she . . ." He took a slow breath. "Is there a problem? You know she and I are old friends. Just friends. That's it."

"Not always just friends. She is your ex."

"Ex. That's exactly it. I don't give you grief over your exes, plural."

"My exes don't live in town. For that matter, my exes are . . . Oh, why do I bother."

"If it's not okay to have friends, we're in trouble. Besides, I thought you liked Darlene. And she thinks you're the greatest. And good for me. She likes you."

"I like Darlene, I do. I just . . . Look, I don't have a lot of history with men and trust. With men, some; with trust none."

"Then I guess we have to make history, because I'm not going anywhere. And I already told you, with you I want it all."

"Then why do you still have your apartment in town?" She didn't say what she was thinking. Did she really want a ring? Was that what this was about? She wondered.

"We've been through all that. I can't sublet, and I haven't been able to break the lease. It's basically just . . . well, a retreat."

"And you need a retreat from . . . from what? From me?"

"Well, yes, sometimes. You, like, well . . . Hey, I don't want to argue. We were having fun, talking about this find, working out our plan of attack."

"*You* were working out our plan of attack."

He threw up his hands in surrender. "Okay, then you call the shots. I'm game. How do you want to do this?"

"Well, you handle the police records, forensics and stuff, and I'll dig into the history, real estate records, people stuff, you know. You study the gun, and I'll study the box."

"Yeah, that's what I was saying."

"You don't get it, Rand. It's about—"

"Control."

"Well, yeah. You can be so controlling, so very much 'I know what I'm doing, so I'll just take charge.' That's you."

"Unlike anybody else in the room?"

Her shoulders slumped. "Maybe this whole thing isn't going to work."

"What whole thing?"

"This." She spread her arms in a sweeping gesture. "Us. A life together."

"That is so like you, always ready to weigh anchor and sail away the moment things get tough. It's what you learned early on. Change hats, get on a bus, and there you are: another beginning, always another."

She could feel the tugging at the corners of her eyes and struggled to keep from crying. Was it anger? Or was it because he was right? Maybe she was the one who wasn't ready to commit. Maybe his hesitance gave her an excuse not to look at her own uncertainty. Maybe she was actually pushing him away. Had it been a mistake to let him in, to let anyone into her real world? "I'm learning," she said at last. "Always learning."

"Hey, that's my line. *Semper tiro.* Remember? My Latin motto."

ೞ Chapter 4

THE BLACK-AND-YELLOW was parked down the street when Shanna pedaled past on Monday morning. It looked as if the driver were asleep, with the seat reclined and the baseball cap now covering his face. Visiting boyfriend maybe? The Smids, in the adjacent house, had a daughter about the right age living at home. Shanna slowed and circled to get a better look inside the car. The driver didn't stir. The remains of a burger-and-fries take-out cluttered the passenger seat, and the rear seat held a military-style duffle bag. Traveling light and traveling alone, she thought.

As she did her second U-turn, she noted the license plate, a four-digit VIP number from Connecticut. No, it couldn't be, she thought. There was no way that past could come into this present. It had to be coincidence, but, just in case, she made a mental note of the plate before she stood on the pedals and sped down Racine Circle for the short ride to the university.

Her emerald green Cannondale had become an extension of her persona and a trademark around campus. Students might cycle around if they couldn't afford a car or disdained walking everywhere, but faculty drove. When she first arrived at Holcomb, the bicycle had been a necessity; now it was habit as well as a mobile declaration of her dedication to environmental causes—and to frugality.

As usual, she parked it in the faculty garage on Old Campus where she would not have to worry about it being "borrowed" by an enterprising student. She backtracked across the sprawling green campus toward Stergeson Hall, the former science building where she had an office and where most of her classes were held. She was early enough that she encountered only a handful of students as she passed the imposing brick exterior of Blendman Hall. She glanced at her watch. There would be plenty of time to prep for her first lecture after stopping in on Dean Havers, head of the school. It was an unplanned detour, but Havers had a reputation for early arrival and late departure. Perhaps the professor would have a recommendation about who to consult about the artsy cookie tin.

℃

Alicia Havers was the university's token female dean, and it said much about the snail-like progression of progressive values at Holcomb that she oversaw the School of Humanities, Arts, and Languages, another Holcomb hodgepodge now housed in one of the least appealing buildings on campus, an ugly, utilitarian structure that was part of what was known locally as the "second wave" of building out, an ambitious but penny-pinching expansion just before the lavish third wave when the university hit the jackpot. The jackpot came in the form of a bequest from its most famous alum, the mega-church preacher and evangelical entrepreneur Reverend Harlan Fairlee. Fairlee had left his fortune to the university, and his name was on two endowed chairs and various facilities all over the campus.

The woman who came out of the Dean's office to welcome

28

Shanna was a walking testimony to what it took to advance this far in the tradition-and-testosterone infused swamp of Holcomb. Tall, broad-shouldered, with a West Point posture and an eyes-front stare, she extended her hand with straight-armed precision.

"Welcome. My secretary has yet to arrive, but may I help you . . . ?"

"Shanna Newsom, history." She returned the firm handshake.

"Ah, yes, Professor Newsom. I only have a few minutes, as you might surmise, but come in, take a seat, and tell me how I might help you."

"Certainly." Shanna followed her in and sat in the chair facing the blank expanse of an antique desk topped by a green blotter and an old-fashion pen-and-ink set that looked like it was for more than just show. "To get right to the point, I was hoping you, or someone in the art department, might help me with the provenance of this." Shanna slid a folder onto the desk, turned it to face the dean, and opened it to the first photos of the cookie tin.

Professor Havers shook her head and closed the folder. "No. Twentieth century, I'm quite certain. sculpture is my field, Greco-Roman. Really, I doubt there is anyone here who would help, not since they took art history out of the arts and made it into history. You should find somebody in your own department." She slid out a desk drawer and started thumbing through a paper directory. "Professor Martine Rossum. Do you want to note her office number? She's in Stergeson Hall."

"I think I know where she is. I should have . . . I am sorry for taking up your time. I should have checked first or emailed."

"Yes, perhaps you should have, but I'm still glad you stopped by in-person. I've been wanting to congratulate you ever since your book came out. I appreciate those who have the temerity to tell it like it is." She stood. "So, belated congratulations,"—she held out her hand again for a shake—"best wishes in your research, and thank you for coming by." It was a precise and perfunctory dismissal.

"Well thank you for your time."

"It was nothing." The Dean glanced at her watch. "Three minutes. Have a pleasant day."

The School of History and Human Sciences was yet another assemblage of academic disciplines thrown together in the aftermath of consolidations and cuts and the reorganization urged by a consulting firm the university had hired to help guide it into the twenty-first century. The supposed savings from simplifying the administration had yet to match the promises of the consultants—or their seven-figure fee.

After the fine arts and humanities were reshuffled and gutted in favor of science and technology, Professor of Art History Martine Rossum, a specialist in modern art, ended up with an office on the same corridor in Stergeson Hall as Shanna Newsom, a quantitative historian specializing in economic history. Their areas of interest had almost no overlap, and their entire relationship had thus far consisted of polite nods at faculty events.

Shanna tapped on the open door of the office and leaned in. "Hi! Professor Rossum? I'm Shanna Newsom from down the hall. Got a minute?"

"Sure, come on in." Martine, a pear-shaped woman in her

late fifties with a pleasantly lined face framed by ringlets of deep umber hair, got up from behind her desk, which was an orderly mess of oversized full-color books that spilled over to adjacent shelves and onto the two extra chairs. "You can move those. Just put them on the floor. I've been doing research for a book. You know the drill." She laughed, a squeaky chuckle.

"How is that going?"

"Slowly, but not entirely surely. I'm not good at writing, at least not this kind of writing."

"You mean, like scholarly writing?"

"No, I mean like cancerous writing, the kind that keeps growing, ever more monstrous and bloated. Poetry is more to my taste and talents, I suppose, paring things down to ever fewer words that say more and more."

"So you're a poet?"

"Only in the voices in my head, or at unguarded moments like this where those voices just blurt it out before I can shush them and avoid embarrassment. Anyway, I'm glad you're here. You know, with our names, I always thought we'd make a great duo for a joint paper. I guess I tend to be in tune with the sound of names as much as who or what they represent. Can't you hear people citing the quote-unquote, classic Rossum and Newsom paper? Or Newsom and Rossum. We should have collaborated long ago. Of course, it's different spellings and, in my case Rossum is sort of an assumed name anyway."

"Oh, really?" Shanna couldn't help thinking about the assumed names in her own life story.

"Well, my father, a Holocaust survivor, was born Able Rothman. He changed his name to Rossum after coming to

America."

"So, you're the other Jewish prof on campus?"

"Well, there's also Drew Marks in computer science, and Nika Solomon in modern languages, but you know, none of us is what you would call very observant, although I was raised pretty conservative. Of course, I'm not counting the Messianics over in the School of Bible Studies. Christian Jews? Jewish Christians? No one quite knows what column to count them in. And you?"

Shanna shook her head. "No, not Messianic and not observant. Candles and challah for Friday night Shabbat dinners, at least when I visit Jewish friends in town. That's about as far as it goes for me."

"Jewish friends in town?" Martine raised her eyebrows. "Not the Lewises down in Taggertsville?"

"Yes, you know the Lewises?"

"Only that they tried to recruit me into their family gatherings when I first arrived on campus. It wasn't a good fit, and I was dealing with too many other . . . well, things."

"So, may I ask, where does the Rossum name come from?"

"Well, when my father emigrated to America after the war, he wanted to make a new life and, in a way, erase the past. The name Rossum pays homage to one of his heroes, the Polish writer Karel Čapek."

"Chappick? I'm not familiar with . . ."

"Čapek coined the word robot, at least with its modern meaning, in his speculative fiction play, 'R U R – Rossum's Universal Robots.' In fact, robot is just the Czech word for worker, and the name Rossum is a play on a Czech word meaning reason or intelligence. My father was a pioneer robotics engineer, even worked on the Mars Rovers, so it was kind of a trademark, an insider's joke. I grew up surrounded by engineers and science fiction buffs who got the reference and thought it amusing."

"And you ended up an art historian."

"Yeah, well, a different form of family tradition in a way. I grew up surrounded by art. My father collected: paintings and drawings, minor stuff, nothing really big or important, nothing that he ever seemed attached to. Every so often new pieces would appear, or one piece would be replaced with another. He was an engineer for whom art was part of the wallpaper. He might rearrange it or sell or trade a work now and then, but he didn't seem to care. In a way, by going into art and not engineering, I was attempting to make a clean break from the past. You know?"

"Yeah, I do know," Shanna said, thinking back to her own clean breaks, except she knew from experience that they were never quite as clean as they seemed at the time. "And what are you doing these days? I mean, besides carrying a Sisyphean teaching load like the rest of us."

"Oh, I'm not rolling boulders uphill this semester. No, technically, I'm on sabbatical, trying to finish a book on the feminist renaissance in tattoo art."

"Tattoos? That's now considered art? I mean, as in fine art. No offense."

"You'd be surprised. Here, let me show you." She turned and ran her finger along the spines of books on the adjacent shelf. She slipped a coffee-table art book from the shelf and flipped through it, opening to a page showing a color close-up of a young woman's back nearly covered with a full-color river-and-forest landscape done in swirls of subtle shading as if sprayed from an airbrush. Brightly colored birds and the face of a dark-skinned woman peeked out from the foliage. "This is by a Canadian First Nations artist who goes by the mononym Ofelia. Most of her work is more abstract, but this better shows off her technique."

"And that's a tattoo? I thought tattoos were, like, all blue-black lines."

"Yes, it's a tattoo. Or really many. A work like this, well, it was completed over several years."

"Ouch."

"Well, it does hurt, but not as much as some people think."

"What got you into studying tattoos as art?"

"Well, in part it's more rebellion. You know, the whole Jews and tattoos thing. Technically, they're forbidden. And then along comes the Holocaust and the millions in the camps the Nazis tattooed with serial numbers. My father never wore tee-shirts, but he would sometimes roll up his left sleeve and say, 'See, I was there.'"

"Have you, er, do you have . . .? Well, I don't mean to pry."

"It's okay. The answer is yes. Here's one." She pulled up the sleeve of her jacket to reveal overlapping images of two flowers. "Moccasin flowers, or Lady Slippers as they're also called, the official flower of my home state, Minnesota—also my daughter's favorite. We got matching tattoos when she turned eighteen. She . . . we're . . ." She stopped talking and rolled her sleeve back down. "It's a long story." She closed the art book. "So what brings you to my office. I mean, I know who you are because of your book and that award, but we've never really talked. Pretty gutsy to be teaching here and then biting the hand, as it were, by writing a book on how Deep

South colleges and universities benefited from slavery."

"Well, Professor Rossum—"

"Marti. Please call me Marti. Otherwise it's going to be Professors Rossum and Newsom, back and forth."

"Okay, Marti, I'm Shanna, and I have something that . . . well, it's probably not exactly in your line of art history, but I thought you might be able to tell me something about it or at least point me toward a source that could help track down its story."

"Sure, what is it?"

"Okay,"—Shanna reached into the tote bag she had brought with her—"it's kind of kitsch, a cookie tin decorated with a replica of a painting signed by the artist."

"Well, let's take a look at it."

"I brought photos of it. I hope that's okay." Shanna handed over a file folder. Mari's eyes widened when she opened the folder. "You recognize this thing?" Shanna asked.

"I don't know. Something like it, maybe. As the lid spells out, it's from Germany, Hannover. The company is Bahlsen, a major supplier of cookies and other baked sweets. The painting is probably turn-of-the-century. I can't read the name of the artist, but must be French. It says Paris. I don't think this is an antique, though, if that's what you were wondering—more like a reproduction for commercial purposes. So what's the story on this one?"

"That's what I'm trying to find out. I've been putting in a garden in my backyard and dug this up. I'm ultimately interested in possible provenance, the when and who of how it ended up buried in my backyard."

Marti's face took on an anxious look. "Where exactly do you live?"

35

"Practically next door, over on Racine Circle."

"Oh, really? Not the house that belonged to . . . uh, Professor Fender?" Her voice finished on a changed note, like a twist of lemon added to a glass of soda water.

"I don't think so. The last owners were a couple of post-docs who were asking too much for it after they finally got real jobs . . . well, wherever they ended up. I don't know how post-docs can afford to buy a house in the first place. I don't think I've ever heard of Professor Fender. What department is he in?"

"No department. He was in Modern Languages before he suddenly retired one step ahead of being stripped of tenure and booted out."

"What was that about?"

"An old story, I'm afraid, and one still too common. Professor putting the moves on students. He . . ." She looked away for a moment. "He was a real piece of work, that one."

"Not to pry, but it sounds like there might be some personal history there."

"Sort of. But,"—she shuffled through the photos of the cookie tin—"let me see what I can come up with about your buried treasure. I should warn you. I'm afraid it's not likely to have much value as a collector's item, what with the rust and dents and scratches, but maybe I can pin down some information of interest."

"That would be great." Shanna got up to go. "You know where to find me if you find out anything. Should I leave the door open?"

"No, you can close it."

As soon as the door was shut, Marti retrieved a magnifying glass from her desk and started examining the photos.

There it was, in the photo showing the inside bottom, just visible as faint tracks, the crude scratched initials. Martine Rossum's hand shook as she set the magnifying glass down.

ઍ Chapter 5

ANOTHER WEEK OF RAND and Shanna passing each other in hallways or sharing snatched meals between marathon sessions of catch-up reading and grading papers brought them to Friday night with Rand busy in the kitchen preparing a special dinner.

"What's on the menu tonight, oh resident chef?" she asked.

"Steak au poivre, seared asparagus with hollandaise sauce, rösti potatoes," he said, wielding the pepper grinder with a flourish, "and a nice brambly zinfandel to set off the steak."

"What's the occasion?"

"Isn't Friday night occasion enough, my Jewish sweetheart?"

"Half-Jewish, maybe less."

"Less, more. Who cares? Any excuse to celebrate, especially as we don't seem to get more than the briefest respite from the academic grindstones these days. So, let's make the most of the time by prohibiting talk of politics."

"Good idea. Of course, these days that's about everything, especially if you count departmental politics. So, a silent meal?"

"Hardly. How's your gardening going?"

Shanna sighed with guilt. "It's not. I've been spending what little spare time I can carve out at the library and searching online, tracing ownership of the house, provenance of that cookie tin, and so on. In the meantime, the half-finished garden is doing its own thing, sprouting a fine crop of local weeds and invasives."

"Might be some edibles out there anyway. I thought I spotted some lamb's quarters. That's a great wild green, better than spinach."

"So, there you go. I guess I'm a better gardener than I realized. And maybe a better gardener than art researcher. I have yet to hear back from Marti Rossum, who said she'd look into the backstory on the cookie tin. Any progress on the Luger?"

"Some. Two of my students recovered a partial print from one of the cartridges, but it looks like the gun itself was wiped before it was packed away. I've got Professor Rolandson in Chemistry supervising a team of students analyzing the paper in which the gun had been wrapped and the surface film residue on the gun itself."

"I'm curious," Shanna said. "What's it worth? I mean, if we wanted to sell it. After all, it is some kind of antique."

"Mass produced antique, if you call something from the forties antique. What is it worth? Depends on a lot of details. I already talked to a dealer in the Midwest who is pretty savvy about Lugers in all their variations. He said it depends on things like whether all the parts have matching numbers, what percent of the surface is still 'blued' steel, stuff like that. To be worth big bucks, it would have to be in excellent condition, with all matching parts and matching magazines, come with an authentic leather holster, and so on. By itself, he says ours might be worth as little as $800 or so, maybe up to $1200. He said he'd have to see it."

"Well," Shanna said, "that's a welcome windfall, considering what we make. I could think of some things to use that on around the house."

"I rather thought we might display the Luger prominently on the mantle, but I can tell by the look on your face how that does not fit with your interior decorating aesthetic. So, your turn again. What have you found about the property?"

"Well, before we bought the house, it sat on the market for over a year. The previous owners, the Merchesons, were asking way too much. They finally relented and dropped to market when the husband was transferred to Singapore, where the wife has family. I dickered with them through the agent and finally just made an offer. I never met them. You know how it is. You can live on the same block for years and never know your neighbors—or at least that's me."

She pulled out her smartphone. "I have a list of previous owners, all five, going back to 1985, all young faculty or silver-spoon grad students. No one stayed for long; they all moved on or moved up. Maybe that's part of why we never know our neighbors. Three houses in the neighborhood have turned over in the year since I . . . since we moved in here." She scowled at him. "What?"

"What? You're scowling at me."

"I'm not. It's just that you have that look, that skeptical cop look. What about?"

"Nothing. Just the 'I-we' thing again. You did move in here. Then I moved in with you. It's your place and—"

"It's our place. That's how I see it."

"See it any way you like. I'm talking facts, history. I

41

thought those were your currency."

"There you go again, throwing that at me."

"Throwing what at you? I'm just saying . . ."

Shanna, not one for loud confrontations, just dropped her hands to her sides and stood there, trying to fight off tears that made no sense to her. She hated that, being brought to what her father had always called her silly irrational tears, which had always seemed to her to be a stupid label. Weren't all tears irrational?

Rand threw up his hands. "Here we go again. What do you want? Do you want my name on the damn mortgage? Is that it?"

"Well, your name is on the damn mortgage for Darlene's restaurant."

"I told you, cosigning was just a formality, to help with the bank when she moved down here from Boston. This is not New England. And even in Boston, there's still a lot of unacknowledged redlining going on. A Black woman, single, from out of state. She was having trouble getting anyone to take her seriously. In the end, it wasn't even about me or my name. Money talks, and lots of money talks the loudest. When she plunked half down on that property, in cash, damned if that bank loan guy didn't suddenly start smiling and talking all nice."

Shanna turned away, starting to pace, giving her a moment to make a surreptitious swipe at her eyes. Even with Rand, she hated appearing weak or vulnerable. "Yeah, I heard you tell that story before, but it doesn't matter. What matters is us. We hardly see each other, and when we do, all we talk about is teaching and students—or now, this damned pistol—or we're fighting. Like now."

"We're not fighting, this is just talking. We were having a discussion about who owned this house, remember?"

Shanna shook her head in slow motion. "Sometimes I don't know what to do with you, Randall McMurphy."

"Now I know I'm in trouble. When you call me Randall, I know." He gave her what she always thought of as his seal-pup look, where his face lost its mid-life lines and his eyes widened and softened into sea-green pools.

"Oh," she said, shaking her head, "you do know how to change the subject without so much as a word." She stopped pacing and came over to where he had been whisking his version of hollandaise sauce. She came up behind him and put her arms around his waist. "Can we leave houses and mortgages and Mauser-made pistols aside for a while? You know, I really miss you."

"What about dessert? I haven't made the dessert yet. Don't you want dessert?"

"Depends. What's for dessert?"

"How about me?" he said, turning around into her arms.

"Okay, I'll take a double order. But, since it's an occasion, let's do dessert first." She took his hand. "Tell the wait-staff that I'll take mine in the bedroom."

❧

It was long after dark by the time they got around to dinner, a quiet one at the kitchen table, with the planned dinner downsized to simple pan-seared steak and a salad that Rand whipped up while Shanna set the table and lit candles borrowed from the dining table. She studied his face by the cold light from over the stove and the waves of warmth from the candle flame. He was younger than she was, but not by much. Still, she could see the sketches of time deepening, adding character to his narrow face, adding more gray to his mustache and flattering streaks to the receding waves of his hair. How did he see her, she wondered. Men develop character; women get crow's feet. Did he hear the tick of a biological clock, or was that just a woman thing? Was he already growing tired of the same face across the table?

He looked over from the stove and caught her eyes. His smile grew slowly. "You know," he said, "you are so beautiful. I keep rediscovering that."

"And you . . . you are so sweet."

"Not beautiful?"

"Yes, beautiful. To me. Is that okay? I mean, I know I'm supposed to see you as handsome, but that's not the word, not my word for you."

"Good," he said. "My mother was always going on about her handsome man. My father was handsome, and my father was selfish and brutal." He brought the steak to the table, deftly divided it, and slipped it onto their plates. "There, easy comfort food. I hope it's okay."

"Looks and smells good. And dessert was yummy."

"Agreed. Anyway, growing up, I never wanted to be handsome. I wanted to be gentle and generous. But, I became a cop and got a lot of that trained out of me. It's not like they teach courses in brutality or selfishness at the police academy, but they certainly don't promote gentleness. And frankly, with survival at stake, it helps to be self-centered."

"That's not how I see you," she said. "You are gentle and generous, but you are definitely self-contained. I still don't understand just why you let me into your life."

"Maybe that's why. Self-contained. Good word. Better than selfish or self-centered or even self-sufficient. Fits both of us, which is why we fit together but also why it might always be a challenge. For both of us." He smiled warmly at her. "I think it's harder for you. Teamwork is the name of the game in police work, so I have more practice. You've been on your own, pretty much, since you were—what?—sixteen, seventeen. And your work: it's library scholarship, lonely digging and thinking."

"I work with others. I have students who—"

"Do your bidding, serve as extensions, roving bots. Face it, you don't have a lot of experience being a real team player."

"Sure, I do."

"How many papers have you co-authored?"

"Well, that one, based on my dissertation. And I give credit to my research assistants."

"So, your advisor gets listed as second author and you give credit to assistants in the little acknowledgements section at the back. That's protocol, not teamwork. But look, don't get all defensive. I'm just—"

"Don't be defensive?"—she cranked up the amplitude—"When you tell me I'm not a team player, you think I shouldn't be defensive?"

"I was just trying to say that I recognize how it's even harder for you than for me. And it's hard enough for me. Plus, you're such a thinker, spending so much of the time inside your head, churning and mixing and stewing. Most of the time I have no idea what you're thinking about. Like right now. What are you thinking about that you're not saying?"

Shanna opened her mouth to speak but said nothing.

"See? If you don't let it out and let me in, then we—" He

was interrupted by the buzz of his cellphone in his pocket. He took it out and looked. "It's a text from Rolandson. He says he has something interesting to show me. I should drop by his lab some morning."

"Lugers. The buried past, loaded guns waiting to be dug up, old ammo, stories that can explode in your face," she said.

"What?"

"You asked me what I was thinking about, so I told you. And now I'm thinking about chemistry. And people. Like you and me." She carefully sliced off a sliver of steak. "Now you know."

❧ Chapter 6

PROFESSOR STIEG ROLANDSON was a head taller than Rand, a decade younger, and had the demeanor of a funeral director. Wearing a white lab coat and a pair of safety goggles, he stood with hands folded watching as two students completed a makeup lab experiment. "Ah, McMurphy," he said, as Rand approached. "Don't mind the ladies here. Or the stink they're making. Mostly harmless. The chemicals, that is. Not the ladies." He did not smile. He gave the two students a keep-it-rolling hand gesture, then half turned and nodded gravely toward a stack of printouts behind him on the workbench. "So, we have something rather anomalous here." He let his safety goggles dangle from their elastic.

"Here? This is about the pistol?" Rand said.

"Well, yes, indirectly. Thanks for picking it up yesterday. I really didn't like having that thing sitting around here." He closed his eyes and continued as if reciting something memorized. "We estimate from corrosion on the container that it was in the ground for as little as three years and possibly as much as eight. We might be able to narrow that with soil samples and rainfall tables; the soil around here tends to be sandy but acidic"—his eyes opened, fixing on a spot at Rand's hairline—"but this is a chem lab not a forensics facility nor is this an ag school."

"No, of course not. But still, that's useful to have a time frame, even a rough one."

"Mmm. Okay, but the gun itself shows very little corrosion, much less than I would expect. So the anomaly is really about the paper in which it was wrapped."

Rand opened his hands. "Do tell."

"Well, it resembles so-called parchment paper or baking paper, which is just paper processed to make it more heat resistant for use in the kitchen. And that's what it apparently is, but in this case it has also been treated with an odd mixture of aromatic and aliphatic amines and mineral salts."

"Which, to the chemically challenged like me, means what?"

"A sort of do-it-yourself VCI."

"VCI?"

"Volatile corrosion inhibitor. VCIs are low vapor pressure compounds that outgas to coat the surface of metal parts and form a passivating layer that slows or stops corrosion. VCI impregnated wrapping materials are commonly used to store or ship metal parts or mechanisms, such as tools, machinery, guns."

"I see, so, a rust inhibitor, right? But what is, as you say, anomalous about this case?"

"This is not commercial VCI paper, which, because it's treated with a mix of somewhat nasty chemicals, is invariably imprinted with a suitable warning declaration of what it's for. Somebody took plain baking parchment, soaked it in a custom-brewed concoction, dried it, and used it to store that Luger. I would say this was a make-do effort by someone who understood a little chemistry—at least from a practical standpoint—had access to some chemicals, and worked with materials at hand. There was also a folded and taped coffee filter filled with silica gel tucked between layers of the treated paper, so you might have missed it. The desiccant probably was scavenged from shipping packets, since there were varied grain sizes. All in all, whoever buried this wanted the pistol to survive in good, usable condition and did a credible if not fully professional job of preservation. They wanted to hide it rather than get rid of it."

"Well, that makes sense considering that it was not buried very deep. I'm guessing they expected to come back and retrieve it."

"Or they wanted it to be found. I mean, you said it was buried in a backyard garden plot, someplace where people would be expected to dig."

"Yeah, you may be right. Thanks for this, Roland. Can I get a copy of your analysis?"

"Here, take this." He handed over the stack from the workbench. "I can always print out another." He glanced toward the two students who had been pretending not to listen. "I better get back to my fledgling chemists. The ladies seemed to have precipitated out a yellow-orange solid from their sample. That's not supposed to happen."

∞

Marti Rossum was already seated, sipping a cappuccino at one of the small high-top tables, when Shanna arrived at the Student Center cafeteria. Shanna waved and nodded from the "Chai and Choco" bay across the food court, then headed for the table with her cup of tea. "I'm so sorry I'm late. Students. You know how it goes. Every time you ask if there are any questions you get stony faces, but as soon as the bell rings, the dam breaks and they avalanche down on the front of the hall, a landslide of the inquisitive—mixed metaphors be damned. Or dammed."

"That's okay. I like my metaphors mixed, preferably with tequila and lime. And yeah, I know what you're talking about. But I don't miss it. Having time for research and reflection is a luxury I could get used to."

"Tell me about it. I'm looking forward to a sabbatical. Someday." She set down her cardboard cup with its dangling tea tag, gave her seared fingers a shake, and pulled out the chair.

"You good with just tea? Maybe a bite to eat? You look like you could use a little something."

"No, I'm good. I'm meeting Rand next for a late lunch. So, were you able to find anything about that art that might be useful? I've been eager to learn more."

"Yeah, I found out some things. I still wasn't able to identify the artist of the original painting, but I finally heard back from the archivist at Bahlsen, the German baking company. The tins were part of a 'nostalgia series' Bahlsen released in 1987 and 1988, with reproductions of vintage art that had originally been commissioned by founder Hermann Bahlsen for promotional posters for his company. He made several trips to Paris around 1900, when the original posters were printed, but the archives contain no information about the artist of the work. So that's it for the provenance of the art."

"And what are you not saying? Any ideas about that particular tin? Where did it come from?"

"I suppose I should tell you. As to the provenance of that particular tin, I can be more precise. I know exactly where it came from."

"You do?"

"Yes, it belonged to my daughter."

"What?"

"If you look carefully at the bottom of the tin, inside, you will see scratched initials, NR, Natalie Rossum. I remember the day she got it. My father had just returned from Germany. His last trip. Of course, we didn't know that at the time." She closed her eyes. "I remember . . ."

❧ Chapter 7

NATALIE BOUNDED DOWN the stairs and rushed to open the front door at the first-floor entrance to the upstairs apartment. "Zayde, zayde!" She leapt up, threw her pudgy five-year-old arms around her grandfather as he lifted her, and kissed him on the neck. Able Rossum hugged her with a measured embrace before lowering her to the floor and carefully shutting the door behind him. "Did you bring me anything, huh?" she said. "Something from . . . from that place?"

"Germany," he said.

"Yes, Germany. Did you bring me something? Did you?"

"Yes."

"What is it? Show me, show me."

"Natalie, enough." Martine stood at the top of the stairs, squinting in disapproval. "Let your grandfather at least get in the door before you assault him."

"But he is in the door. Already. And I didn't salt him."

"Well you certainly peppered him with demands." It was a game they played, tossing random wordplay into conversation. Natalie had caught on early and was surprisingly good at it.

"I was,"—she scrunched up her face in concentration—"just shaking him for . . . oh, I don't know."

"Good try, kid," she said, descending the stairs carrying a

plastic basket of dirty laundry. "Next time you might go for something like, say, 'a shakedown'. Now that would have been clever."

"What's a shakedown?"

"That's when you try to force somebody to give you things. Like what you were doing." She set the basket down. "And father, welcome home." It was said with a certain polite formality. "How are you? How was your trip?"

"Good. Long."

Martine stared at him. His return after such a long absence drew attention to his idiosyncrasies. He could be talkative, but never about feelings. Asked a technical question or talking about space or engineering or when he worked on a NASA project, he could go on for hours. Ask him how he felt and the answer was rarely more than a word or two.

Natalie inserted herself between them. "Did you fly on a big plane, zayde?"

"I did, my little Natalie, I did. I flew on a brand new Airbus 300. It's such a big plane that it can carry hundreds of people and can fly thousands of miles, all the way across the ocean."

"Is it as big as this house?"

"Well, not as fat but much longer, like almost as long as . . . as from here to the Swinberg's house."

"That's long!" she said as she sidestepped to see if he had anything behind him.

"Looking for something?"

"Yeah, what you brought me. You said you brought me something."

"I did. And I did." He twisted to face her as she tried to sneak around behind him.

"Then why don't you give it to me?"

"Natalie!" It was a sharp rebuke in Martine's almost whispered disciplinary growl.

"But . . ."

"But nothing. Your butt is going to get a present if you don't stop pestering your grandfather. Let him at least come up and have some coffee before your shakedown."

"But . . ."

"You heard me. Why don't you go to the kitchen and pick out a special mug for your grandfather while I bring him up?"

"Ooh, ooh, I know just the one." Her face lit up.

Abel watched his granddaughter as she scrambled up the stairs. "You didn't ask if I wanted coffee," he said to Martine as he followed her up to the apartment.

"When did you ever refuse coffee?" she said, leading him down the short hall to the front room. She set down the laundry basket and gestured toward the worn sofa.

"Last week, in Germany. That's when." He placed the bag he carried at the back and sat on the edge of the cushion. "Too strong, bitter. Brought back bitter memories."

"Well, I hope my coffee is more to your taste."

"I'm sure."

"So, how was your trip? Success?"

He nodded. "I met with some engineers from Krupp."

"The coffee grinder company?"

"Now maybe. Then, the munitions manufacturer. I know . . . knew some engineers there who . . . who once worked on . . . control mechanisms, guidance systems, what's called dead reckoning."

"Dead reckoning? The dead can reckon?" She grinned at

him, a tense, closed-mouth smile.

"Navigation by dead reckoning," he said, launching into his talking-down teaching mode that indicated his annoyance over something she didn't already know. "If you know where you started, your speed, bearing, and travel duration, then you can figure out where you are now. There's no GPS on Mars or the moon. A robot rover has to know where it is."

"You're always out there, up there, somewhere else. Mars, the moon, Germany, always after something."

"I reach for something better."

"And the Germans, Krupp, they know better about that stuff than NASA?"

"I knew these guys, also from Siemens, very clever about ruggedized, simplified components, the sort of thing needed for a robotic rover. I thought we could catch up and talk shop over *bier und wurst*."

"And did you?"

"Some. The beer and sausage were good, and I got a few fresh inspirations about designing solid state accelerometers, technical stuff. You wouldn't be interested."

"I would," Natalie said, bounding into the room carrying an oversized coffee mug imprinted with the NASA logo and the slogan "Failure is not an option."

"All right. Bring me that mug filled with black coffee, and I'll teach you all about piezoelectrics and micro lever arms, okay?"

"Mama, zayde's going to teach me about pizza electrics if I get him coffee."

"Well, you sit down on the sofa with him, and I'll get the coffee. That way it will all still be in the mug when the mug reaches him."

Abel was midway through an attempt to explain about acceleration to a bright kindergartener when Martine returned with the coffee. Already growing impatient, Natalie interrupted his lecture. "But what about my present, the one in the bag behind you?"

"You'd prefer presents to physics?"

She nodded with enthusiasm.

"Okay." He handed the bag to her, a sealed duty-free bag that was obviously an airport afterthought. Natalie tore it open with enthusiasm.

"What is it?" She held up a decorated metal box with a stylized painting of a chubby baby playfully dipping a cookie into a goldfish bowl. "Is it a baby doll?"

"Open it and see."

She struggled to pry open the tin. "Can you do it for me, zayde?"

"I can, my Natalie." He lifted the lid and held out the open box for her.

"What are they?" she said, a look of disappointment spreading on her face.

"Sweet biscuits, called cakes or *keks* in German. We would call them cookies. Go ahead, try one. They're good."

"Did you eat one already?"

"I had a sample at the airport."

Natalie looked skeptical as she reached for one. "They don't look like regular cookies. Cookies are round and have chocolate chips in them."

"Some do. Go ahead, see if you like these. If you don't, I'll eat them up so you can use the box to keep your treasures in."

Natalie took a cautious bite from a corner, smiled and

nodded, and stuffed the whole rest of the biscuit into her mouth.

⨂

In the morning, Natalie proudly displayed the empty tin to her mother. "See, I can put treasures in it now."

Martine shook her head. "Don't tell me you ate all the cookies. Let me see your tummy. Oh, my goodness, but you are now a butterball full of butter cookies. So, what treasures are you going to keep in it now?"

"It's too small for my Pooh Bear."

"What about the necklace I gave you for your birthday?"

"The one with the star?"

"Yes, the Star of David."

"Is that a treasure?"

"Yes, a very special treasure."

"Okay." She scrambled up the stairs to her room.

⨂

Bringing herself back to the present, Martine shifted her gaze from the stain on the cafeteria table to face Shanna. "Anyway, the cookie tin was a gift to her from my father, who brought it back from Germany on one of his many trips, his last, as it turned out. After Natalie devoured the contents in an overnight orgy—she never was one for much self-restraint—she used it to keep letters and postcards, mementos, little trinkets. Tell me, was there anything in it when you found it?"

"Yes . . ."—Shanna hesitated, wondering whether she should trust Martine—"but it wasn't correspondence."

"What did you find? I mean, it would have been something of my daughter's, whatever it was."

"Do you think so? Even if the tin was really the one your

daughter had, that doesn't mean she was the one who buried it."

"Well, I would say it probably does, since it disappeared around the time my daughter disappeared. I thought she might have taken it with her."

"Your daughter disappeared? What happened?"

"I don't know." Martine started to choke up. "I haven't heard from her in years, not since she left, and I haven't been able to locate her. After she left, I even hired a detective. He traced her to New York and then to Paris, but the trail went cold there." Martine closed her eyes. "It's more painful than you could imagine. I don't even know if she's still . . ."

"I'm sorry. I'm not sure if I should tell you what we found in the box. I certainly don't want to add to your pain."

"No, tell me, please." Martine leaned forward, a beseeching look in her eyes. "Anything from . . . any part of my daughter. It would mean a lot to me."

"Maybe. Maybe not."

"What did you find?" The words came out slowly and the voice had turned anxious.

"A gun, a German Luger."

Martine's face became a mask, fixed, as she stared past Shanna. The silence between the two women stretched into many tense seconds. Shanna broke the silence. "You know anything about the pistol?"

"No." It was said with little conviction. "It couldn't be . . . not Natalie. She wouldn't have . . . couldn't have."

"What about your father? You said he made trips to Germany. Maybe on one of those?"

"I told you, he was a Holocaust survivor. There's no reason for a survivor to have a German handgun. Why?"

"That's what I'm asking you? And if the tin was your daughter's, why would she have a vintage handgun?"

"As I said, my father was a survivor of the camps. Maybe he acquired it before he and my mother left from France, although why or how I have no idea. My father talked very little about the war. He told stories, some, but they were—I don't know what you'd call them—sort of condensed, simplified. You know, like, this happened and that happened, then I met your mother when France was liberated, just after she was caught and just as she was about to be sent to the camps. End of story." She stared into the foam atop her cappuccino. "My father was always talking, but almost never about himself and never with much emotion. He was like a lot of typical . . . well, you know . . ."

"Are we talking about men here, typical males of the species?"

"Typical of the engineering species, at least the engineers I met while I was growing up. If you asked my father a question about electricity or robots or rockets, he had reams to spout on about. If you asked him about himself or his past, you'd get a few words of summary. It was all, I suppose, just too painful.

"My mother wasn't much different, at least with me. I would overhear the two of them talking for hours in their bedroom, usually in French, sometimes in German, almost never in English. My dad was fluent and spoke English with hardly any accent save for a few odd words, but my mother's English was more limited and heavily accented, and she never seemed fully comfortable using what little she knew. She wanted me to learn French, but my father stopped her from teaching me and wouldn't let her use it around me. In reaction, I insisted my daughter learn French, which she loved. I tried to pick it up on my own, but I was never good with languages. Or math. Mostly I'm a visual person. I think in pictures and textures, shapes and colors."

"That's how you got into art history?"

"Not exactly" She shook her head with an almost embarrassed smile. "I got into art history because I couldn't draw and I couldn't paint. I didn't even bother trying sculpture. I was drawn to it, actually. Like poetry, it's about removal, cutting away until what is left is beautiful, the essence stripped naked."

"Yes, I remember you mentioning that you wrote poetry. But you didn't take that route."

"I did for a while after a writing teacher told her students never to tell the story of a rock rolling downhill. I understood what she was talking about, but I rebelled, writing a poem called 'Rock Rolling Downhill.' She thought it was quite good, but by then I saw adulthood and responsibilities lurking around the corner. Still, I love art and kept looking for a way to be part of it. As I said, I'm a visual thinker. So art history was a way out, a way to do something I wanted . . . and to give the middle finger to my father."

"You weren't close with your father?"

"Oh, we were close, all right, especially after my mother died. Maybe too close. He could be very . . . well, controlling, to the point of suffocation. My mother was quite a bit younger than he was but died long before him. All the years when I was growing up, she looked almost as if she—how can I say this?—as if she had just emerged from the camps, a fragile, half-starved waif, so slim that it was hard to imagine she could have born two children."

"Brother? Sister?"

"Brother, the anointed awaited son. But he died when he was four, years before I was born. I'm named after him, the long-sought replacement baby. He was Martin, and I'm Martine, perpetually measured against his ghost. 'Martin would have done this at your age,' my father would say. 'Martin was so good at math. Did you know that he invented his own number system when he was four.' Of course I knew; it had been shoved in my face over and over again. When I was seven and learning long division, my father told me that Martin would have been doing calculus by that age. Stuff like that. I was always a big disappointment to my father, all the more because my mother so embraced and encouraged me."

"She did? I thought you said she didn't talk much."

"You don't need to talk much to show love, and she so loved me. I think she was lonely, although she never complained. She was very . . . very subservient to my father, who sometimes seemed to me to treat her more like a domestic than as a wife. I saw very little affection between them. I'm sure they loved each other, but their life together seemed more like a contractual arrangement than a marriage."

"And you have a daughter."

"Yes, I have a daughter. And your unstated next question, that you might be too polite to ask, is about my husband. I have a daughter. I do not have a husband. I've never been married, and there was only one man in my life, who turned out not to be who I thought he was. Enough said." She looked Shanna directly in the eyes. "Your turn."

"Okay. We have more in common than you might think. I've never been married, but I do have experience with men who turn out not to be who I thought they were. No kids, though."

"And Rand? Who you're having lunch with later?"

"Randall McMurphy. He lectures in sociology. Adjunct faculty."

Martine laughed. "You can sound a little like my father did, with his telegraph-speech answers and *Reader's Digest* life stories."

"Well, yeah. I assume most everyone in the department knows we're a couple. We don't hide it, but we try not to flaunt it either. This is a Southern university, and the residue of its distant origins as the Holcomb Bible College is a sticky film still coating most everything. Dean Tingerly has made it clear he has no problem with our, uh, arrangement, but, although it is the twenty-first century in most of the country, this is Holcomb University in Taggerts County. There are people on the faculty or in the administration who are stuck in earlier times and would resent us being too flagrant about our lifestyle."

"And Rand, he's the detective, right?"

"Well, yeah. I guess you could say that. He actually was once a police detective, in Boston. And New York, if you count a brief stint after nine-eleven."

Martine nodded. "So, the rumors that he—and you, I guess—still do a little private-eye stuff on the side, are they true?"

Shanna was wondering where this was all going, so she just nodded noncommittally.

"I'd really like to find my daughter, or at least find out, uh, what happened to her. I would hope you can understand that. Anyway, I'd like to make a deal. I would like the cookie tin back, if that's okay; I'll even pay you for it. You can keep the Luger; maybe it's worth something, but I don't want it anyway, definitely not. I do wonder if you and Rand maybe could help me track down my daughter."

"You know, the gun may have been involved in a crime. You don't know down what dark alleys this might lead."

"I . . . I understand. But maybe you can shine some light down the right dark alleys, at least to find my daughter."

Shanna let out a long breath. "Okay, I'll have to check with Rand, but we'd certainly need more details about your daughter and all. What can you tell me about her?"

"I've told you some. She was never one much for self-restraint: threw herself at boys as soon as she discovered them, changed interests and passions as often as she changed her socks."

"And she was at Holcomb? What was she studying?"

"Yeah, she was at Holcomb because faculty brats get preferred admission and reduced tuition. And she resented it. She was determined to keep as far away from me academically as possible. She started out pre-med, but switched to nursing in grad school. She was nearly finished when she . . . when she split. Now, I just want to find her, find out what happened. If you can help . . ."

"I'll run the idea by Rand and see what he thinks." She glanced at her watch. "Speaking of which, I better get moving. Can you send me an email with whatever you know—or suspect—anything you think that might help? Do you still have the name of the private detective you hired? It might be useful for us to contact him."

"Someplace. I'll pull together what I can, but I'd rather not email it. I'll slip it into your departmental mailbox." She reached out her hand. "Thank you, Shanna."

Shanna held Martine's hand between hers. "No problem, Marti. I haven't done anything yet, but I'll try."

As she started to leave, Shanna noticed a student on the way out, baseball cap turned backwards, sporting the logo for the New Britain Rock Cats. Shanna was not much of a baseball fan, but she remembered the minor-league team from her time in Hartford, a time that might as well have been on a different timeline; it was not part of this life.

As the student turned to head down the hallway, she caught the glint off a trucker's wallet chain dangling below the edge of a bomber jacket that was a couple of sizes too big. She fought to keep from drowning in the tsunami of memories that came flooding back.

∽ Chapter 8

RAND, AS MODERN as they come but old-school when it came to courtesy, stood as Shanna approached the table at the Faculty Club. The dining room—with its somber wood-paneled walls, subdued lighting from vintage fixtures fitted with clear open-filament bulbs, and scattered white-draped tables—was all but deserted in the midafternoon lull. "You okay?" he said. "You look like you just saw a ghost."

"I may have. Or maybe I am one. If not now, soon."

"What happened? I thought you were meeting with Professor Rossum."

"I was. But afterwards on the way over here I spotted that kid, the one with the Mustang that we kept seeing around Racine Circle. This time I saw him from the back, leaving the caf at the Student Center. His baseball cap . . . it was from the New Britain Rock Cats."

"Never heard of them."

"Hartford-area double-A team. I've actually been to a couple of their games. Guy was a fan."

"Guy. You mean . . .?"

"You know who I mean. I still don't like to say his name. He was an evil, violent man, and he deserved what . . ."

"Look, it's probably just some student who happens to follow this minor league team."

"But remember, his car had Connecticut plates. It was hanging around the house. And he was wearing that cap."

"So, he's a new transfer student, maybe, nosing around, curious. Not much of a mystery about a kid from Connecticut with a cap from a Connecticut baseball team, now is there?"

"Don't just dismiss me like that," she snapped back at him. "Don't be another Jess."

"It's Rand, Shanna. I'm Rand." He took her hands. "This is not Hartford, and I'm not the guy whose name you won't let yourself say. Except when it slips out like that."

She chewed on her lower lip and glanced around to see if any others of the few guests in the Faculty Club dining room had noticed. "I'm sorry. This really shook me. We keep seeing that car, and now . . ."

"Look, we can run a make on the plate if we see the car again. Okay?"

"We don't have to see it again. I noted the license plate. It's . . . darn, I didn't write it down, and now I suddenly can't remember it. Except it was only four digits, like a vanity plate or a VIP. And it was a palindrome, like 7007, except that's not it."

"Four digits, so we only have to check out, like, 10,000 plate numbers."

"No, I said it was a palindrome. There are, uh"—she squeezed her eyes shut in concentration—"only ninety palindromic numbers of four-digits not starting with zero, and we can cross out the nine with identical digits because I would have remembered that, so eighty-one. But not 7007."

"How the hell did you do that? You know, you can be scary when it comes to that higher math stuff."

"This isn't higher math, it's just arithmetic. You just multiply the number of—"

"Don't tell me. You'll fry my brain circuits. I forget that you are such a math whiz. Anyway, can you get me a list of those numbers? I'll have a buddy run them and we'll see what comes up." He noted she was thumb-typing on her smartphone. "What are you doing now?"

"Writing a script to generate the list for you. It's much faster than typing out all the numbers. There, I just texted it to you."

"And there, I forget you are also a programming whiz."

"I'm no whiz. It's easy, just step-by-step logic."

"Step-by-step I know very well, and logic is my middle name, but programming . . .? Anything beyond 'Hello world' in Python, and I get lost. I barely squeezed by with a gentleman's C in my required programming course by cutting and pasting chunks off the Internet and then changing the names of variables."

"So you cheated, you plagiarized."

"I wouldn't call it that. The instructor said we could use pieces from the code library. I just borrowed from a bigger library." His phone buzzer burped. "There, I have your list. Now watch this. This is where I flourish, as I was explaining. Cut-and-paste, then a little preamble to Judd saying we're looking for a Mustang, tap 'send', and we're off and running." He turned the phone face down on the table. "That's how I roll."

"Who's Judd?"

"Judd Whitland, a friend of Darlene's who works up at the Mass RMV, does occasional favors. It's Massachusetts. Civil servants there have a long history of a certain—what shall we say?—sloppy flexibility when it comes to doing their jobs."

"So, yet another friend of Darlene."

"Look, let's not start, not here, not now. Let's just eat and catch up." He scanned the daily menu sheet at his place, then looked up. "I saw Stieg today, and he had some interesting stuff. What about you? Did you get anything from Professor Rossum?"

Shanna was thinking she got a lot from Martine, more than she expected. "Yeah, I know where the container came from."

"Really?" His face brightened. "Do tell."

"It came, originally, from Marti's father, Abel Rossum. The cookie tin was a present to her daughter, Natalie. The daughter is now grown up and a no-show, but presumably she had something to do with burying the gun. I think there's a lot more to the story, but it will take spending more time with Marti before she'll be ready to share it."

"Curious coincidences. You go to Holcomb's only resident art historian and she just happens to know the provenance of the cookie tin. How's that?"

"Local story, local history? Maybe it means nothing more than luck."

"Maybe. At least we now have names to start some more serious digging."

"And we have a time frame. Natalie disappeared some nearly seven years ago, so we can presume the gun was buried about that time, maybe by her."

"That agrees with what Stieg told me about the chemical analysis. Three to eight years, he estimated. Also said the gun had been wrapped in paper that had been treated with chemicals to inhibit rust. So, the gun was not just being buried to get rid of it. It was meant to be in good shape when it was dug up. And whoever prepared it knew something about chemistry, but it was not a standard mix of chemicals, maybe just a kitchen cabinet catchall."

Shanna scanned the daily menu sheet, ticked the first box and circled "hot tea, lemon" at the bottom. She waited until Rand finished marking his sheet. "Marti wants us to help find her daughter, or at least find out what happened to her. She said she'd pull together materials that might be useful. I didn't make any promises."

"It's a no-brainer. We're already following up on the box and the buried gun. Part of the same case. Maybe we should bring Darlene in. She's good with cold cases. She might be able to contribute. What do you think?"

Shanna stared at him, mouth open, eyes narrowed.

"I take that as a no. You know, you really need to work on this thing you have about Darlene. She is not a threat."

"I don't want to work on this thing about Darlene. I just don't want to have to deal with her or the history you have with her. I want a future. I've had enough of the past, of past lives. I just want to get on with being Shanna Newsom and having a life."

Rand cocked his head, his brow knit. "Look, I understand about you and your so-called 'past lives.' I know you've been through a lot and had to run away from who you were in order to survive. But I don't think this, what's happening right now, is about history, personal history or otherwise." He waited with an expectant look on his face. When she said nothing, he nodded slowly. "This is about kids, isn't it? This is about the fact that Darlene and I had a kid together. It's the elephant-in-the-room topic in our relationship. That's what this is really about."

"No. No way. That's not what this is about. And don't turn your amateur psychoanalysis on me. And why are you grinning like that?"

"It's the way I grin whenever someone protests too much. Listen to yourself. You don't want me to do the psychoanalysis, so just do it for yourself, like you do almost everything else. You are the DIY queen of Holcomb University, hell, of the whole state. And you call me self-contained, self-sufficient?"

"You left out self-taught, self-defined. How about self-centered, self-absorbed?" She started to laugh quietly. "Who is protesting too much? My god, what a pair we are. And yes."

"Yes what?"

"Yes, I want kids. I want them with you. I want them while there's still time. I don't know how I'll do as a mother, but I already know you'll be a good father."

Rand's head drooped. "What kind of a father? A father who lost his son."

"That wasn't your fault. You weren't even there."

"But I should have been there."

"You know, Rand, sooner or later you have to forgive yourself."

"Do I?"

"Yes, because you can't start over with me until you settle that piece of the past."

Rand signaled to the student waiter standing by and trying not to look too attentive while shrugging off total boredom. "So, that's my piece, is it, what I have to come to terms with?" Rand said. "And what is it that you have to come to terms with from your past that you never told me about?"

The waiter approached, a manufactured smile swiftly pasted in place. "Yes, how can I help."

"We're ready. Here." He handed the two menu checklists to the waiter, who looked to be a lower classman working on his first beard. As soon as the waiter retreated, Rand reached over and took Shanna's hands. "So, my Shanna, are we ready for new beginnings?"

"Always beginning. Damn. And somehow it always means ending something, letting go."

"That's how it works, my amateur philosopher." His hands curled around hers.

"That's how it works, says my amateur psychologist. As you say, *semper tiro*, always learning. We're all amateurs. Only one shot at a lifetime, no off-Broadway trial run, no work-shopped rehearsals, no apprenticeships. We just do it."

"Well, except for those of us who start over from scratch, reinvent ourselves, rewrite the play in the middle of the run."

It was talking in code, metaphors saturated with private meaning, and it was too much for Shanna, who fought back tears and struggled to suppress the surging tremors in her face. As she closed her eyes, the tears finally flowed, and the images tumbled in, old movies of the high life in the Manhattan finance whirlwind before the planes hit the Twin Towers, clips of the low life in Hartford, snapshots of cooked books at a dodgy construction company, cinema trailers featuring the faces of men who had used her or betrayed her and who she believed she had left behind, for once and ever, but who still lurked in the shadows at the edges of her thoughts.

Rand waited, waiting for her to choose the window and the words, waiting for her to make the choice.

"Where do I begin?" she said, eyes still closed, still seeing ghosts.

"Here, now. Anyplace, anytime."

She opened her eyes to find herself across the table from the man she loved. "There are things, things I never told you."

"Whatever it is, you can tell me. When you're ready."

"How can you be so infuriatingly wonderful?"

"Because that's what you are to me: infuriating, wonderful. Back at you."

She sucked in a deep breath and exhaled slowly. "I was pregnant. I wanted the baby, even though things were already down the toilet with . . . with Jess. He said no way. When I told him it was my choice, he said that it was his choice and started to beat me. I got away, but after . . . after he was killed, I knew he was right. I couldn't walk away from that life and start a new one as a college professor if I was dragging a kid along. I did the pill thing. For two days, it felt like I was going to die, and I did, a little. At first. Then I put it behind me and never looked back, except I'm still haunted by the what-ifs." She wiped her eyes with the corner of her napkin. "Marti—Professor Rossum—this whole thing has brought it all back to me, because she managed to do it. She was a single parent and made it through grad school and onto the faculty while raising a kid. That could have been me. I could be here with a son or daughter."

"Maybe," he said. "But maybe then you wouldn't be here with me. I might have run for the nearest exit when I found out you were a package deal. Just the idea of having a kid again scares the living shit out of me."

"Me too." She looked up with a forced smile as the waiter approached with their lunches.

"Two Blond Pizzetta Specials, one coffee, black, and one Earl Grey tea with lemon. Enjoy."

Rand glanced at the two pizzettas and grinned at her. "See, we really are so much alike. Well, except for that tea thing you have."

"Tea thing? Do realize how many kinds of tea there are? Infinite variety. Coffee is just coffee, mainlined caffeine."

"There's lots of different coffees."

"Yeah, like roasted coffee, over-roasted coffee, and burnt coffee. Or coffee with milk, coffee with too much milk, coffee with steamed milk . . . the list goes on."

He shook his head slowly and gave her a wink. "Just enjoy your pizzetta and your oh-so-refined tea."

"We have stuff to talk about."

"We always have stuff to talk about, but we are not always eating at the Faculty Club, so let's put aside life's big themes for half an hour and just enjoy the interlude."

"If we put aside the major life topics, we'll have nothing to talk about. It's all major life stuff."

"Only if we make it that." He took a sip of coffee. "Or we can make it easy."

"Easy for you to say. I mean, are we going to turn my garden discovery into a big deal and try to find Marti's daughter, or do we leave rusty cookie tins alone?"

"Already decided, as I said. A no-brainer, since we're already on the case, we might as well see it through. And as to the kids question, that's already settled, too."

"What?" she said, a shocked look slowly taking over her

face. "How is it already settled?"

"Look, we're both terrified. We wouldn't be so scared if we didn't want it so much. So, it's settled." He picked up a wedge of his pizzetta and took a bite.

Shanna stared at him, mouth open, ecstatic and furious with him at the same time. "You . . ."

"I know, infuriating and wonderful. Back at you."

∾ Chapter 9

WITH ITS EXPOSED roots and rocky out-croppings, the woodland trail that wound up and around Speen's Hill at the back of the Holcomb campus took concentration to negotiate at a run. Rand had introduced Shanna to the trail with it's rewarding glimpses back over the campus, and they now often ran it together, schedules permitting. The narrow, twisting route was not conducive to conversation, but Shanna preferred company when trail running through the woods. She was confident that she could take care of herself, but there were stories of abductions and assaults, though none in recent years. Now, with their heavy teaching loads, she and Rand had found it all but impossible to do their work-out runs together. Still, she kept up her routine.

Habit was the heart of Shanna's sense of control over the chaos that ever threatened to encroach on her carefully composed and orchestrated life. With or without Rand, she would run five days a week, rain, shine, or winter wind. For other women she knew who ran regularly, it was usually about keeping in shape, warding off the tummy of time, or even for some, running in desperation to outpace the inexorable clock of mortality. For Shanna, it was about rhythm, the nested rhythms of the minutes and days, the beat that allowed her to sustain the illusion of security. Ever since

Rand had entered her life, those rhythms had become syncopated and the illusion more elusive.

After her last class of the day, Shanna made a quick change into her running clothes, did her warm up stretches behind the Wernor Athletic Center, and headed across the open field for the break in the trees that marked a shortcut intercepting the main woodland trail higher up. Within yards after reaching the trees, the air became cooler, and Shanna picked up her pace to build the heat in her muscles. The roots and rocks were slick from a cool rain shower earlier in the day, and she ran, head down, watching just ahead, concentrating on balance and placement to a degree that suddenly seemed unnatural rather than the familiar comfort and mindless precision of a good run. She looked up in time to see another runner approaching along the main trail just short of the intersection with the cutoff on which she ran. It was no one she recognized from campus and not a regular runner. He ran in jeans with a somewhat stiff-legged splay-footed gait. His baseball cap, now facing visor forward, carried the comically menacing mascot of the New Britain Rock Cats.

Shanna froze. She lost her balance as her right foot twisted off a damp rock at the trail edge and sank into a slurry of forest-floor detritus. She landed hard on her left hip and slid down the steep embankment. The figure above her looked straight at her before taking the turn at the cutoff, heading downhill toward her.

Shanna struggled to regain her footing, then started scrambling straight downhill, through the trees and off-trail brush. Her pursuer was not nearly as agile in the rough as she was, and Shanna was first to reach the bottom of the hill and the open field behind the athletic center. Despite the pain in her hip and ankle, she sprinted across the closely mowed field to the back gate. As she carded herself into the track-and-field facility, she glanced back in time to see her pursuer turn around and retreat back up the hill.

℞

Shanna paced outside the lecture hall, waiting for Rand. "You okay?" he said as he finally pushed through the double doors.

"He came after me, up on Speen's Hill." The words sputtered out of her. "It was him, I know. How many people around here have Rock Cats merch? Tell me. It's got to be somebody after me. Has your motor vehicle guy come up with anything yet?"

"I haven't heard from him. I'll ping him, but it could take him some time to run all the numbers, since he has to sneak it into his regular work without drawing attention from a supervisor." Rand slipped out his phone to send a text message. "Oh, wait a minute. There is a text from Judd: no subject, no message, just an attachment. It's a snap of a computer monitor. Hmm. Surprise, surprise, he found three Mustangs among those Connecticut vanity plates in the list. Let me zoom in on this. Okay, we have Columbo, B. T., Messing, A. L., and Thibault, J."

"Thibault? That's impossible." She put her head in her hands. "He's dead."

"Who's dead?"

"Jess, Jessup Thibault. The guy, my Guy. Only it looks like he's no longer dead, and, see, he's come back for me. My other life didn't end. It's caught up with me. Except it isn't him, can't be. This guy is half the size that Jess was."

"Wait. Chill out, Shan. Maybe whoever he is, he's using Thibault's car. The car's not reported stolen."

"I don't know." She shook her head, the look on her face mixing panic with resolve. "I'm beginning to think I may have to get away, start over, another beginning. And I have to get away from you, before you get caught up in my life, that life."

"Slow down, darling. I'm already caught up in your life, and you're in mine. But what is this all about?"

"It's about survival, and maybe the less you know the better off you are. I did some things in that other life."

"I know about all that. You told me."

"You know about that, but not all of it."

"Then tell me the rest. We're in this together, no matter what. I keep telling you, I want it all with you, the good, the bad, all of it, all of you."

"Are you ready to leave all this,"—she looked up and down the hallway—"to start over with a different life somewhere else, maybe not even in this country? Are you ready for something like that, because that's what it might take, that's what it took for me to get here, walking away from another life, another me, fabricating a new life out of whole cloth. Those . . . those people have long memories, very long."

"Calm down, don't get so far out ahead of yourself. Let's get back to the house, sit down over some hot tea, and sort through what happened. I don't think this is quite the place to go into panic mode."

"It's not panic and it's not a mode. This is . . . this is my life, always beginning, starting over. I did it before. Manhattan. Hartford. I left those lives behind, reinvented myself. I guess I can leave this life behind."

"And me? What about me? Can you leave me behind?"

Shanna stood, mouth open, ready for words that wouldn't come to her. She was fighting for composure when a student approached from behind.

"Doctor McMurphy, do you have minute?" The voice was female, Southern, with a hint of Florida-coast Hispanic. "Could we talk? Maybe in your office?"

"I'm in the midst of something," Rand said. "Sorry. Just send me an email."

"I did. I keep doing it. I just would really like to talk, like. It's . . . it's important."

Shanna surreptitiously wiped at her eyes as she turned to find a petite young woman with black-and-blond streaked undercut hair looking surprised and disappointed. "Hello," Shanna said, a smile growing as she nodded. "Oleander Walston, right?"

"Olee," she said. "I was hoping to get to talk to Professor McMurphy. I didn't mean to interrupt anything. I mean . . ."

Rand's eyes shifted between the two women. "It's all right, Olee, but whatever it is, let's handle it through email. Okay?"

Olee shook her head in an almost microscopic oscillation. "Fuck," she said under her breath as she started to walk past them. "I should've known better than to even try. You guys, you're all alike." She picked up her pace and strode quickly toward the exit.

"See," Rand said to Shanna. "That's the student I was telling you about, the one that keeps trying to see me in private."

"She's got an agenda, all right, but I hate to disappoint you. I don't think she has the hots for you, and I don't get the feeling that she's trying to negotiate for better grades."

"And how do you figure all that?"

"She didn't flirt, didn't once touch her hair, and she didn't have that look. No, her look was worry, not want. I think she has a problem, one she figures you might be able to help her with."

Rand looked skeptical. "Really? Maybe I should . . ."

"Maybe you should."

"But we were headed home. We really need to talk. That's what you said."

"We do, but I also need some time to think."

"I know what those words mean, my Shanna Grace. You'll drop it and later tell me it was nothing, and we'll be right back to the beginning again. As always."

"No, we'll talk. I promise."

His eyes narrowed, but he nodded in agreement. "Okay, I'll see you back at the house. Take my car."

"No, that's all right. I have my bike."

"No. That guy from Connecticut is still around. Take the Civic. And remember about what's in the . . ." He left the rest of the sentence unfinished.

"I'll be careful. Don't worry about me. We can talk later. You go see if you can find out what your student is worried about."

"Probably her quiz grade."

"Oh, I think it's a lot more than that."

ɞ Chapter 10

SHANNA WAS ON HIGH alert again as she crossed the parking lot. Approaching the Civic, she pressed the button on the key fob and checked her surroundings once more before getting in and starting the car. At the East Campus exit she turned left toward Racine circle, slipping smartly into the now heavy traffic heading into Taggertsville. She could not stop herself from repeatedly checking the mirror. Not until she pulled into the drive at the house did she allow herself to start to relax.

She jumped at the touch of something cold against her neck.

"My, you are the nervous type." The voice was high and hoarse. "Now what would you have to be so jumpy about? What, this little thing?"

In the mirror, Shanna saw a small gloved hand gesture with Rand's pistol.

"Nice of you to leave this. And lucky me, the lock on the glove compartment is broken. This'll make the story ever so much easier to write. The boyfriend's gun. His prints, I assume. How's he going to wiggle out of that?"

"Who are you? What do you want?"

"You know fuckin' well who I am. You ran a make on my car, even."

"Thibault. How the hell . . .?"

"You think your boyfriend is the only one with registry connections? Since you left, there's been a few shuffles up in Hartford. No one accesses those record systems without triggering an alert that goes right to the right people. That was the last straw, what you and your boyfriend pulled. You always think you're so fuckin' smart, changing your name and everything. Didn't work, did it, Louise?"

"I'm not—"

"Shut up, Louise. Let's go into the house without any funny business. Nothing like what you pulled on my brother. Now, just shut up and let's go inside without making a scene and have a nice little talk about old times."

Shanna's mind sprinted through options. If she made a move now, it might get the neighbors' attention, but it was also likely to get her killed before anyone could do anything. With the gun nudging her, she started toward the house thinking about what was in it and how she might take advantage of what she knew. She stopped. The muzzle jabbed her painfully in her back. "No, we better go around back," she said. "More private, no neighbors to notice."

The slider from the deck into the kitchen was unlocked. As they entered, Shanna jammed the slider closed on Thibault's outstretched arm and made a dash for the small bedroom that was now the home office she shared with Rand. She jammed her desk chair under the door knob as she grabbed the big packet off Rand's desk and dumped the contents. The Luger was in a large zip lock and the magazine and remaining ammunition were in a smaller one. I hope this still works, she thought, as she ripped the bags open. She was still trying to slip bullets into the magazine when the chair fell to one side under the onslaught of body slams from the other side of the door.

She jammed the partially filled magazine home in the handle of the Luger. As the door gave way and Thibault tumbled into the room, Shanna remembered to thumb off the safety. She landed a vicious kick to the head before Thibault could stand, then stomped on his outstretched right arm, sending Rand's pistol spinning across the bare floor and under the bed. "Stay down," she snapped, pointing the Luger at him. "I'll shoot. You know I can and I will."

"With that antique?"

"With this antique." As she held it she smiled. "This antique, I'll have you know, is actually a beautiful piece of German engineering, as my boyfriend would say. Now who the fuck are you, because you're not Jess Thibault, that much I know."

"No, you bitch, not Jess. You took care of that when you offed him."

"I . . . I didn't kill him. I . . ."

"Don't lie to me, you fuckin' bitch. I saw you shoot him. I was hiding in the next room. I saw you."

"Who are you?"

"You don't remember me? It's me, Jenn, his kid sister. I was home sick from school when you came over that last time. I heard. And I peeked around the corner just as you shot him. I ran out the back to tell uncle Frank next door, but I couldn't find him at first. By the time we got back, both of you were gone. You'd finished the job and . . . you know about when they found the body. I've been trying to track you down ever since."

Shanna was looking at the wiry young woman whom she

had thought was a boy, but her mind was slipping into the past, picturing the Thibault house, with its gables and climbing ivy, and the dining room with its long polished table. Jess had been talking crazy, about changing their carefully concocted plans. When she told him no way, he had grabbed her and began punching her to the floor. He didn't know she had started carrying a gun, and before he could continue, she pulled it out of her jacket and fired up at him. He crumpled and screamed, doubled over in pain. She got up and stood over him. "Don't fuck with me," she had said. "As you limp through the rest of your life, remember that. Don't ever fuck with me." She had left him like that, doubled up on the floor in a pool of spreading blood. That had been the last time she saw him.

Shanna looked at the skinny, baby-faced woman in front of her. "I didn't kill your brother. That must have been the Forte crew. They thought he—"

"I saw you kill him."

"I knee-capped him. He was alive when I left him, though I wouldn't say alive and well. If he was gone when you got back from looking for your uncle, whoever did him must have heard the shots and taken him away to finish the job. I know how he ended up, and I can tell you, I had nothing to do with that." She took a deep breath and tried not to picture the shipping crate with his dismembered body stuffed inside to rot. "But now, I have a real problem, which is you. You know who I am and that I was once someone else. That's not good."

The sound of the front door opening startled both of them. Jenn Thibault scrambled toward the doorway as Shanna raised the Luger and squeezed the trigger.

Click.

Shanna was trying to figure out what had happened, as the woman ran out through the back and disappeared into the dusk. The cocking lever! She remembered Rand pulling it back. She was just tugging it up and back when Rand entered the bedroom.

"Hey, be careful with that. You know what happened to our deck railing." He looked around. "What the hell has been happening here?"

"She got away. Out the back."

"She? Who are you talking about?"

"Jenner Thibault, Jess Thibault's kid sister. She's the one who's been stalking me. She saw me shoot Jess and has spent years trying to track me down."

"Hang on there. I always thought you had nothing to do with that guy's death."

"I didn't. I didn't kill him. I shot him in the knee with a peashooter of a little handgun. It was enough to teach him not to play games with me but not enough to finish him off." She gestured with the gun in her hand.

"Hey, careful with that thing." He reached out for the Luger, which she turned and handed to him. "You shot the guy? I thought . . . I think we have a lot of things to talk about, but first, let me retrieve my Glock from the car and check out behind the house."

"It's not in the car; it's under the bed. He . . . she had it. I tried to shoot her with the Luger."

໖

As Rand came back in through the back slider, he tucked his Glock into his waistband. "No sign of her. We should call the police and get a bulletin out on her car. Shouldn't be too hard to spot a black-and-yellow Mustang with palindromic plates from Connecticut."

"No, we're not going to do that."

"Shanna, this is serious, real. We gotta call this in."

"No. She knows. She knows who I am. That makes her a threat to both of us if she talks to the police. I don't know what to do about her, but we can't get the police in on this."

"Then what are we going to do, launch our own private manhunt?"

"Or get out of town as soon as possible. In the meantime, we need to be on guard."

"On guard?" Rand gave her his you-gotta-be-kidding look. "You mean more vigilant than normal? Like in normal for you?"

"Look, you knew what you were getting into with me."

"Not when I got into it, but now that I know, I guess I'm stuck with you." He looked down at his hands. "I'll admit I'm scared, and I'm probably crazy, but I'm with you." He took her in his arms.

Shanna shuddered for a second, then finally let go of the tension and allowed herself to melt into his strong arms and to feel his big hands sliding over her body. It was a primitive response to a close call, but pressed against his body, with the pressure of his growing erection on her belly, she started getting turned on. "I want you in me."

He didn't argue.

As they made desperate and hurried love in their shared office, the house was being watched through binoculars from the trees just beyond the reach of the floodlights on the rear deck.

༄

Shanna rubbed morning sleep from her eyes as she entered the kitchen. "Smells wonderful. Is there any aroma on earth that beats bacon on the griddle?"

"I can think of some close seconds, but I'm not in the mood for debate." He gave her a broad grin. "Your tea's on the table—English Breakfast—and the eggs will be done in a minute. Then let's talk over a quick breakfast before we have to leave for classes."

"Are you sure? Maybe we should cancel, take a sick day to sort out things."

"No, we're better off where there are lots of people around. I've already alerted Gus Creller at University Security to be on the lookout for Thibault around campus." He sat down and started in on his breakfast. "I'm betting," he said between bites, "she's carrying, and I'm betting she does not have a concealed-carry permit. And who knows what the local finest can turn up once they look into her record. I know you don't want the police involved, but Gus is chill and I think we'll be all right." He wolfed down the last of his bacon and eggs. "We better stick to schedule, as my sweetheart always says, helps keep entropy at bay."

Shanna was thinking that entropy and disorder were the only unstoppable forces, but she nodded. "You think I should start carrying?"

"Maybe. We can look into it. As I now understand, you already know how to use a handgun, even if you don't know the meaning of *geladen*." He winked at her.

"You know," she said, "it's all a false sense of security: the campus cops, a handgun, crowds."

"What isn't?" he said. "It's all about the sense of it, that feeling of confidence that allows you to move forward. That's the only security on offer in the real world."

"Mmm. Maybe. And here I was just starting to think there might be room for the real thing in our future."

"There is. We just have to stick close and stay open. I better get my stuff together and get over to my office. I have a meeting with that student at nine."

"That student? Are we talking about the young woman with the worried look?"

"Yeah. I caught up with her yesterday, and you were right. She does have a problem. Something to do with a faculty member—male, of course—and maybe inappropriate advances, but I don't know the details yet. She wants to talk with me because I know the law, so maybe it's complicated. And she seems to trust me. I'll find out."

"I'll go in with you. I don't want to stay here alone. I can hang out in the library until my class. There are always others around."

"We really need to report this whole thing," he said. "We should have done that right away, last night."

"Right, like to the local Keystone Kops?" She smirked. "They're going to help? No, it just risks bringing the whole life of Louise tumbling back down on top of me, and then where am I? Where are we? Nobody now at the university besides you knows my backstory, and I'll do almost anything to keep it that way."

"Does that include getting rid of Thibault? It's hard for me to picture you killing anyone."

"Not so hard for me. What would you do to survive? How far would you go? You keep a handgun in your car. I assume that means you would be ready to use it if necessary."

"If necessary. But I was trained that deadly force is a last resort." He looked up suddenly.

"What is it?"

"Outside. A few of my students from Intro Forensics." He glanced at his watch. "I forgot I told them to show up first thing this morning. I was going to have them go over the back deck as if it were a crime scene and when they find it, see if they can recover the bullet from the railing. Then later I'll have them do ballistics to confirm it was fired by our Luger. Change of pace for a class that was spending too much time listening to me drone on. I hope you don't mind. I can put it off if you want."

"No, it's okay. I do wish you had told me, but, actually, having a bunch of your students in my backyard is comforting. Who knows, they might even find something from our night visitor. I'll let you go supervise while I get ready. Then I'll ride in with you."

Rand dumped his dishes in the sink and opened the back slider. "Good morning, guys. I'll be right with you."

"No prob, Professor." Tariq Wei, whose name and face said his family story was complicated, was the self-appointed spokesman of the group of volunteers. Tightly wound Fran Seeborg was off by herself, pacing in impatient circles, while Bobby-Jo Janowitz was intent on Tariq as she played with her red hair. Rand turned back to Shanna. "Love it how the group dynamics play out." She nodded, turned, and headed for the bedroom.

"All right, people," he said as he stepped onto the deck. "We're going to pretend this is a crime scene where there has been a shooting. We'll walk the grid looking for shell casings and bullet holes, and we'll see if we can recover any bullet and work out the probable trajectory by sight. Okay?"

"Okay, Professor. Should we just start?"

"Yeah, divide up the area and holler when you find any-thing. I'll be right here if you need me."

The three students debated how they would divide up the work, then started the slow examination of the backyard. Fran, who had the section of the deck nearest the sliding door, quickly found the splintered hole where the bullet from the Luger had embedded itself in the railing. Rand called the others to leave off their searches. He showed them how to use a rod in the hole to eyeball the trajectory before demonstrating how to extract the bullet doing as little dam-age as possible.

He bagged the bullet, labeled it, and set it aside. "You might as well finish the job. Just pick up wherever you left off."

He was flipping through messages on his phone when Tariq called out. "Should we do the same thing with this oth-er one?"

"What other one?" Rand stepped off the deck and walked over to where Tariq was stooped, pointing at one of the pres-sure-treated support beams resting on the footings.

"This one. Isn't that another bullet hole? Looks different, but I thought . . ."

Rand bent in close. "You thought right. It does look like a bullet hole, but not as recent. See the darkening around the edge and the dirt in the hole."

"Want me to try extracting it?"

"Ah, I think I better do this."

The entry hole was clean, and Fran and Bobby-Jo, were quickly able to use a rod to get a bead on a chest-high spot at the tree line. It took some time to dig out the bullet, which looked like another 9 millimeter parabellum round, like the one he had accidentally discharged when trying to disarm the Luger. "Good work, people. Tariq, you finish walking the grid, while you two check out that spot at the tree line. And keep a lookout for shell casings."

Rand slipped the two labeled poly bags into his pocket, and went back into the house. Shanna was waiting at the kitchen table. She looked up from her notes. "How did it go?"

"Curiouser and curiouser," he said. "We found a second bullet embedded in the deck."

ᴀᴏ Chapter 11

WHEN RAND ARRIVED at his office after dropping off Shanna at the library, Olee Walston was sitting cross-legged on the floor beside the door, thumb-typing on her phone. "You been waiting long?" he said. "I thought we were set for nine o'clock."

"We were. I just didn't want to miss you. Or keep you waiting." She scissored herself erect and slipped her phone into the back pocket of her slashed-knee jeans.

"Well, then, come on in." He unlocked the door and held it for her. "Grab a chair and tell me what this is all about. Are you in some kind of trouble?"

"It's not me. I can handle myself."

"I'm sure you can. So what's the problem?"

"Can we close the door?"

He shook his head. "Ah, 'fraid not. Not if it's just you and me talking. Doesn't look good. But don't worry. You saw how deserted we are at this hour back here in the slums the school sets aside for us part-time scholars. No one is going to hear. So, what's up?"

"It's . . . it's a friend. She's pregnant."

"Why are you telling me? Does this look like Student Health Services?"

"Because you know about legal stuff. See, I'm pretty sure I

know who the father is, and he's . . . well, he's one of the professors."

"Then your friend should take this up with him, shouldn't she. And if she has a complaint against him, she should file it with the university."

"That's the problem. She'd never file against him. I'm the only one she's told. She's in love and thinks he's in love with her."

"Doesn't matter. Such relationships between faculty and students are strictly forbidden, even if it's supposedly consensual. University policy is clear on this."

"But, I'm wondering about the law. I mean, do I get in trouble if I, like, say something? And if I make an anonymous report, will it be taken seriously?"

"I think a report could be made in a way that would be taken seriously."

"I don't know. I don't trust people, and I trust, like, schools and stuff even less."

He smiled. "But you're trusting me."

"That's different. You remind me of my brother. He's a cop, too, probably the only good one I ever met."

"Well, I would say most cops are good."

"Not in my world, not where I grew up. Cops were the ones my dad was always dodging. My brother is why I'm talking with you, since you were a cop, but you're not anymore, plus I see how you are with students. You seem to care."

Rand nodded. "I try. What made you think all cops are bad—your brother excepted? Where did you grow up? Not around here."

"South Florida. How much time you got? It's a long story."

"I got the time if you do. Tell me. If you want."

"Well, my mother was Mexican-American, and my dad was a lost soul, a grifter and drifter from Louisiana who semi settled down and fed his family by fishing, mostly illegally. He'd disappear on his little fishing boat—sometimes for days—and come back with ice chests full of fish, specialty premium stuff to sell to restaurants, plus spiny lobsters. They were the easy pickings compared to what he had to get with his spear gun. The lobsters, you just pick 'em up off the bottom. Not worth much, nobody seemed to want 'em then, so we ate 'em. Lots."

"You grew up poor but eating lobster all the time?"

"Trash food. To this day, I can't stand lobster or crab in any form. You grow tired of it. Didn't matter however many chiles my mom would cook it with. I'd complain, but I was hungry, and my father would raise a silent hand to shut me up. In my first sixteen years, my father might have said, like, sixteen words to me and my brother. Then he made up for lost time."

"What happened then?"

"My mother was in the country illegally. They deported her. My brother and me were about to leave for school this one morning when the immigration people just showed up to haul her away. They wanted to know where my father was. We lied, said he was at the store and would be back any minute. We were afraid he'd get in trouble and we'd end up in foster or something. I could see by this guy's face that he didn't believe me, but they really didn't care. If my father wasn't around, they'd have to wait until some social services people showed up for us, and they wanted to just get on with doing their job of wrecking families, keeping America safe from illegals. Know what I mean?"

"I guess I do."

"Yeah, well, Ramone and me were really scared and didn't know whether we should get to school like everything was fine at home or wait for my father to come home."

"You keep saying 'my father'."

"Yeah, well he was. Ramone's dad was my mom's first. Hector. She talked about him sometimes with Ramone when my father was out, but I never met him. Anyway, we go to school, pretend everything's cool. We're back home and my father still isn't back, which either meant it was a good trip and he just kept fishing, or it was a bad day and he was still trying to catch something.

"Finally he arrives, smelling of salt-spray and sweat and fish, with one ice chest full of spiny lobster and a single grouper. Bad day. He was not happy. Went to the kitchen looking for mama, comes back, looks at us, and says, 'Where?' Not a man of words, as I said. We told him, and he started screaming at us. It was our fault, he yelled, because we had wanted to go to school and pretend like we were normal, like other people, instead of just working the boat with him like he wanted. That's how the immigration people found out, he claimed, why they took her away.

"I swear, he screamed at us for a couple of days, non-stop, wouldn't let us go to school, not even out of the house. Then one morning he grabbed his spear gun and diving gear, went down to his boat, and took off. He never came back. A month later they found his boat in Cuban waters with the ice chests empty."

"What about you and your brother?"

"He had just turned eighteen and was about to start

community college in the fall. Ramone was smart and quick on his feet. He petitioned the court and managed to get custody of me. We squeaked by for the two years it took him to get his associate's degree, then he joined the local police force, and I got a scholarship to Holcomb. Haven't been home since. Can't afford to travel."

"You haven't seen your brother?"

"We write. But he's not much of a writer. Not a talker, either, like my father in that. I think he's got a girlfriend, and he sends me a few bucks now and then."

"Can I ask? How do you get by now?"

"My scholarship, and"—she laughed—"I mooch a lot, plus I work in the library. I see your wife in there quite a bit."

"We're not married. Not yet."

"That's what my father always said. 'Not yet,' he'd say, as if he ever intended to. Ramone's dad never married my mom either. It's a guy thing, I guess."

"For some, I suppose. But look, back to your friend and the faculty member she's involved with. What do you want to do? Do you want to tell me who it is?"

Olee glanced toward the open door. "You're right. It's probably none of my business."

"I didn't say that. If you want, I can deal with this guy. If it's true, that he's sleeping with a student, I can report it, start an investigation."

"If it's true? That's the way it always goes, isn't it? I already told you, Sandi . . . I mean my friend, is pregnant by this guy."

"Okay. Do you want to tell me who it is, or do you want to make a report yourself? Or convince this Sandi to do it?"

"What if . . . will I get in trouble? I can't afford to lose my scholarship."

"You won't."

"Okay, I'll tell you. But you have to leave me out of it. Okay?"

"Okay, but I will have to do my own checking before I risk making a false accusation."

"There you go again. Nobody believes a woman. I told you what happened."

"I believe you, but remember, I was a cop, and we go by the book. Your brother would probably understand. Okay?"

"Okay." She dropped her head, then raised it to look Rand squarely in the eyes. "It's the chemistry guy, the tall one. I saw her with him and she talks about him."

"You mean Stieg? Professor Rolandson?" Rand laughed. "That's . . ."

"Is this funny?"

"It's just a little hard to picture. I hadn't thought of him as the type."

"What does that mean? What's the type?"

Rand put up his hands in mock surrender. "I didn't mean anything by it. I suppose there isn't a look that can identify a predator. At any rate, I'll start working on it, I promise. And I won't bring you into it. No one has to know how I first found out. Okay?"

Olee pushed her chair back and stood without speaking. "I hope," she said after several seconds, "that you really are like Ramone."

"Your brother?"

"Yes."

"Well, if that means can you trust me, then I am like Ramone."

ೞ

Stieg Rolandson was wrapping up a lecture on organic chemistry when Rand showed up at the back of the classroom. Rand watched closely as a covey of students approached the raised demonstration platform at the front to ask questions or plead for time extensions. None of the young women seemed noticeably pregnant. As Rand walked forward, Stieg looked over the heads of the students and gave him a solemn nod.

Rand waited until the crowd cleared out before ambling down to the front of the lecture hall.

"You're back soon," Stieg said. "More forensic chem questions?"

"Not really, more like personal questions." Stieg looked him in the eyes but said nothing, so Rand just continued. "Should I just cut to the chase?" Stieg raised his angled eyebrows in answer, leaving Rand on his own to hold up the conversation. "Okay, so, are you sleeping with one of your students?"

"No." He started stacking his lecture notecards. "Is that why you came here?"

"Yeah, pretty much. But I've heard that you're having an affair with one of your students, knocked her up."

"No, I'm not having an affair. Are we done here? I have a meeting to prep for."

Rand was watching Stieg's face intently, but there was no tell, no twitch that might say he was lying or nervous. "Does the name Sandi Besslar mean anything to you?"

"Yes."

"And?"

"And what? She was in my Special Projects Seminar last

year. Very bright, enthusiastic about physical chemistry. She dropped out."

"Maybe she dropped out because she got pregnant."

Stieg inhaled slowly. "I didn't know she was pregnant." He stuffed the notecards into the pocket of his lab coat. "And now I must be going. I'll make allowance for your being an ex-cop and pretend this interrogation never happened." He started to walk away, but Rand reached out and took his arm. Stieg looked down at Rand's hand with evident disapproval, and Rand let go.

"We're friends, Stieg. I would hope we'd be honest with each other."

"We played poker together three times, Rand. You asked for my help with some slightly skewed investigation about a vintage handgun. That's it, the sum total. Oh, yes, and now you confront me with an accusation."

"It wasn't an accusation, it was—"

"An inquisition then? Call it what you will, but next time get your stories straight before you start impugning the reputation or integrity of a colleague. That's what I am, a colleague, not a friend, certainly not after this." He looked down at Rand, eyes narrowed, then stepped down from the platform and marched out the side door.

Rand stood in the empty room for several seconds, a look of puzzlement on his face. When he looked up toward the back of the room, he noticed that someone had entered the lecture hall while he and Stieg had been talking. It was Olee Walston.

"He's lying," she said, as he passed her on the way out.

He stopped and turned. "What do you want me to do, accuse a colleague of lying?"

"Talk to Sandi. Obviously you figured out who she is."

"I'll think about it?"

"You'll think about it. I've heard that version of a copout more times than I can count."

"Not a copout. I'll think about it."

The knock on Shanna's office door startled her out of a murky waking dream. She slid open her desk drawer and laid her hand on the Luger, checking that the engraved tab was protruding, that there was a round in the chamber. This time it was ready. "Yes?"

"It's me." It was Rand. "You all right?"

"Uh, yeah, just doing some thinking." She silently slid the drawer closed.

The doorknob rattled. "You going to let me in? Or should I just stand sentry duty out here."

"I'm sorry." She rose and opened the door for him. "I'm jumpy, just being cautious. Thibault knows who I am and would have no problem tracking me here. After all, she let herself into your car while it was parked in the South Lot."

"It's okay. Maybe we should get you a handgun."

"I already have one." She reached back over the desk and opened the top drawer.

He leaned forward to look in. "Not exactly what I had in mind, something you could carry in your backpack and keep handy. Maybe like a Sig Sauer. The little P238 even comes in colors."

"Designed by men, no doubt, who think women want to make a fashion statement with their deadly self-defense. Like those idiot industrial designers who came up with a line of pink power tools."

"And what color would you want?"

"In power tools or pistols?"

"Well, let's go with self-defense now and save do-it-yourself for later."

"Black, like yours, same ammo. The Glock 43 got good reviews."

"So, you've been researching this."

"Damn straight. You don't think I want to depend on that damn Nazi antique, do you? It's just what I had at hand. That's how I do life. You play the hand you're dealt. Well, until you can swap decks or pull an ace from up your sleeve."

"Speaking of card games," he said, "I don't think I'll be playing poker again with Stieg Rolandson."

"Why not?"

"According to our dear Oleander Walston, he's been having an affair with a student. I confronted him about it, he denied it, and then icily dismissed me."

"Stieg Rolandson, the chemistry professor? The one the students call The Undertaker?"

"The very one. So, your crack about Oleander being pretty but dangerous was on the mark, but not for the reasons you might have thought at the time."

"Who do you believe? Was he lying?"

"Oddly, I don't think so, although I'll admit he's a hard one to read. I haven't talked with the student yet. Olee thinks I should."

"And what do you think?"

"You know me. It's hard for me to just drop something without pursuing it to some kind of conclusion."

"Yeah, I remember that about you." She sighed. "So, what are we going to do about Jenn Thibault. I don't think a restraining order would mean much, and I don't see how we can live like this, jumping at every knock on the door or dodging shadows for the indefinite future."

"I still say we should go to the police."

"And what will they do? I've been reading up on stalker cases. Sooner or later, the police back off and then the ex-boyfriend or whoever finishes the job. I'd rather be proactive on my own."

"Well, then, we need to look at a bunch of little things that might make a difference, like varying our routines, installing an alarm system, getting you your own handgun. I've already put the campus police on alert. To get a conceal carry permit, you'll need to take gun safety training."

"I already signed up."

∞ Chapter 12

SHANNA WAS JUST opening her office when Marti Rossum came down the hall, pumping her short legs to catch up. "Sorry I haven't gotten that material together that I promised to you," she said. "Maybe it was all a bad idea. Besides, it's suddenly become hectic for me, even if I'm not teaching."

"No problem. I have plenty on my plate as is."

"It sounds like we could both use a little destressing. How would you . . . ah, you and Rand . . . how would you like to swing by for drinks at the end of the day. Nothing fancy or special, just get a chance to unwind."

"That sounds very appealing, but I'll have to check with Rand. He's got this insane teaching load this term. Where do you live?"

"It's 19 Parkridge Drive. It's only a few minutes up the road. You'll see the Parkridge sign just past the Weberton turnoff. Can't miss it."

"Okay, I'll text you one way or another after I hear from Rand."

"You're welcome to come over either way, plus one or not."

"Thanks. I'll let you know."

∞

Shanna turned in at the carved granite sign that marked the

entrance to Parkridge Estates, a Southwest-themed development of upscale homes. Parkridge Drive turned out to be a meander with frequent speed bumps that would have made it difficult to exceed the "strictly enforced" speed limit. At number 19, a modern two-level with a faux adobe exterior and a detached three-car garage to one side, Shanna pulled into the circular drive and stopped at the front entrance. She was thinking that not all Holcomb professors were as poor as church mice, when Marti opened the front door and beckoned for her to come in.

"Perfect timing, Shanna. Welcome. Rand couldn't make it?"

"He sends his regrets. He's behind on marking papers and changed his mind at the last minute, which does tend to be his style."

"Well, we girls will just have to make the best of it. I hope you like strawberry margaritas, as that's what I have waiting on the deck out back. Of course, I can come up with something else. Wine, bourbon, Tito's Handmade, name your poison. Just don't ask for a Cheerwine Shot. I'm a Minnesota transplant and I go only so far to fit in with the local drinking morés."

"A margarita would hit the spot. And speaking of which, this is a nice spot. Quite the well-groomed community. Beautiful house."

"I moved up and out after my father died. Selling his house in Minneapolis brought more than expected and, well, real estate down here is much less expensive. So, I figured Natalie and I might as well. These days, I kind of rattle around in a house that's way more than I need. Not sure what the next move will be, but I hold onto the place because

. . . well, a part of me still clings to hope that Natalie might return. Anyway, come on in. I'll show you the place."

The interior was finished in hacienda styling, all exposed beams, textured plaster, and dark-stained wood accents, with furnishings to match. The walls were everywhere arrayed with artwork—mostly oils and watercolors, some pencil drawings—many recognizable to Shanna as early twentieth century modernism. She approached the nearest wall, stopping before several works, looking for names she might recognize. "You have quite the gallery here," Shanna said.

"Inherited, not all to my taste, but my father collected art, which was one of the early influences on my own interests. Did I tell you that story? For him, it was background, something he did. And he was always collecting, mostly obscure, minor works, mostly smaller pieces like these. There was a also a certain amount of turnover. I don't think he cared much for or about any of the pieces. In any case, he made some savvy investments and left behind a bigger estate than I would have expected. All in all, he was always somewhat of a mystery. In most ways." She stared in silence at the painting in front of her, a portrait of a young woman done entirely in blue-gray shades.

She faced Shanna with a social smile. "Shall we repair to the back and a little relaxation?" Marti gestured toward the French doors opening onto a spacious deck facing a walled-in back yard.

෮

After the second margarita, the conversation turned from departmental scuttlebutt to Marti's daughter, Natalie.

"She was always smart and strong. As a mother, I felt like I was running to keep up and largely at her mercy. She had ways of getting what she wanted—with me, with her grand-father, and with men in general, at every age. She adored her grandfather, although she cooled toward him when she reached middle school and became really negative about him after he died."

"She studied here at Holcomb, right?"

"Yes. She started out in pre-med, but then back-peddled to go into nursing. I never quite understood what sent her down the various rabbit trails she followed. At one time she was going to be an astronaut, then a chemist, then she got into art preservation and restoration. All her passions were passing, but total and all-consuming while they lasted. Boys, too. She fell in love fast and moved on with equal speed."

"And she took off with some guy, right?"

"She did. Preston Fender,"—she sucked in air and scowled—"a middle-aged professor of French and German, who, if the stories sifting down from the administration are to be believed, stood accused of sexual harassment. I des-pised the man, and I don't understand what Natalie ever saw in him, much less why she would run away with him. He must have been some kind of Svengali." Marti stared into her nearly empty glass and looked to be on the edge of tears. "I should have seen it coming. She was spending more and more time with him, some project, and we were fighting and arguing almost daily. And then . . . gone without a word. She just vanished, disappeared from the planet. I . . . I try not to think of the worst."

Shanna cocked her head and looked into Marti's eyes. "I can scarcely imagine how hard it must be."

Marti straightened her shoulders, drained her glass, and forced a smiled. "But I didn't invite you here to share a good cry. How about another drink and a change of topics."

Shanna placed her hand above her glass. "Thanks, I'm good, gotta drive home. But help yourself. And tell me more about your book. How's that going?"

"Oh, let's not go *there*. Enough about me and art and family history. What's doing in your life? How are you and Rand?"

"Rand and I are doing well, as well as can be expected given that we hardly see each other. You know how it goes with the end of the school year and everything is hitting at once. Rand and I are both looking forward to slowing down over the summer, maybe helping you get back in touch with your daughter. Oops, didn't mean to . . ."

"That's okay. I keep intending to put together a packet for you, but, well, as you can see, it's still an open sore for me. But I'll get to it, I promise."

"No hurry. When you get the time."

∞

The next day, a thick packet from Marti Rossum was waiting in Shanna's faculty mail cubby. The open mail slots in the lounge, mostly used for flyers and other low-priority material, were certainly not more secure than email, but it occurred to Shanna that at least this way there would be no digital trace in the university's email system. Perhaps that was the logic behind Marti's insistence on physically passing the material.

It was tempting to open the envelope immediately, but Shanna knew how easily she could be drawn into the hyper-focused pursuit of puzzles. She detoured to drop the package at her office before her second lecture of the day, a heavily revised version of one of Professor Freedman's sessions from his "World at War" history course. She had finally given up trying to follow his terribly dated syllabus and had begun to slip in topics of her own, shifting the emphasis from names, dates, and battles to social, political, and economic impacts, particularly drawing on the work of her fellow quantitative historians. The results had been mixed. Weekly quiz scores were trending upward, but class attendance had declined.

Earlier in the day, Rand had advised her to bring back more of Freedman's graphic slides from key battles. "Images of exploding bombs and bloodbaths are a lot more engaging than crosstabs of numbers," he had said, rubbing it in.

"That's a very male perspective on class engagement."

"Look at the demographics. Whose taking your course? I'd bet it's mostly guys."

"You'd lose the bet. It's about an even split."

"Well, then, that's probably because you're teaching it, a draw for your fangirls."

"Maybe, but then I seem to be disappointing pretty much everyone with my lectures."

"You're being hard on yourself. You've been shoehorned into someone else's subject, and it's just not you. You need to find a way to make it your own."

"So says the adjunct instructor whose by-the-book courses come straight from the can."

"Ouch. Now that hurts. I don't have time for a lot of customization, what with carrying not only my regular course but also two that I've never taught before."

At the time, she had given him a poor-poor-boy pout and a hug, nudged him toward the door, and then immediately set about sorting through her PowerPoint deck and restoring some of the Freedman photos of trench warfare for the afternoon lecture.

∞

Shanna dragged herself up the stairs and down the hallway after a lecture that had staggered from one awkward moment to the next. The last minute shuffle of her slides had thrown off her timing, and she had to rush through the last third of the lecture, the part that she considered the most important. At least she had the packet of material from Marti to look forward to.

The office door was unlocked and the envelope was not on her desk. She had a moment of panic as she tried to remember exactly what she had done when she had swung by the office earlier. She was sure she had left it atop the desk, but now she went through all the desk drawers and even riffled through the filing cabinet. Had someone come in and taken it? It was inconceivable that cleaning staff would have touched anything on her desk. Besides, they never came in until after eight at night. No, she must have misremembered or misplaced it. What could she do? She certainly couldn't tell Marti, "Oh, I can't find all that material on your missing daughter. Any chance you have copies?"

She started a top-to-bottom search of the office. It took her all of fifteen minutes to examine every box, shelf, drawer, and cabinet in the small room. Nothing.

Now you've really done it, she told herself. You must have left the door unlocked, maybe open, and some student walking by must have grabbed it on impulse. A fat manila envelope? What a tempting object. No that made no sense. As she mentally sorted through scenarios, her sense of panic rose to a pounding crescendo.

Her head was in her hands when Rand walked in carrying the envelope. "Interesting stuff. Hope it's all right with you that I grabbed the thing to get a head start on making sense of this case. You must have been in a hurry, because you left the door ajar."

Her face reddened from embarrassment and irritation. "You know, you almost sent me into a tailspin. I couldn't find the envelope and couldn't imagine what might have happened to it. I've been beating up on myself for misplacing it and tearing the place apart trying to find it."

"Sorry. I figured you would guess I had it."

"You should've left me a note or something."

"Yeah, I suppose, but I also assumed I'd be back here before you finished your lecture, but I got caught up in reading all the material and thinking about what happened."

Shanna took a deep yoga-inspired cleansing breath. "Okay, you're forgiven. This time. So, what's it all about."

"Take a look yourself, come to your own conclusions, and let's compare notes tonight. I have two more classes to teach." He crossed to the door, then turned back. "This could be messier and more complicated than we thought."

"Isn't it always?"

"The way of the world," he said on his way out.

Shanna pushed her notes for the next class to one side and slid the contents of the envelope out onto her desk. There were three color-coded file folders, each about a quarter inch thick. The green one, labeled PI, contained invoices and correspondence from one C. T. Deverell, Licensed Private Investigator. Shanna whistled at the amounts in the invoices. How many on the faculty, even full professors, could afford to sustain such expenditures? Then again, she wondered, what would I be willing to sacrifice if it were my daughter who disappeared?

She studied the reports, fourteen in all, each filling several single-spaced pages with detailed chronologies and observations that added up to little of any substance. C. T. Deverell was a thorough investigator but a master of uninspired, wordy, and often ungrammatical reporting. Natalie Rossum had last been seen on campus "in the company of which with one of the professors, later identified as one A. Preston Fender, Professor of Modern Languages." Natalie had withdrawn the maximum daily limit from her bank account on three successive days "by the means of a single ATM machine in Taggertsville" and was later identified as having purchased a bus ticket to New York using cash. Airline records showed that three months later she flew to Paris on the same Air France flight as "one said A. P. Fender, presumably the aforementioned Asst. Prof., Mod. Lang." "Subsequent to arrival in France, said professor did rent/lease a single-bedroom apartment unit located in the 17th Arrondissement section of the city of Paris, France." Apparently, Natalie and the professor lived there together, but neither had been seen by neighbors after the first few months and the apartment was "discovered to have been abandoned at some prior point of time when eventually and finally accessed again by the landlord after expiry of the lease and/or rental agreement occurred."

The bottom line was that the circumlocutious and grammatically challenged detective Deverell had been unable to track them further "possibly aggravated by linguistically and/or cultural barriers making effective engagement with appropriate local informants, civilian or otherwise, not infrequently uninformative." Shanna smiled at the thought of a somewhat clumsy private eye stumbling around Paris unable to speak French.

The blue folder contained a mix of news clippings, screen shots of articles from the Web, and photocopies of family photos and documents, including immigration papers for Marti's parents, Able Rothman and Marie Halévy, birth certificates for Martin and Martine Rossum, and a court decree making official the change of surname from Rothman to Rossum. The birth certificate for Natalie notably omitted the name of the father. There were a few photos of Able and Marie and a plethora of pictures of Natalie at various ages documenting her growing resemblance to her mother as she got older. A printout of the faculty page for A. Preston Fender included a formal headshot of a boyishly handsome man with dark curly hair and thick eyebrows to match. Fender, who grew up in Vermont, had studied at the Université de Montréal and done his graduate work at McGill. So, the French connection deepens, Shanna thought.

The news stories included local coverage in the Taggerts County Chronicle and the student-run Holcomb Clarion about the scandal involving Fender and accusations of inappropriate behavior with students, varying from sexual innuendo to a full-on affair with an unnamed student. Shanna assumed the student was Natalie.

Suddenly inspired, Shanna turned to her computer and accessed the Holcomb historical archives. Using her faculty access, she opened the archived faculty directory for the year before Natalie had disappeared and searched for Fender. A familiar address leapt off the screen. His listed residence was on Racine circle where she and Rand now lived.

Why had he not shown up when she had checked for previous owners? She did a mental face-palm. Apparently because he had not been an owner but a renter, maybe under an informal arrangement that didn't show up in any of her searches. That was the problem: she had allowed herself to fall into the lazy habit of using straightforward searches of official sources and databases instead of creative research outside the check boxes. What else might she learn if she opened her eyes and widened her search?

She glanced at her watch and cursed. Ten minutes until class and she hadn't done any prep. Well, Shanna, she told herself, that's what you're good at, winging it, making it up as you go along. Besides this is your course and you've done it before. Make it an interactive session, turning the tables and getting the students to talk about the readings. Whatever. Get them to pose questions for themselves. Maybe you should do that too, oh smart one.

As Shanna gathered up the folders to restore them to the envelope, some inkjet-printed photos slipped out of the third folder, the red one labeled "AFTER." They were copies of vintage photos, one that appeared to be an outdoor close-up headshot of Able Rothman as a younger man, a military-style building, like a barracks, artfully blurred in the background. The man's head was turned slightly, his eyes focused in the distance. A shadow fell at a diagonal across his face. It had the feeling of a carefully posed and composed art photo more than a snapshot, and there was something disturbingly familiar about it, not so much the subject but the technique, which showed acute attention to light and shadow at the same time as being at a remove from the subject, as if it were not a person but an object in a still life.

She recognized that form of artful detachment, the studied style that she knew from growing up with a father who was an award-winning photojournalist, acclaimed for his compelling portrayal of real people but himself a misanthrope for whom human beings were objects, subjects to be preserved in silver halide, museum pieces to be fixed on paper but not understood.

The other picture, a printout of a grainy and streaked wartime photograph, showed a group of prisoners with their American GI liberators. With one exception, the unsmiling prisoners were emaciated and unkempt. A man with a relatively clean face and fuller cheeks, stood at the back with a hand on the shoulder of the ragged reed of a girl in front of him. On his bare left arm at his side, his tattooed prisoner number was partially visible. It was hard to be certain, but it did look like the man could be the young Able Rothman. Shanna turned it over. A scribbled note read "them" and below, in Marti's poster-perfect lettering: "in stuff Natalie left behind. Why?"

∞

Shanna's last lecture of the day had been a chorus of chaos. Maybe I'm losing it, she thought, as she headed back to her office. Maybe I can't play 'Let's Pretend' like I used to. She knew part of her problem had been her eagerness to get the class over and get back to the mystery of Natalie Rossum. As she carded the lock on her office it winked red at her before she noticed that the door was slightly ajar. Did I do it again and leave the door open? she thought. No, I was sure it was closed and locked. Who else could open her door? Admin? The custodial staff. It was times like this that she wished she were already carrying a compact handgun with her. But even

Rand didn't keep his Glock on his person. What would Rand do?

Feeling self-conscious about it, Shanna stepped to the side, flattened herself against the wall, and cautiously toed the door open. Through the widening gap, she could see that her office was a mess. Books and papers were scattered on the floor, and the secure file cabinet where she kept her interview transcripts and coding sheets, was now on its side, battered but still unopened.

She backed away and trotted down the hall. As soon as she rounded the corner, she reached for her cellphone and called Rand. The call was rejected. Who next? Should she finally risk calling the police? Maybe the Campus Patrol. Rand said he had already clued in Gus Creller. She didn't know Creller's direct line, though, and she was hesitant to use the campus emergency line, which would log the call. The fewer records of what was happening, the better.

She tried Rand again, but he didn't pick up. She was about to call the hotline when a panting, pot-bellied figure in campus-patrol khaki rounded the corner. Shanna recognized Gus Creller.

"Somebody hassling you, Professor?" he said. "The alarm net reported your office lock being out of order, maybe forced open. I just alerted Professor McMurphy like he asked. Let's check it out."

"I already did. Someone broke in, but I don't know if they're still there."

"Then let me check it out. You wait here." He slipped his Taser from its holster and sauntered toward her office. "Hello? Anyone there? You can come out, but no funny business. Ya hear?" It was almost comic as the cautious but casual Gus rocked his way toward the half-open door. He released the safety on the Taser, held it at the ready, and stuck his head in the door. He pulled back, smiled at Shanna, and said, "All clear." He pushed the door fully open and waited for Shanna. "Looks as if you got some organizing to do. You know what they say: messy office, messy mind. Ha ha. You think they took anything?"

"Hard to tell. Whoever did this really trashed the place." And here she was, in that place all over again, with the dark destroying forces bringing disorder to her ordered life. "I hate this," she said.

"I know you do," came the voice from the hall. It was Rand. He stepped over the books littering the doorway and gave her a reassuring smile. "And thanks, Gus. I'll take it from here. And if you can, you know, could you minimize things in your report. It would be much appreciated. You understand."

"I do indeedy. No need to even ask. I already know where you're coming from, so no problem. I'll just leave you to it. And I'll let Engineering Services know they need to fix that lock. If you stop by Campus Security when you can, Professor Newsom, we'll reprogram your keycard and the lock. Oh yeah, do let me know what you find, Rand."

"Will do." Rand closed the door after Gus and leaned back against it. "Well, we know she's still around. But I don't get what this is all about. Why break in? Is there something she's after, something you have from . . . maybe from your Hartford days?"

"The only thing I still have from my Hartford days is the nightmares. And now a nemesis, or so it seems."

"All right, let's see if anything is missing. I'll help you

straighten up. I know how much you hate undoing the big messes."

A sudden realization flashed over Shanna's face. She stepped gingerly around books and papers to get to the other side of the desk and open the top right drawer. "Well, we know she took at least one thing. The Luger is gone."

☙ Chapter 13

AN HOUR OF SORTING, stacking, and refiling convinced Shanna and Rand that, besides the Luger, the only thing missing was a box of assorted energy bars Shanna kept tucked away in the top left desk drawer. The envelope with its three colored folders was recovered, contents intact, from under an avalanche of history and economics journals.

Rand surveyed the mostly restored room. "I don't think she was actually after anything in particular. Unless she was after the Luger."

"Why would she be after the Luger?"

"Well, this is a longshot—no pun intended—but my students found another bullet hole in our deck, possibly made some time ago and fired from maybe the tree line behind the house. I don't know. Maybe Thibault has some connection with the Luger being buried back there, but I'm just playing with possibilities. My bet is that the Luger was a bonus find that she grabbed on impulse, like your granola bars. This was really all just to keep you off balance, to let you know she was still around, watching, always able to get to you whenever she wanted."

"Thanks for being so reassuring. I'll really sleep well tonight." She rested her elbows on the desk and lowered her chin to her hands. "What are we going to do? If she can just waltz into my office or the house or your car any time she feels like it . . . We can't live that way. I can't live that way."

"No, we can't, but there are things we can do. Let me work on this. I'll get a perimeter alarm installed at the house, and I'll add my own bit of extra security here, including an internet webcam inside your office. I have favors I can pull in with the community to up the surveillance and the stakes. And, we'll set a trap. I think your nemesis, as you call her, has more balls than brains. In the meantime, our strategy will be to never be alone, to always be with people, in the open."

"Oh, great, just the prescription for your average moderately agoraphobic introvert."

"Don't worry, I think I can rise to the occasion."

"I meant me."

"I know you did, sweetheart. I know. Just reminding you that, in so many ways, we are two of a kind. I think we should eat out tonight, not at home. We can grab those files and drive out to Dahlia's. It's probably booked solid, but I'm pretty sure we can get a table." He winked. "It helps to know the right people."

"Yeah, the right people. Like Darlene. Again."

∞

Dahlia's was a destination dining spot on a rise just off the highway out of Taggertsville. The only gourmet restaurant truly worth the accolade in all of Taggerts county, it served creative reinterpretations of classic comfort food, with a fusion of Asian and Caribbean influences. The place was busy for midweek, although there were a few scattered tables still open. The moment Shanna and Rand entered, Nareem, the maître d'hôtel, with his toothy smile and tucked-back dreadlocks, made a beeline for them and welcomed them enthusiastically. "So good to see you Rand, to see you both," he said. "I'll get your favorite table set for you right away. And I'll let Darlene know you're here." Thanks to Rand, they were instant insiders, which thrilled Shanna—and pissed her off.

She and Rand were noshing on an appetizer plate of finger-size vegetable fritters with assorted spicy dipping sauces when Darlene Shirley emerged from the kitchen. A tugboat of a woman in her black-bordered white *chef de cuisine* uniform, Darlene steamed straight for their table. Ignoring Rand, she stopped in front of Shanna, let a toothy smile flash in her cocoa face, and spread her arms. "On your feet, girl, and give us a hug. It has been too long, too long."

Shanna stood, smiled, and stepped in for a perfunctory hug, but Darlene folded her into an extended embrace that reminded Shanna of the woman's soft strength. "Yes," Shanna said softly, "it's been too long. I . . ."

"No excuses now, girl. And no excuses needed. You're family here, like it or not, and that's that." She let go. As Shanna sat down again, Darlene swept up the menus from the table. "You won't be needing these. I'll take care of you tonight." She turned to Rand and winked. "Nice to see you, Randall. Bennet says he's been schooling you behind the bar. You wouldn't be interested in getting your license so you can slot in now and then tending bar on busy nights now, would you?"

"Sorry, I already have a night job. You forget that my day job means nights of prep and grading homework. Shanna gets to have a TA to help with that, but us adjuncts, we do it all on our own."

"You braggin' or complainin' now?"

"Little of both."

Darlene nodded toward the envelope on the table. "You bring some of that homework with you?"

"No, this is something else, a cold case we're working on, a disappearance."

Darlene put her hands on her hips in indignation. "You workin' a cold case? Without me?"

"Hardly. We're here, aren't we?"

"Well, good then. I'll get back to the kitchen, but when it comes time for dessert and coffee, you gotta scrunch over and make room for me so you can fill me in and I can tell you where you all are going wrong. Okay?"

"Okay. But we're going to have to do some real scrunching to make room here."

"You sayin' anything about what I think you're sayin'? Listen, mister, I've actually been takin' off the pounds."

"I know, Darl, I know. I just meant, well, this is just a two-top."

"Okay, if it'll make you more comfy, I can have Jakey slide over another two-top so's you won't have to scrunch none at all. Okay?"

Rand laughed. "Okay. Now, any chance we can get something to eat in this joint?"

Darlene chuckled and gave him a rabbit punch as she passed him on her way back to the kitchen.

Shanna leaned back in her chair and gave Rand her patented Buddha smile. "What?" he said.

"Nothing. I was just noting the way you two so easily slide into routine, ragging on each other like old buddies."

"Yeah. Old buddies. That's what we are, buddies."

"I get it. And you're right. Darlene is no threat to me. She's just a reminder of what I don't have with you."

"Not yet, maybe. But you and me, we're only on year two. Give us time."

"Let's hope we have it. Time."

"Now don't go burrowing down dark holes, not tonight. Tonight we feast on Darlene's best, and we focus on somebody else's problem. Whatever happened to Natalie? That is the question for tonight." He reached for the envelope and slid out the folders.

⁊ↄ

Dinner was a groaner of small plates stretching out for hours until the restaurant was nearly empty. After a lull, Jakey Tamler, a freckle-face local working his way through Holcomb as a busboy, came over. "Hi, Professor Newsom," he said. "I'll get you another table so you all have plenty of room."

"Thanks. Uh, which class are you in?" she said. "I'm sorry, the classes this spring are so big, it's hard to keep track of everybody."

"No prob. I'm in two of your classes. EconHis and World at war, but you probably wouldn't remember me. I'm usually late for class because of the bus schedules, so I slip in at the back."

"Oh, yeah. Now I recognize you. Look, if you are having trouble with assignments or anything, just come by my office. Anytime."

"Thanks, but I'm managing. Not enough sleep, though." He slid an extra two-top into place, whipped a fresh tablecloth on and smoothed it just as Darlene arrived with a tray.

"Thanks, Jakey. You can knock off now. You don't wanna miss your ride." She started unloading the tray. "Double espresso for the ex-cop, smoky blend tea for the professor—

see, I remembered—and Meyer Lemon and Ginger Sorbet with Carob Glaze for all."

"Nothing to drink for you?" Shanna asked.

"I've been swigging so much coffee all evening that I got the float-away jitters already." Darlene grabbed a chair from another table and plunked it at the extra two-top. "Bring me up-to-date on this here cold case. I been peekin' at you all hunkered over those folders and papers and such. Got my curious up. What's it about?"

Rand gave her a quick summary of how they got the case, what they knew so far, and what they were still puzzling over. "So, mostly, we still don't know a lot. We got this Luger that we now no longer have, but it's never been registered and doesn't show up on any law enforcement or collectors databases. Thanks to Shanna, we now have a connection between our house where the Luger was found in a metal box, the missing Natalie Rossum, and this Preston Fender, who used to live in the house and taught at the university. Fender departed under a cloud of sexual scandal, and apparently Natalie went with him."

"So, it's another case of that old teacher-student hookup story." Darlene shook her head sadly. "And then what?"

"The trail went cold in France," he said.

"Or, a dear dumb detective named C. T. Deverell dropped the ball," Shanna added. "We don't know much else."

"Well, look, you two have a lot to deal with. Why don't I follow up on Deverell, see what I can find out about him on the QT from the PIs I know, okay?" Darlene eyed Shanna. "And you, girl, you are good. But you need to play from strength. History is your beat, numbers are your thing. Let me and Rand do the cop stuff. You look at the history, look where history was. You know what I'm saying?"

Shanna, a serious smile on her face, nodded. "Yeah, I think I do. And thanks."

"No thanks needed, girl. You're family. We sisters take care of each other, cheer each other on, you know."

Shanna laughed at the thought of a skinny white woman and a big Black woman claiming to be sisters. "Okay, sis, we're good."

"Now, speaking of taking care of each other, what's this I hear about some Hartford brat threatening you?"

"Rand told you?"

"Of course, but I already knew. I know Gus Creller, I know the local dispatcher, hell, I know half the cops and most all the ex-cops in the whole damn county. Word gets around. Which gives me an idea."

Rand waited but Darlene didn't continue. "I'm all ears," he said.

"Yeah, we know, Dumbo, but you can't help you look like Alfred E. Newman. Anyway, why don't we turn up the heat on our Mustang-driving missy? Any wants and warrants?"

"No, Jenner Thibault is clean, practically the only member of the entire clan who is."

Shanna leaned forward. "Look, I know what it's like in those circles. Things up there are so corrupt that maybe someone scrubbed her record somehow."

"Now that I doubt," Darlene said, "but it doesn't matter. Look, here's what we do. We just whip up some new reasons to bring her in. Hell, we don't even have to make it up. I'm going to bet Gus has some security camera footage of your girl around your office. If she drove to and from, her car probably was caught by a gate camera. We can leak a story about a possible former student that the Campus Patrol would be interested in talking with, alert the public to be on the lookout, et cetera. Turn it into a grand mystery that gets people talking and eyeballing. Idea isn't to actually get her, but scare her off. We turn on the floodlights, and that cockroach has to go to ground."

"Until she switches clothes or cars," Shanna said.

"At least it buys us some time while we figure how to put some better barriers in place." Rand spread his hands. "Or find a way to neutralize the threat."

Frown-lines creased Shanna's face. "When you say 'neutralize,' I hope you're not thinking like I think you're thinking."

"We do what we have to do. You already offed one of the Thibaults."

"I didn't. I told you I didn't do it, and I was telling the truth."

"I know that, but you did set him up. You set the gears turning that eventually ground him up."

Shanna looked from Rand to Darlene and back, but there was no judgement there. Rand took her hand. "If we can find a way to get her to give up or back off, we will. Darlene's idea of a PR blitz to scare her away is a good place to start. Then we'll see. I don't get the idea that Jenn Thibault is the brightest bulb on the string. It might take less than you think to scare her off. My guess would be that her problem-solving prowess goes only as far as hightailing it north."

"Maybe." Shanna sighed. "Let's hope. But persistence trumps prowess most of the time."

✿ Chapter 14

DARLENE KICKED OFF her scheme by calling Aretha Barley, a rising Black star at the largely white-bread Taggerts County Chronicle. "I can give you a scoop," Darlene told her, "about Holcomb, a story with some legs. It's yours if you're willing to trust me and can promise anonymity."

"What do you have?"

Darlene told her.

Aretha's measured breath was audible over the phone. "I need some way of confirming the story."

"You can try the usual sources at the university, but they are likely to play dumb. However, I can give you an inside hook to the story if you can promise them anonymity, too."

"Okay, as long as I know I'm not just trafficking tales. I'm really trying to make it on the hard-news side of the business. I had enough of the features and flab when I was working on the podcast piece of the operation here."

"You know me, girl. I can promise you this is a real story, even if your 'usual sources' at Holcomb might deny it."

"All right, give me your insider, and I'll see about the story."

"Anonymity?"

"Sure, who do you have?"

"How about an ex-cop and a university professor?"

"Really? Those two? Okay, you got it. I produced a piece on Shanna Newsom after her book came out, back when I was working for Fuentes. Newsom's good, the real deal. And I know Rand from other stories. Local hero guy, right? Once took a bullet to protect a kid. So let me get on it and see what flies."

The Chronicle ran the story and it flew—faster and higher than Darlene and the crew had expected. The rest of the local press—community cable, one TV station, and a weekly freebie—starved as usual for real news of the region, quickly picked up the "leaked" story. Straight-faced denials by Gus Creller and the honest ignorance of the Holcomb University spokesperson only served to fuel a fever of speculation.

Spottings of the Mustang, mostly mistaken, started immediately, but then stopped just as abruptly. Rand prevailed on his out-of-state sources to confirm from turnpike toll cameras that the Mustang had indeed headed north. Since there were no actual police bulletins, Jenn Thibault was able to make the trip all the way back to Hartford unmolested, but Shanna and Rand were not celebrating her departure. Accelerating academic demands in the approaching end of semester made it difficult for either of them to carve out time for themselves, much less to chase cold cases.

කිට

Rand was in his office early, head down in grading quizzes, when Olee Walston pushed open his office door and leaned in. "Got a minute?" she said.

"Uh, sure, I suppose." He slipped the exam papers into his desk drawer. "Come on in, and—"

"I know, leave the door open."

"Right, thanks. Grab a chair."

"I don't need a chair, this is quick. I just wanted to tell you I didn't report the guy. And Sandi is . . . well she left school. I don't know where she is now. I checked with someone I know who works in the bursars office, and they say she withdrew. Maybe she went home. So, as you guys always say, now the thing is academic."

"Maybe not, the world is full of repeat offenders. We don't get a lot of them here at Holcomb, but we've had our share."

"Yeah, like that Fender guy who left in a hurry a little before I arrived. Except, I think he was a switch hitter. Anyway, I wish you could do something about Sandi and all."

"I can't do anything formally without a complaint or evidence, but I do plan to be keeping an eye on a certain chemistry professor."

"I suppose that's something, you being a cop and all."

"Ex. Like I said, ex-cop. Speaking of which, how's your brother? Florida, right?"

"He's okay, I guess. Doesn't write or call much. He's kinda preoccupied, I guess, has a new girlfriend."

"And you?"

"Yeah, I got a new girlfriend, too." She grinned. "Thanks for asking. Don't say anything to anybody. You know how Holcomb is, still sorta squeamish about, well, people like us. Giti and me have talked about starting a student LGBTQ+ support group."

"That's great. This place needs to do more to back up the brochure copy about its dedication to diversity."

"Yeah, but, well, we're busy with classwork and trying to find a place together off campus and . . . well, you know how it is. Like you and your lady."

"Like me and my lady?" His eyebrows twitched, stopping

somewhere just short of a scowl. "Like how?"

"Didn't mean anything, just, you know, priorities, who comes first. Anyway, thanks for listening to me and thanks for trying. I hope . . . I hope it all works out right, the way it should. I mean the chem guy. I hope he doesn't . . ." She shifted the weight of her backpack. "Anyway, I have a physics exam, so . . ." She shrugged and started to leave.

"Hang on a moment," Rand said. "What was that you said about Fender, something about being a switch hitter?"

"Well, yeah. I heard some of the sisters always thought he was queer, like maybe it was some guy he was hittin' on who blew the whistle on him." She shrugged again, shouldered her backpack, and left.

৪৩

Shanna struggled to complete the answer key for the final exam in History 207, World at War. She needed to get it off to her TA so he would be ready to begin grading the tests, which included several last minute additions, extra credit questions that were Shanna's way of giving floundering students a bonus shot at a passing grade. She liked throwing out memorable tidbits that might stick to student gray matter, such as the fact that the Luger, arguably the most famous German pistol, had actually not been designed by a German but by an Austrian, Georg Luger. She was posting the finished answer key to the secure dropbox when she noted incoming email from Lina Schlüssel.

Earlier in the week, Shanna had been musing over what Darlene had said to her about using history, about using her tools, and something like "go where the history is."

Where the history is? Lugers. Germany. War records. The Germans were notorious for being meticulous record keepers, but Shanna already knew from teaching Freedman's course that many civilian and military records from the war years had been lost or destroyed. Rand had tried using police databases and a chain of connections to sources in Europe, but had not been able to track down anything more about the Luger other than where and approximately when it had been manufactured, which could be deduced from the serial number. According to the audit trail she was able to follow, it had been manufactured by the Mauser factory in Germany in 1942 and then not a trace until it appeared among Abel Rossum's effects.

Shanna was acquainted with a few historians in Germany whose work was remotely related to hers in that they studied the use of slave labor. In their case, it was mostly about the Nazi regime during World War II, particularly the ways in which forced labor often backfired or proved to be an economic disadvantage. Munitions produced by concentration camp laborers were often sabotaged or deliberately manufactured out of tolerance or subtly damaged in handling. A shockingly high percent of shells jammed in rifles or failed to fire. Starving, overworked laborers always produce less and make more mistakes, even without deliberate sabotage. Moral issues aside, factories staffed by forced labor were often failures in one way or another.

As an historian, Shanna had composed a query about her interest in Lugers and one Luger P08 in particular, then sent it off to Schlüssel and a couple of other academics she knew of. Now she clicked to open the email that had just arrived from Berlin. What time was it there? Already nearly the end of the day. She read the message.

Thank you for your email. I remember your very good

paper in Proceedings ICEE2, the Second International
Conference on the Economics of Exploitation. Please
pardon me that my English is not very good.

I remind that military records for the years 1939-1945
are incomplete and some are harder to access than
others. In the case of this particular Luger, we are fortunate. I was able to trace the serial number to a successive run of numbers that had been issued to a particular unit, a detachment of officer engineers working
at Peenemünde. I will try to get a roster of that unit. If
so, it may be possible to identify the officer to whom it
was issued.

These records are not available in digital form as internet
files, so I will have to in person do the search, but I am
already doing other research at the Federal Archives
at Berlin-Reinickendorf, so I will do my best. I am sorry
that many of the records of the Waffen SS are among
the lost.

I am interested to read more about what you are studying. As you know, the work on the V1 and V2 rockets
at Peenemünde was supported by underground factories using prisoners from the concentration camps, so I
assume that is why you are asking me. I am curious to
know about this particular officer's pistol and the connection to your work.

I hope I can help. And I hope we can meet someday.

Mit den besten grüssen,

Lena Schlüssel, Dipl. Geschichte

Shanna was wondering whether it was possible that Able
Rothman had been among those prisoners who had been
working at one of the underground factories making rocket

components. Could that be what spurred him to go into engineering and to work for NASA?

She was drafting a reply to Lena Schlüssel when she suddenly realized she had never done even a simple background search on Rothman under that name. What was his full name? It was in the materials from Marti. She flipped through the folders and found the court decree changing his name. There it was: Abel Zechariah Rothman. Distinctive enough to make for easy searches, she thought. She entered it in quotes at her go-to site for historical research, one that simultaneously queried a variety of primary online sources.

The results page painted quickly: date and place of birth, where he went to high school, college, club memberships. Shanna stared at the page with just a handful of postwar entries in the short time before Abel Rothman had become Abel Rossum, but it was the earlier ones, from before the war, that puzzled her. She picked up her cellphone and called Marti Rossum.

"Hey, Marti, got a minute?"

"Lots of them. Have you found anything?"

"Something, maybe. I thought you said your father was a Holocaust survivor who immigrated after the war. He was Abel Zechariah Rothman, right?"

"Yes, that what the records say, although he dropped the Zechariah when he changed his name. Simpler, I guess."

"Well, I'm looking at a screen full of search results that says he was born in Duluth, Minnesota, in 1920. That makes him a U.S. citizen. He majored in modern languages, specializing in French and German at the University of Minnesota, and was vice president of a Francophile club there, but there's no record of graduation. What gives? Is this the wrong Abel Zechariah Rothman? Do you know more of the real story?"

"Like I said, my father told stories in synopses, details deleted. I think he did once mention he was American, which is how he was able to jump the queue and get here so fast with Marie after the war ended. But he had been a prisoner, in a concentration camp. He lost his passport or something and ended up being caught in a roundup of Jews."

"And he never talked about growing up, about his family?"

"Not really. They were visiting over there, I guess, visiting relatives, and then things went sour, and the whole family were grabbed by the Nazis. Or something like that."

"But they were U.S. citizens."

"Yeah, but they lost their passports or they were confiscated or something. Like I said, my father didn't like to talk about the past. I assumed it was all just too painful, the horrors and all, so I respected his reluctance. Still, every so often he would say something, out of the blue almost, as if he suddenly remembered something, a verbal tic that compelled him to throw in a sentence or two. When I was young, I would ask him questions, but as I grew up and learned that his evasions and elisions made it fruitless, I gave up trying to make sense of his story."

"I take it you never got into the genealogy craze. You know, where did I come from, who were my ancestors, that sort of thing?"

"I suppose I absorbed it from my father, a sort of avoidance of antecedents and ancestors. He was uninterested to the point of outright denial."

"People have pasts, Marti, often more complicated than we realize. That's something I know about and can understand. Believe me. Not everyone wants to dig up old dirt. But, would it be all right with you if I did a little digging myself? For all we know, it might lead to something useful in learning what happened to your daughter."

There were seconds of silence over the phone. "I suppose."

"I won't do it if you object. It's a longshot anyway."

"No, you can go ahead." It was said almost with a sense of surrender. "Just please tell me what you find."

"Of course. But can I ask what your hesitance was about?"

"You can ask, but that doesn't mean I can answer. I confess I don't really know what it's about. Call it ambivalence. The truth is, I just have always had this feeling about letting sleeping dogs lie. As an art historian specializing in the twenty-first century, I don't do a lot of digging in the deeper dark, the way you do. In my specialty, the past is measured in decades. The darkest secret I've bumped into was about how one well-known tattoo artist in Oregon ran off to England with the secret formulae for the inks his mentor had used. Real dramatic stuff, huh?"

"Depends on what happened afterwards."

"Lots of slamming and trolling on the Internet, but no death threats, at least not yet. Anyway, good luck with your research. I look forward to hearing what you find. Or at least I think I look forward to it. Bye for now."

Shanna set her phone down. With the last of her grading keys now posted to her TAs, she could let herself take a break—a short one. She switched to her favorite site for genealogical research and started looking for Abel Rothman's family. The birth record took her to his parents, Ira Nathan Rothman and Beryl Judith (nee Spitzer) Rothman. After a half hour of easy searches and lucky finds, she had a fairly complete picture of a rather sparse family tree.

Abel was an only child born to older parents. The 1920 census entry included the newborn Abel, the father, Ira, age 46, and mother, Beryl, age 32. Beryl died of cancer in 1941, and Ira died less than six months later of a heart attack, both still at the same address in Duluth at the time of death. They couldn't have been in Germany during the war, visiting relatives or otherwise. Abel Rothman was already an orphan before he returned to the United States, which could explain his never looking for his family, although there was at least one cousin still living. Beryl had a younger brother, Hyam, whose youngest daughter, Chava Spitzer, never married, was shown with a last known address in Menomonie, Wisconsin. Shanna made a note to figure out an angle for contacting her.

But now there were new mysteries, new questions. Abel Rothman had been majoring in modern languages and never graduated, but after returning with Marie to the States, he had become an engineer who started working on the American missile program only a couple of years later. How had that happened?

Online material on Abel Rossum was abundant, owing to his prominent role as a robotics engineer associated with the space program, but the stories were inconsistent. The Wikipedia page said he had an engineering degree from McGill in Montreal, while an obituary in the *Minneapolis Star Tribune* said he was a graduate of the University of Minnesota. Some more poking around convinced her that the Wikipedia entry was wrong. University of Minnesota records confirmed that Abel Rossum had been awarded a master's degree in engineering in 1947 with a double major in electrical and mechanical engineering. How was that possible? Completing a double-major master's in only a year? The man must have been a genius.

Maybe he was. There was a string of patents attributed to him starting in 1948 and continuing until shortly after his retirement. Many were too technical for Shanna, but she could get the gist of some of them. The first, issued shortly after he finished his double degree, she was able to figure out: an improved mounting for a navigation mechanism that could be used in self-guided aerial vehicles. It had been classified initially—presumably because it had military applications—but later declassified and published.

Shanna sent off another email to Lena Schüssel, thanking her for her reply and asking whether it was possible for her to check records of the underground factories for a particular prisoner. She cited the number that, according to Marti's notes, had been tattooed on Abel Rossum's arm.

Before leaving the office, Shanna returned to searching for Abel Rothman. On AllClassmates.biz she located a copy of Rothman's high school yearbook for the year he graduated. She purchased a one-time access for an unreasonable fee and clicked through to the Rs. She stared at the page of stiffly posed photos of girls in high-collared dresses with hair in wavy rows and boys in jackets and ties with slicked back hair. It was hard to imagine that the round-faced dweeb looking out at her beneath his well-oiled but still kinky hair would, a few short years later, become the man she had seen in Marti's photos of her father.

๛ Chapter 15

THE MAIN DINING room at Dahlia's was deserted but already arrayed in readiness for the next day's lunch crowd. From the back, at the only four-top not perfectly squared and set with a white table cloth edged in signature mint-green, Darlene gave a high sign to Shanna and Rand. Although the restaurant was closed on Mondays, it was still a working day for Darlene and some of her staff, and it also gave the three of them an opportunity to consult without the distraction of customers. "Do you ever take a day off and just put your feet up?" Shanna asked as she sat down opposite Darlene.

Darlene gave her a what-you-talking-about look. "What would I do on my day off?"

"Something fun."

"This is something fun, testing and tasting new menu items, tweaking the workflow, training up staff. Besides, we close for a month every year to give us all a break. Although, I usually spend much of the time visiting chefs I know, checking out rising stars in the culinary scene. Hey, what can I say? Food is what I do, it's me. The only other fun thing I do is cold cases, like this one. And it's beginning to be a fun one."

"Did you get anything on this Deverell dude?"

"Yeah. Some people around here and up in New Jersey

remember him as a bumbler who could never shut up, a private investigator who had a way of stringing clients along even though he didn't deliver much. And then, bingo, he struck oil or something, maybe playing the ponies, which he did frequently. Anyway, he packs it in and retires to Cyprus, or so they say. I'm seeing what I can learn without having to get on a plane. I'm a feet-on-the-ground gal all the ways through, although I don't mind flying for food if I have to. Come to think of it, I know somebody in Cyprus, in Nicosia, who is doing really fun inter-ethnic stuff with Greek, Turkish, and Israeli influences, so I could make it work if we need to put boots on the ground. But not now, can't get away until our August break."

Shanna was taking notes. "You know when Deverell retired to Cyprus?"

"Yeah, and you'll love this. The job for Professor Rossum seems to have been Deverell's last gig. He doesn't find the daughter but he does find some money. Makes you kinda wonder, huh?"

"Can you keep on it?" Rand asked. "Maybe see if we can get an address or some notion of the source of his sudden wealth?"

"I'm on it already," she said, giving Rand a fist bump. "And what's this about new forensics on the missing Luger?"

"Yeah, I had some of my students play crime scene investigators at the house. They recovered a bullet embedded in the deck framing that proved to be a match for the one I, shall we say, 'test fired' when we first got our hands on the Luger."

"Do you think Thibault shot at the house after she made off with the Luger?"

"It doesn't look like it. This wasn't a recent discharge, maybe from years ago."

"There are only two possibilities," Shanna said. "Before or after. It wasn't used while it was buried. Obviously."

Rand grinned at her. "Well, it could have been dug up and buried more than once, but that's just dancing more angels on the head of a pin. Which means it would have to be Natalie Rossum or a companion if it was not a recent discharge, otherwise it's gotta be Thibault."

Darlene was shaking her head. "Leaping to conclusions, detective. We don't know whether Natalie—or some associate—buried the box. We only know it was her box and she disappeared at roughly the same time as the box went underground. Very roughly. And speaking of which, wouldn't there be a missing person report? Did you check?"

Rand nodded. "I did. And when I didn't find anything around the time Professor Fender left the university, I told Shanna to ask Marti Rossum."

"And?"

Shanna shrugged. "She said that at the time she didn't see it as a missing-person matter. In her mind, Natalie had run off with the schmuck. To her, it wasn't a matter for the police."

"And you buy that?"

"I did, but now that I'm wearing my cold-case hat, I'm thinking she might have any number of reasons for not reporting it to the police."

Darlene squinted in concentration for a moment. "I'm wondering about the partially loaded magazine. Did you count the rounds when you first got your hands on it?"

"Yeah, the magazine was half empty, that makes four,

plus the one in the chamber. So five."

"All right. Let's assume the magazine was full when it was inserted. Unless the Luger already had a round in the chamber when the magazine went in, that would mean that three rounds had been fired before the gun was buried. Your students accounted for one round fired into your back deck. Two to go. Maybe worth another more thorough search around the house and yard."

"Maybe," Rand said. "Could be anything. Target practice? Test firing to see if the gun still worked? Lots of possibilities, lots of room for speculation."

"You did check to see if a Luger was involved or suspected in some incident around that time—gunshot wounds, the like."

"Of course, that was one of the first things I looked into. Nothing definitive turned up, not in the area, anyway. I could start checking out-of-state, but the wider we cast the net, the more likely we are to end up with by-catch."

Shanna had a puzzled look on her face. "Hang on. Let's stay focused local. Where does one get ammo for an antique collectible?"

"It's not an antique round," Rand said. "Sometimes it's called nine millimeter Luger, but the nine-by-nineteen millimeter parabellum is a popular round, one of the most widely used and widely available today. It's also known as nine millimeter NATO, an international standard, which says a lot, and it's used in many different firearms, including my Glock. There must be dozens of companies making nine millimeter ammo."

"Where would you buy it locally?"

"Fairson's Gun and Tackle in Taggertsville, for one, or just go online. Couldn't do that back up in Massachusetts, of course, but down here, you just need to be twenty-one to buy ammo, mail-order or in-person."

"And what if I needed only a few rounds?" Shanna asked.

"A box of nine millimeter is fifty rounds. By the box is the usual rule. I don't know if Fairson's would break a box."

"I think I'll drop in on Fairson's this week."

Darlene excused herself to go solve some kitchen crisis with her pastry chef, leaving Shanna and Rand to nosh on several samples from the day's trial runs of new versions of crab cakes. "I like the old ones," Shanna said. "I understand why Darlene has to keep changing the menu, but it's supposed to be comfort food, familiar. Why do you chef types have to always keep messing with stuff?"

"Maybe because that's what makes it fun for us. New. Beginnings. Like relationships, those electricity-charged early days. Remember?"

"Me, I like sticking with a recipe that works." She raised her eyebrows and gave him a silly grin.

"Are we talking food or people now?"

"Yeah."

∞

The asphalt in the half-empty parking lot at the edge-of-town strip mall was cracked, and the verge by the road was weedy. Trying not to act nervous, Shanna strolled across the pavement toward Fairson's Gun and Tackle, a brick-fronted store flanked by a pizza joint and a martial arts academy. As she entered Fairson's, a spring-loaded bell above the door jangled, and a balding man in a snap-pocket plaid shirt looked up and smiled from behind the counter at the back.

Shanna was wondering whether to meander up and

down the aisles first or make a beeline for the counter when the man called out, "Can I help you, ma'am?"

"Maybe, I think so." She walked over. "I'm looking for bullets for an old gun. It's a Luger."

"Really? Can do, but maybe you should consider moving up to a more modern piece. I can show you some really nice handguns for self-defense. Or just for shooting fun."

"I think I'll stick with the Luger. I inherited it," she improvised. "I just want to try it out, you know. What would I use."

"Well, before you try it out, better make sure it's in firing order. You could bring it in. I could take a look at it, give it a cleaning."

"That's all right. A friend already made sure it was in firing order, as you say." She suppressed a smile as she thought of Rand accidentally blasting the railing of their back deck.

"Okay. Plinking, target practice? I'd recommend these." He pulled out a box from the cabinet behind him.

"That looks like a lot of bullets. How much would that cost?"

"That would come to"—he tapped keys on a calculator—"$58.66 with the taxes."

"Ouch. More than a buck a round. I only need, like, only enough to try it out. Couldn't I just buy, say, ten?"

"Sorry, store policy, we don't break boxes. Some specialty ammo comes in smaller quantities—at higher prices, of course—but this kind of stuff, we only sell by the box, box of fifty, and a lot of our customers prefer to buy by the case, 500 or 1000 rounds at a time."

"Really? I guess you can tell, I don't know a lot about guns—just got my carry permit—but . . ."

"You gonna carry a Luger around with you?"

"Not really. I have a friend who thinks I should get a Sic Sawyer P-something-or-other."

"Sig Sauer, maybe the P238 or P938. They're very popular with the ladies. Here, I can show you. I even have the P938 Rainbow model in stock. It's really beautiful, multicolor, takes the same nine millimeter Luger ammo."

"I don't think so. Don't you ever have anyone coming in asking for a smaller quantity of ammo, maybe like for an older gun, like an antique Luger."

The man laughed. "Yeah, we get, you know, newbies every once in a while. In fact, if I recall, I even once had another lady come in here, years and years ago, with the exact same question as you. I remember, she also had a vintage Luger and wanted just a handful of rounds."

"Really? What did she do?"

"She ended up buying a box of the cheapest training ammunition. I remember her because she did the weirdest thing. After she paid for the box, she opened it up, grabbed a handful of rounds and dropped them in her purse, then walked out. Left most of the box on the counter. I yelled after her, but she was out the door, just like that." He slid the box on the counter to one side. "I can do the same with you, if you really want to throw away money. I'd be happy to sell you a box of training rounds, let you take only what you need, and I'll use the rest on the shooting range."

"Let me think about it. I'm at Holcomb, and I for one don't have money to throw away."

"Now that's really funny. It just came back to me. She said something like that. She was at the university, too, and pleaded poor. I always thought you people were, like, had it

149

made, being professors and all. Funny, thinking of what once was the Bible College not taking care of its own."

"Yeah, funny that. See you."

As Shanna drove back to the university, she was thinking that Marti Rossum might have some more explaining to do.

ᏂᎤ Chapter 16

ROSSUM WAS NOT in her office. Shanna was standing by the door composing a text message when Marti rounded the corner with a loose paper stack in one hand, her keycard in the other. She waved the papers in Shanna's direction. "More of the usual interdepartmental detritus," she said in explanation.

"Further proof," Shanna said, "of how far behind the times we are." At Holcomb, the administration still insisted on paper for many things instead of just distributing everything by faculty email. It was never consistent and seemed to depend on who wrote the memo or the mood in the Dean's office, so faculty always had to check both inboxes, real and virtual.

"Did we have a meeting?" Marti asked.

"No meeting, not scheduled, just passing by. I was about to send you a text."

"You still can, you know. Seriously. That's what our students do. They're sitting across from each other in the caf and texting back and forth. I never understood."

Shanna laughed. "It's contagious. Rand and I have even caught ourselves texting each other when we were both in the house. It's only one floor and the walls are like paper. We could have a conversation from one end of the house to the other without hardly raising our voices."

Marti opened her office door. "Well, come on in if you want, or you can continue to text me from the hallway. I've got nothing on my calendar except working on my book. I'm watching the end of my sabbatical creep up with every day I cross off my calendar, and I'm barely halfway through my manuscript." As she led the way, she pulled a spare chair from the side. "Have a seat. And what's up? Find anything new?"

"Maybe. Trying to sort out the murky Rothman-Rossum origins. And still trying to track down what happened to your daughter, of course. I was over at Fairson's Gun and Tackle this morning." She waited for a response that didn't come. "Know the place?"

"Ah, in Taggertsville? Is that one of the shops in that dump of a strip mall on the other end of town?"

"You know it?"

"I've been by it, I think. A couple doors down is Sergio's, Taggertsville's only tattoo parlor. Sergio is smalltime but a talented artist who keeps up on modern technique. Why?"

"Hmm. The manager at Fairson's says he remembers a woman buying ammo for a Luger some years ago. Said she was at the university."

"Holcomb's a big place. Would it be surprising if someone looking for ammo was from here?" Marti started casually rearranging papers on her desk as if she were not really interested.

"But for a Luger? And this particular woman did something that made the manager remember her."

"Do tell."

"I thought maybe you might tell me about it."

"Are you thinking I bought ammo for the Luger? Why would I do that?"

To Shanna, Marti's tone was evasive. "That's what I'm wondering, and that's why I'm asking you. If we're going to be able to help find out what happened to your daughter, you're going to have to be straight with us."

Marti stared at her in silence.

"So, forgive me if I'm too blunt, but what haven't you told me about your daughter, the Luger, or Professor Fender?"

Marti lowered her hands to her lap. "I think maybe it's time you drop the case. I asked you to help find my daughter. I didn't ask you to do family genealogy, and I certainly didn't ask for you to start accusing me."

"I'm not accusing you of anything, just trying to find out what happened. Did you also ask Deverell to drop the case?"

"He wasn't getting anywhere. As I said, he traced Natalie to Paris and then lost the trail. What was the point? You've read his reports. Why keep paying for empty verbiage?"

"Good question."

"Well, we can leave it at that." Marti stood up behind her desk. "And you can return the material I shared with you. And the cookie tin. I'd ask for the Luger, too, but I understand you already managed to lose that. Mostly though, I want that tin back. I have so little of Natalie's."

Shanna was mentally sorting through scenarios, trying to make sense of the sudden change in Marti. "Of course, I'll bring everything in with me tomorrow. When should I drop it by?"

"Any time before noon, would be fine."

"Okay, first thing in the morning." Shanna rose and started to leave. At the door, she turned. "You know, this is not the sort of thing that Rand or I would just walk away from. We don't like leaving things unresolved. Just because you're no longer interested—or cooperating—doesn't mean we're not still interested."

Marti stiffened. "I asked you as a colleague and friend to drop it. If that's not enough, I may have to consider other options."

Shanna weighed her own options and decided it was best not to say anything more. She nodded gravely and left without another word.

☙

As usual, the door of Rand's office was open, and Rand was at his bare desk mousing around, squinting in concentration, his face made pale by the light of his monitor screen. Shanna hesitated, then gave two knuckle raps on the door jamb. He looked up. "What's brings you down to the departmental slums, Shan? I could have come up to your digs. You look like someone with a lot on her mind."

"Yeah, you're right. I just came from Marti's office. We've been fired."

"I didn't know we were hired."

"You know what I meant. She wants us to drop the case."

"Well, that clinches it, then. No way."

"Yeah, I agree. I'm really bothered by Marti's sudden reversal. I thought I could trust her, that she trusted me, but now ... I 'm beginning to wonder about what role she played in her daughter's disappearance."

"Me too. But why, then, would she ask us to dig into it."

"She didn't ask us to dig into it; she asked us to help find her daughter. I think in her mind our mission was supposed to be narrow and focused, but then we did our usual thing and started asking all kinds of questions."

"And how are we doing on the answers?"

"Not as well as on the questions, but I think I've narrowed it down to either Natalie or Marti who bought the ammo for the Luger."

"Wow. You're a regular Columbo."

She stuck her tongue out at him. "Look, what I meant is that I confirmed it, and, based on my visit to Fairson's Gun and Tackle and now my chat with Marti, I'm pretty sure it was Marti, not Natalie. Anyway, let me tell you about my morning." She gave him a two-minute rundown of her field trip and conversation with Marti.

"Okay," he said. "We have a suspect, but we actually don't have a crime, unless something sinister happened to Natalie, which we don't know. But why would the prime suspect first hire a detective and second set loose a couple of cold-case amateurs on the trail?"

"Good question," Shanna said. "I think we need to go back to basics. Do you know the first law of research in economic history? Follow the money. Also the first law in politics. And life. So, we have at least two way pointers. First, we have an associate professor at an underfunded college hiring an expensive but underperforming private detective and paying him to do little or nothing. Second, we have said detective ostensibly suddenly retiring in quasi luxury. And these events are linked, at least in time. So, I would say you and Darlene should amp up your pursuit of detective Deverell, and I'll start looking into the financials of Professor Rossum."

ॐ

After cutting short her last lecture of the day, Shanna returned to her office, closed the door, and resumed her online research. She settled on a scattershot approach, going after everything she could find on anyone connected with the case, including Natalie, Marti and her parents, as well as Professor Fender. By the time Rand swung by to ask if she wanted a ride home, Shanna had uncovered a much richer picture.

"Here, take a look at this timeline I put together." She walked over to her whiteboard that was now heavily marked up with red lines and black lettering at odd angles. "Let's start back here." She tapped at a point about a third of the way across.

"Abel Rothman survives the Holocaust, hooks up with Marie Halévy, they are married while still in France, but, within a few months, they immigrate to the States where Abel gets hired by Minneapolis Honeywell, who pay for him, newly hired and just arrived in the country, to get his master's degree at the University of Minnesota. This guy was hot shit from the moment he landed here, going on to work for several major aerospace contractors, eventually playing a role in helping design the Mars rovers."

"So?" Rand was unimpressed. "The guy was smart and competent. So what?"

"Maybe nothing, but he settled in so quickly that it's almost as if the path were greased for him. On the other hand, he never placed himself front-and-center, although he seemed to have been well-respected among colleagues in his niche of engineering. He never actually worked for NASA itself. There are a couple of archived articles in the Twin Cities papers making passing reference to him that link him to Wernher von Braun and other German rocket scientists brought over after the war to advance our missile and aerospace program, although he never seemed to have been a feature player, more like a walk-on." She tapped on the timeline. "And then there's his death."

"And?"

"He died unexpectedly as the result of cancer that went undiagnosed until it was too late. He also died intestate, which surprised me considering he was such the methodical type, and his estate went through probate court. Turns out he left behind a lot more than one would expect from a successful but not stellar engineer, including a rather extensive art collection worth who knows what. Everything went to his daughter, who appears to have used the proceeds from the sale of his house in a suburb of Minneapolis to pay cash for her new place here. As to what happened to the art, most of it seems to now be lining the walls at Marti's place. I couldn't find records of sales—the art world is not known for its attention to record keeping—but three of the paintings were reported stolen in a breaking-and-entering a few years back, shortly before the disappearance of Natalie."

"Might she have taken them? Could that be what this is about?"

"It's a possibility, but for insurance purposes, they were only valued at a few thousand each. Neither the police nor the insurance investigators could find the perpetrators, who left behind no prints or anything. The neighbors reported seeing nothing unusual and no one heard anything. The *Chronicle* reported that the door lock had been jimmied. Maybe you can get the police report and see if there's anything else. Anyway, the paintings never surfaced. It's another thing I'd like to talk with Marti about, except I don't hold out much hope of her being candid with me anymore."

"What about Natalie?"

"Maybe it wasn't about Deverell's incompetence as we thought. For all intents and purposes, she disappeared after Paris. I tried all kinds of variations on her name and searched all manner of records, but nothing. Zilch. She never appears again in social media, news, never used her credit card. Nada. Natalie Marie Rossum seems to have dropped off the face of the earth."

"Can't happen. Unless she went off the grid. But where? In France? Why? What was compelling her?"

"Something she knew but shouldn't, maybe? Something others would be after her for?"

"It is damned hard to disappear completely in the modern world of digital surveillance. Look, even you were tracked down. If Jenn Thibault can find you, certainly we can find what happened to Natalie."

"Go ahead, be my guest. Give it your best shot. Maybe you have access to records that I can't reach, but after Paris, Natalie Rossum does not exist."

"That makes no sense, unless she was killed or abducted or . . ."

"I checked death records in France, and you already used your sources to determine that her passport had not been used again after she entered France. And where does that leave us?" She flashed him a raised-eyebrows grin.

"Are you stringing this out to see if I can guess? Just tell me where you are going with this."

"She must have gotten a new name, like me."

"Why would she do that?"

"Maybe because she was running away from something

and wanted a fresh start. Remind you of anyone you know?"

"Okay, but how are we going to track that. She would have to fake her death or something, and then we might have no way of uncovering her new name."

"Only if she were clever enough and sufficiently motivated, if it were a matter of survival. I'm making a guess that this was not a life-and-death matter for her, and I have an idea what happened."

"Your audience is spellbound."

"Remember, we have two disappearances. Preston Fender also vanished, except that in his case there are tracks, and we now know where they end. Turns out Fender died in Paris that same year. A court finding lists his next of kin as—wait for it—survived by his wife, Natalie Fender. Apparently, they got married in Paris."

"Hang on. This is really getting weird, because our Oleander told me she thought Fender was queer."

"Maybe, but he married Natalie in Paris."

"So we're looking for a Natalie Fender?"

"Good guess, but nothing else popped up for Natalie Fender."

"What about other variations on her name she might be using, like her middle name, Marie?"

"Tried that. Some false hits for Marie Fender, but clearly not our girl. Yet we do know something else about her. She's Jewish, and her mother once said that Natalie was the more observant. So, I started wondering what her Hebrew name was. If we were on good terms, I could just ask Marti, but we're not. She and Natalie would have been living in Minnesota at the time, so I thought maybe there might be an announcement about her bat mitzvah in the Jewish press or a synagogue bulletin, and, sure enough, I found a little local news item about both Natalie and her mother becoming bat mitzvah—together, no less—at Mount Zion Temple in St. Paul. Natalie's Hebrew name is Tal, so I started looking for Tal Rossum. No luck. But when I searched for Tal Fender, I got hits. In Jerusalem, Israel."

"Wow, you found her."

"Not quite. That trail also ends abruptly, at least for what I could access."

"Well, maybe we should look for other combinations with Tal over recent years."

"Do you have any idea how common the name Tal is among Jews, especially in Israel? Like a lot of Hebrew names, it's ambisexual, a girl's name but also sometimes used for boys. And then we have all the Anglicized variants, like Talia. No, I went down that garden path and was just overwhelmed by hits, too many to sort out. So, once again, I'm at a loss, but at least we have a possible country to target."

"Maybe she changed her name again. What if she did the same thing twice: married and then took her husband's surname."

"I'm way ahead of you. I checked every female Tal who got married in Israel in the last five years. None of them was a match."

"What if she got married, but not in Israel. She was an American, after all, not an Israeli."

"Wait, that does give me one more idea. In Israel, marriage is under control of the Orthodox Rabbinate. Only two full-fledged Jews can have a Jewish wedding in Israel, and there is no such thing as civil marriage there. You have to have all the paperwork proof of Orthodox conversion or unquestioned ancestry up the maternal line, all up to Orthodox standards."

"What do people do if they don't quite fit the definitions or don't have all the papers?"

Her face lit up. "They go to Cyprus," she said, walking over to her desk and launching a browser. As Rand waited expectantly, she rattled away at the keyboard. "Dang. Seems the marriage records are accessible in Nicosia but are not available online. It's not like we can just hop over there to check the records in person. Besides, it's just a guess, could be a wild goose chase."

"There might be another way, and maybe we can hit two geese with one stone. Remember, we also have that lead on Deverell retiring to Cyprus, and Darlene says she knows someone in Nicosia."

"Okay, we hand this off to Darlene and her vast foodie network."

ᏸ Chapter 17

DISRUPTION HAD BECOME the new norm. Since the intrusion of Jenn Thibault, many of the daily details in Shanna's life had changed. It was not just major changes like Rand now keeping his handgun with him rather than in his car or that she had gotten her carry permit and kept her new Sig Sauer with her. It was also the minor things, such as having swapped their traditional spots at breakfast. As Rand poked away at his pepper-fried eggs with blue cheese, he periodically looked up to scan the backyard through the slider and would occasionally glance at the window over the sink where a display reported on the newly installed silent perimeter detector. Neither the swap in places nor his darting visual check-ins had been planned. They were the autonomic responses of a former police officer, a means to sustain situational awareness.

For Shanna, whose sense of safety hinged so much on staying in control, on sustaining routine, the small changes were deeply unsettling, and she carried a relentless load of background anxiety. When Rand's cellphone buzzed on the table, she stiffened and went on alert.

Rand turned the phone over to check the caller ID. "I better take this." He rose, stepped out onto the back deck, and closed the slider behind him. When he returned, Shanna was staring at her unfinished breakfast. "Not everything has changed," he said, smiling down at her.

She looked up from her daily bowl of yoghurt topped with strawberries and corn flakes and turned toward him. "What?"

He stood in the open slider. "Nothing. You. Morning habits. Echoes from the past." He paused with a distant, thoughtful look. "The call was from Julio Arnez. Remember him? He's now plainclothes. I asked him to look into the police report on the Rossum art theft. He told me he pulled the file, but when I asked him for a copy, he said we better talk."

"Well that sounds heavy duty."

"Yeah, not the sort of thing I'd expect from Julio. I mean, he's a straight-up guy, decent cop, hardly the mysterious type."

"You going to talk with him?"

"Yeah, we're meeting for coffee this morning. It'll be tight between lectures, but I think I can manage."

"You want me to talk with him? I have a pretty open schedule today."

"Mmm, probably not. It's like a cop-to-cop sort of thing. He and I don't have all that much of a history, but I think he likes me. I should be the one to go." He grabbed his mug from the table and gulped down the last of his lukewarm coffee. "And speaking of which, I better get ready and head out soon. You okay with getting yourself to campus today? I mean, we haven't heard a peep from or about Thibault, so it should be okay."

"Yeah, should be. Don't worry about me. I'm a big girl, and now I'm a big girl who carries. Thank you again for that. And you picked my favorite color: black."

Weberton, the two-horse town just over the county line to the west of the university, was best known among locals for its string of old-style motels and for Betty-Jo's, a breakfast and lunch spot that featured seventeen variants on omelets, over-the-top house-made pastries, a panoply of panini, and "bottomless" coffee mugs. For caffeine addicts and sugar-and-fat fans it was a favorite morning and noon spot, but between ten and eleven it often fell into a lull to become a quiet corner just to sip and swap stories.

Rand pushed through the screen door at the entrance, gave a boy-scout high sign to the waitress who glanced his way, and headed for the booth at the end where Julio Arnez waited.

"Hey, bro," he greeted Rand with an outstretched hand. "Long time."

"Yeah." Rand did the down-shake and high-grip of old buddies before sitting down opposite. "I'm sorry I don't have much time this morning. I'm kinda frazzled these days."

"No problem. I just thought it better if we chatted and I didn't have to explain more about pulling that file."

Rand smiled and raised a finger as the waitress walked by. "Just black coffee, thanks." She nodded and gave him a skewed smile that signaled she was disappointed by the small order. "So, what's the story on the great Rossum art heist?" he said to Julio.

"It's interesting, and still unsolved. Here's the rundown. Broad-daylight B&E, lock on slider jiggered with pry bar or tire iron just after the housekeeper and gardener left and before the professor gets home. Perp appears to have made a beeline for three small paintings in the guest bedroom, breezing right past all the stuff in the living room, some of it worth more, or so I'm told. The prof discovers the broken lock right away and calls it in, but doesn't mention missing paintings until days later. Our ever-diligent Detective Aingsly checks for prints around the place, but the only ones found are the prof, the daughter, and the housekeeper, and no sign of anything being wiped. Aingsly suspects the housekeeper, who happens to be Black, to which Aingsly remarks 'surprise, surprise' in his regular racist way. 'Course I'm not one to judge a fellow officer, but at least this time he never finds anything to confirm his biased suspicions. Besides, I'm thinking why would the housekeeper jimmy the lock when she's already inside?"

"Unless she wanted to throw suspicion off her."

"Yeah, I thought of that, too."

"So, maybe an inside job? Fake a robbery to get insurance?"

"Ah, but there's a note attached to the file, from the insurance company. The owner filed a claim and then withdrew it. There was no payout. Now, why would anyone not try to collect on insurance if the paintings were really stolen?"

"You thinking of reopening the case?"

"Yeah, like you think I got time for that kind of tail chasing? I got all I can handle as is. But I thought, since you were already interested and doing your amateur sleuthing thing again, you might want to keep on it and keep me posted. But I also thought, maybe these might be friends of yours or your lady, or something, and you might want to just let it pass. Which is why we're just having a conversation over coffee and why I'm not giving you any copies of no files."

"I see. Appreciated. I'll let you know if we find anything

for you." His coffee arrived, and he checked his watch.

Julio grinned. "Hey, McMurphy, relax. At least drink your coffee. Nothing's so important you don't have time for a cup."

"You're right. It's just that both Shanna and I are flat out these days."

"How is she? I read those stories that someone from out-of-state might be stalking her. Then nothing. What happened?"

"Just stories, Julio, just stories."

"And how are the two of you these days?"

Rand's face brightened. "We're good, Julio. We're talking about making it official."

"Wow! Congratulations. Have you set a date?"

"No. I haven't even asked her yet, not straight out, you know, so don't go spreading it around. But it'll happen, and sooner rather than later. We're not getting any younger."

"None of us are. I'm happy for you, I am. I just hope it works out better for you than me. Sonia and me split."

"Sorry to hear that. You have kids, right?"

"Two, two boys."

"Ooh, that can be tough."

"Yeah, well, we are trying to work that out." Julio took in a long slow breath, held it, and let it out through pursed lips. "Hey, you know, county's getting a new public safety building? Construction starts adjacent to the hospital this June. Should be a real improvement for the county."

"Yeah, big improvement," Rand said, playing along with the quick change of topic. Over the next twenty minutes, Julio finished his coffee and bear-claw pastry, Rand slurped from his bottomless mug that the waitress topped-off twice, and the two of them shifted into the well-practiced male rhythm of talking about trivia as if it were all-important. When they ran out of sports talk, car talk, and county government gossip, they settled the bill.

As he left for his car, Rand got a text message from Darlene. "No news is bad news. Call."

It wasn't until the end of the day when Rand was in Taggertsville picking up gardening supplies for Shanna that he realized he hadn't called Darlene. He decided to take a detour. When he arrived at the restaurant, Darlene was doing paperwork in her "office," a battered bare four-top butted up against a gray three-drawer metal filing cabinet tucked into an alcove off the kitchen. Her laptop and a small printer were plugged into a power strip dangling from a wall outlet. "Hey, Rand, what you doing here? You never called me back."

"Sorry, Dar, it's been one of those days. I was already in Taggertsville and figured I might as well go the extra mile and maybe mooch a bit to eat while getting your news—or lack thereof. I haven't had anything but coffee all day. I'm so wired I could send telegrams from my shaky fingertips."

"Well then, pull up a chair and I'll get Yvonne to put together some nibbles for you. Be right back."

Darlene returned in a few minutes with two salad plates heaped with finger food. "Try your shaky fingers on this." She put one of the plates on the corner of the filing cabinet nearest him and the other plate next to her laptop.

"Thanks." He picked up a pastry-wrapped chorizo chicken sausage and took a bite. "Mmm, as always you're a magician in the kitchen."

"But not in Nicosia. I am beginning to think the Bermuda Triangle is actually not in the Caribbean; it's in the Mediterranean. Cyprus is some kind of black hole. People go there and"—she blew on her finger tips—"they vanish."

"Sounds like magic to me."

"Maybe malevolent magic. Deverell moves there—supposedly—and then disappears. The sous chef from the place in Boston, goes there on vacation, falls in love—with the island and with a Greek Cypriot girl—and starts his own restaurant. Does pretty well, but at some point the place closes and now he, too, is AWOL. I talked with the former absentee landlords, if yelling and gesturing over Zoom with strangers who speak little English can be called talking. They didn't seem to have a clue where the two now live, and they have no interest in helping with our investigation. So, that's the news tonight." She popped a stuffed mushroom in her mouth as punctuation. "You"—she dabbed at her mouth with the corner of a napkin pulled from her pocket—"wanna stay for dinner? Too bad Shanna's not with you. A night out could be good for both of you."

"Thanks, but I should head back. I don't like her to be out of my sight for too long."

"It won't be long. Finish your starters and let me get you some real food. You still worried about the Thibault girl?"

"In the background, yeah. I keep my eyes open and my ear to the ground. But there's been not so much as a peep or a footfall since she left. Something's not right. I don't see Thibault as one to scare off or give up so easily."

"I know people in Hartford. I could have them do some recon for us."

"You know people in everywhere, Dar."

"Well, not in Nicosia, not anymore."

∞

It was still twilight when Rand pulled in the drive, but the new motion-activated floodlights on either corner of the house were already on and the house was silhouetted by the floods in the back. Shanna's Cannondale was parked under the overhang at the side of the garage. Rand felt for the Glock in the small of his back and slipped out of the car warily without closing the door behind him. He walked to the front door and worked the thumb latch. It was unlocked. Inside he found Shanna, pistol in her lap, sitting facing the door.

"Don't do that, Rand," she said.

"Do what?"

"Take off for Dahlia's without telling me, then come tip-toeing in here with that look on your face."

"And what look is that? Is it a tummy-satisfied look? Because I had to pick up something in Taggertsville and Darlene had said she needed to tell me something, so I just kept driving. While she was telling me that Cypress is some kind of black hole that swallows people, I grabbed something to eat, my first chance today. There, now you have the complete entry in my diary for today."

Shanna was irritated, but she also recognized her reaction was irrational. "I . . . I just need you to be here, and I kept waiting for you to call. And . . ."

"What happened? Why are the lights all on with you sitting there fully armed?"

"Three guesses, and the first two don't count."

"Thibault? Or Thibault? Or maybe Thibault? She's back?"

"Not in person, but there was a package in the mail postmarked from Hartford. The return address is on a street that doesn't exist. I checked."

"You didn't open it, did you?"

"Of course not. It's out back, sitting in the middle of my flourishing weed patch."

"Well, let's take a look."

"Shouldn't we, like, call somebody? Like the bomb squad or something?"

"Maybe, but not yet. Let me take a look."

ᘍ

Rand slipped on a pair of his ever handy exam gloves and walked a full circle around the red-and-blue printed flat-rate Priority Mail packet before picking it up and turning it over.

"Be careful. Maybe you shouldn't pick it up."

"You already did. And it's been through the mail, stamped, scanned, tossed into bins, loaded onto trucks, piled with other packages, sped along on conveyor belts, et cetera and so on. It's not going to explode if I pick it up." He stepped back onto the deck and held the packet up to the floodlight. "Dang cardboard is too thick to see through." He set it on one of the glass-top side tables and ran his hand back and forth over it, pressing lightly. "There's definitely something in there, but it's too small to be a bomb, and I don't feel anything that suggests there's circuitry in there."

"And now you're the bomb squad?"

"No, but we all get some training. Enough to know whether to call the bomb squad, and I say no. Grab a pair of kitchen shears for me, will you?"

He was gently shaking the packet when she returned with the shears. "Thanks." He started to slice open the bottom.

"You know there's this zipper thing at the top. You just pull that red tab thingy and . . ."

"I know, but that would be expected, so, instead, we do

the unexpected, just in case."

She took an involuntary step back as he finished the cut, then pressed on the edges to make the sides bulge. "Well," he said, peering in, "it's just a message." He tilted the envelope and let the contents spill into his hand and held it out for Shanna to see. Two nine-millimeter rounds were held between strips of sticky tape. "Looks like she's returning the ammo from the stolen Luger. Now, the question is whether that's a warning or a declaration of disarmament."

"What do you think? She's not letting go. She's telling me she'll get me." Shanna squeezed her eyes shut as tears formed. "What are we going to do?"

"It's a felony to mail live rounds like this. We could—"

"Get serious."

"Okay, then maybe I have to go to Hartford, send a message or two myself. I mean, she's just a kid. How tough can she be."

"She's a Thibault. Do you have any idea how vicious that whole clan can be? No, I don't want you going to Hartford. I don't want you stirring up that nest of vipers. And I don't want you leaving me."

"I'm not going to leave you. Ever." He passed the bullets back and forth between his hands as he stared into the harshly lit backyard. "Maybe we're going about this thing all wrong. We are acting as if Thibault was the problem, but why is she a problem?"

"What do you mean?"

"Why is she after you?"

"Because she thinks I killed her brother."

"Exactly, but you didn't. So the problem is that the murder of Jess Thibault is unsolved. Ergo, solve the mystery, problem goes away."

"Are we back to us heading for Hartford."

"No. Again, we're making this harder than it needs to be. I've been so busy, I haven't logged into the net for months."

"Are you talking about Icey Cold or whatever that guerilla group is?"

"I am. IceColdSolutions. It's one of the best cold-case amateur networks in the world. If I can get some of those terriers to bite, they won't let go until they chew their way through. If they find the real killers, Jenn is off your case."

"I don't know. This is the mob we're talking about, corrupt officials, doctored records. What's a bunch of online amateurs going to do with a decade-old unsolved mob murder."

"Maybe more than you think. Worth a try anyway, and it could be good to know we're not alone in trying to do something."

Shanna was thinking this was so typical of the two of them. She always assumed the worst and prepared for it; he was always the optimist, or at least the hopeful one. Did they really have a future? She wondered. They were so different. Was the fact that they both had started over from scratch at one point in their lives a foundation for a relationship? And now, I want kids. Am I going to end up a middle-aged single parent? She raised her eyes to find Rand looking at her, the love and caring so clear in his blue Irish eyes.

"You okay?" he said.

"Yeah, just wondering about the future, our future."

"It's a good one. And long, like the whole rest of our lives."

Shanna fought against the anxious tears bubbling up from some remote hidden part of her, a part that so desperately longed for permanence, for predictability.

He squeezed her hand. "You know what I've been think-ing about? I've been remembering what it was that you were saying about Jews and Cyprus."

"You mean that it's a favorite wedding destination for Is-raeli couples who don't fit the standard?"

"Yeah. There's always another way—for them, for us."

She held her mouth half open as a flood of feelings washed over her. "What are you saying? I mean . . ."

"I'm saying we're as non-standard a couple as they come. You're Jewish, sort of, maybe can't even prove it, what with all the rewrites in your life story. I'm a nominal Catholic who's been running from that papal past most of my life. We fit the profile. Nonstandard to a fault."

"Are you saying . . ."—she barely dared to let the thought form—"asking me . . . I mean . . ."

"I am. Will you marry me, Shanna Grace Newsom, love of my life by whatever name you go by?"

She started laughing and crying at the same time. "That has got to be a Guinness record for oddball proposals. I mean . . ."

"We're oddball. What do you expect? That's why we have to go to Cyprus to get married."

"And spend our honeymoon chasing missing persons and searching for lost paintings?"

"Why not? It's us."

"You are . . ."

"Wonderful and infuriating. We already settled that. So what is your answer. You never answered. What will it be, Shanna Grace Newsom?"

Tremors shook Shanna's lower jaw. "I . . . I . . ."

"You can say no, if that's the real answer, but you need to

understand, I'm not giving up and not going away, no matter what."

"Then yes. Yes, Randall Sean McMurphy, or whatever your name really is, yes, I will marry you. In Cyprus, in Taggertsville, or wherever. But not whenever. I want it now, before we change our minds, which we have a record of doing rather more often than most people."

"Cyprus, then. I've heard it can be very romantic and so full of history. And mystery. We can disappear for a while, and come back different, a new beginning. Mister and missus."

"How we going to manage that. We finish the term and after a week summer classes start."

"How about this? We wrap up our work early, submit the paperwork, dot-dot-dot, and just split. All this administrivia crap is done remote anyway. I'm sure Cyprus has internet access. We persuade Tingerly to schedule our first lectures for the end of the first week. All told, we can probably manage to squeeze out fifteen days, maybe twenty."

"And we just fly to Cyprus on a whim?"

"It's not a whim. We're getting married. Plus, we have a lead on what happened to the professor's daughter, maybe some stolen art, and a disappearing detective."

"And that has to be a new high in honeymoon weirdness."

"It's us. We get off on digging into stuff. It'll be fun. And Darlene assures me we're in for some good food and wine, even if her ex-sous chef has fallen off the map. Let's do it. Let's get married in Cyprus."

"I've only been out of the country once before, when we went to St. Thomas."

"St. Thomas doesn't count. It's a U.S. territory."

"Okay, then never been out of the country. What about you?"

"Canada. Almost doesn't count, although my Canadian friends would take exception. Politely, of course. Let's do it."

"I don't know. How will we pay for it?"

"Credit cards, like everything else. It's about time we ran up a little credit card debt. It's practically un-American for us to pay off our cards every month."

"I don't understand Greek."

"Neither do I. What about Turkish? It's a divided island."

"Stop kidding around. I'm serious. How am I going to learn a new language in a couple of weeks?"

"I suspect they've had their share of ignorant Americans who don't speak the language. We'll manage, hire a guide if necessary." He was almost bouncing with enthusiasm. "And I love you. And we're getting married."

Her face suddenly clouded over. "This is familiar. You pushing me, dragging me. I don't know."

"Me? Who's pushing who here. You're the one who buys a house on her own and then starts talking family. I'm talking about a getaway and buying plane tickets. I'm not in your league, Shanna, not even in your league. You're the one who gets scared and suddenly is ready to chuck it all and start over with a new name, a new life."

"I'm not ready, never was, but sometimes there's no choice." She looked up and gave him a grim smile. "We do what we have to."

"How did we get from 'yes, I'll marry you' to talking about doing what you have to?"

Shanna let out a sharp sigh. "It's not the same for you, for men. For us there's all this stuff tied up with being married and the whole contract thing and . . ."

"I want to marry you, but I already told you, with or without, I'm sticking it out, kids and all."

"And now we're talking kids. How do we do this, Rand? How do we keep complicating our lives, every decision, as if it were all tied up together in one big mess, like a knotted ball of string?"

"Because it is, because that's how life works. Most people pretend as if each step, each choice, were a thing unto itself, separate and unrelated to everything else in their lives. They do that because they can't face the complexity of the real world, where everything is contingent on other things and every choice is tied up with uncounted other choices."

"I'm like that, like those other people, at least in that way. I can't deal with everything at once."

"Then don't. First we go to Cyprus, then we get married, then we come back. See? One small step at a time."

Her laugh came out in quiet puffs. "You're a cheater. You know that? You use trick logic and wordplay and shifting definitions to win arguments." She wiped tears with the back of her hand. "You are so . . ."

"I know. Already said, goes without saying. Now, let's start organizing for our trip. One step at a time. Easy."

ঙ Chapter 18

THE FOOD COURT was a froth of students grabbing midday meals. Shanna, nursing a chai latte, was there precisely because of the safety of the crowd. As she sipped the milky mix, she was unsure whether to pretend she didn't notice Marti Rossum dodging students looking for an open table. The matter was settled by Marti making a beeline for Shanna. "You expecting anyone?" Marti nodded toward the empty chair opposite Shanna. "All right if I sit here?"

"No, please do." It was a ritual response, but Shanna was wondering what the agenda might be.

Marti unloaded her lunch tray, walked the tray over to a rack at the side, and returned. "I'm sorry about . . . about all that stuff about your investigation. It's all pretty unsettling to me. And I'm not sure what I want."

"I understand."

"You say that, but I think you and I are very different. I really don't like looking too closely at the past. It was one of the things that came between Natalie and me in the later years. She was always asking questions that I couldn't answer or didn't want to answer."

"You mean about family stuff or bigger stuff?"

"Both. She wanted to know about her father—who he was, what happened to him, why I wasn't married—all that stuff. And ancestry, where we came from, you know. She also asked me the questions she had wanted to be able to ask my father."

"All pretty normal, I would say. But that's not you?"

"No. But also yes. When I was younger I wanted to know more, but later, as I got closer, I realized maybe I didn't want to see too much. At some point I came to the conclusion that my father's redacted past maybe served some purpose. When Natalie started getting more and more curious and I was less and less forthcoming, she turned to Preston Fender, who was conveniently fluent in both French and German and, as it turned out, also an amateur genealogist. Not to mention sexual predator. I . . . I hate the man." Marti closed her eyes.

"It's okay." Shanna was thinking about what they had learned had happened in Paris. Now's not the time, she told herself, save it for later. "I understand."

"I really don't think you do. Fender was not just some older professor grooming my daughter by pretending to be interested in helping her sort out her family's past. To me he was part of a parade of predatory professionals, a type, a trigger. He reminded me too much of Natalie's father."

"He was on the faculty here, Natalie's father?"

"Not here. Before. When I was an undergrad. Xavier was so charming, so interested, so warm and attentive. And we seemed to share so many interests: art history, European politics, progressive jazz, Rome-style blond pizza, early morning walks along the Mississippi. And then I got pregnant, and then I learned I was only the latest in a line of liaisons, and soon I learned that no one was going to help me or do anything about him. It was a different era. So I cut bait, transferred to another school, and proved to myself I didn't need him, didn't need another man, didn't need any man."

Shanna nodded in sympathy. "I get it."

"Do you? I was nineteen and my life, the life I thought I was having, was over. Back to square one, beginning from scratch."

Shanna chewed on her lower lip as her own past started rolling in like a fog bank. "Yeah," was all she said.

Marti carefully repositioned her cutlery before continuing. "I lost credits when I transferred, and I lost the respect of my father, at least for a time. That was the end of a lot of things. No more fraternity parties, no more dishing with the girls in the dorm, no more romantic walks and talks with a man I thought was really interested in me for more than sex. Soon I was in my own dumpy little apartment, changing diapers while listening to books on tape, putting up with my father's scorn whenever he would visit. That changed when Natalie was a toddler and started talking. My father was quite late to fatherhood and not too bad with kids up to about six or eight. He had been that way with me, too, until what I came to think of as The Gap Years, where he was off in his world and uninterested in a schoolgirl. Then I was a teenager and my mother died and he got interested again. He would take my face in his hands and say I reminded him so of Marie, so beautiful, like her. My parents had never seemed, you know, close, but he missed her and I felt sorry for him. And . . . I imagine you can guess where this line is going."

"You don't have to talk about it if you don't want to. I think I do know where you are going. My father's brother . . . well, let's just say my uncle got very interested in me after my bat mitzvah, and not because of some religious turning point."

"I didn't have a bat mitzvah when I was a girl. Another story. Like I said, my father was Jewish only in the most nominal sense. My parents would go together to High Holiday services, but my father was never much of a people person and he scorned ritual, so neither the social nor the ceremonial elements of the community appealed to him. He was always a generous supporter of our synagogue and benefactor to Jewish causes, but that was the extent for him.

"My mother was the religious one in the family. I dropped out of Hebrew school after she died." Marti took a deep breath and turned to her bowl of soup. "Chicken soup. Cures everything. That and booze." She savored another spoonful. "This is not even in the same league as my mother's, which she made with a French flair—caramelized onions, fresh herbs—but this is the best the food court offers. Sometimes I feel I'm a soup woman in a burger and fries world. Anyway, between Natalie wanting to stir up the past and her getting involved with Fender and . . . It was all just too much. And it still is."

"Yeah, I'm beginning to get the picture."

"Good. I really do want to find out what happened to Natalie—and I'm terrified also. This stuff about origins, where we came from . . . it can be so simple for some people. I envy them, the people who can trace their families back generations and can sit down with the oldest living relatives to hear the stories firsthand or read diaries or study old correspondence. At the same time, I'm not convinced that knowing is always better than not knowing. I always . . ." She stopped abruptly. "What about you? You never say much about yourself. What about your father?"

Shanna could read the red flag signaling that Marti had reached the edge of her comfort zone. "My father was a photojournalist," she said, "award-winning, picked it up serving in the Navy in the war. My mother died when I was young, so I, too, was raised by a single father, also rather distant. And I have a complicated past, some of which is best left in the past. So, I respect your reluctance and your privacy. I just want to help you find your daughter."

"And I want to know how the story comes out, but I'm afraid to keep reading. What happened, why was Deverell never able to find them after tracking them to Paris? How could they just disappear? I want to know what happened, but I want the story to come out right. Can you understand?"

Shanna was thinking that even when we write the stories ourselves, that doesn't always mean they come out right. "One way or another," she said, "if we want to read the story, we have to be willing to accept what's written, being ready to face reality and pursue the facts wherever they lead. Which is what we've been doing in tracking Natalie and Fender and Deverell, and right now those tracks are leading to Cyprus."

"Cyprus?"

"Yeah, turns out your private eye retired there after finishing his work for you. He came into some money, somehow."

"Really? And you found that out already, on your own?"

"Rand and I, with some help from his friend . . . our friend Darlene. Another ex-cop. She runs a restaurant on the other side of Taggertsville. It really wasn't all that hard, though, just basic research skills."

"Well, I'm impressed. So, uh,"—Marti's face tensed—"what else have you found?"

Shanna worked her mouth in uncertainty over what to say. Stick with what's certain, she told herself. "Much of it's still tentative, we need to confirm things, follow up on hunches. Once we know what's what, we'll share it all with you. If you want. But neither of us like passing on rumors. You understand. He's a detective-type and I'm an historian, so we tend to wait until we know for certain before publishing—or making accusations."

"You can't just give me a summary? At least tell me what you do know."

Shanna hesitated. She understood Marti's curiosity and wanted to get back on good terms, but she also knew the risks if she and Rand were on the wrong track or couldn't follow through. "Okay, this much we do know. The Preston Fender story ends in Paris. He's dead."

"Fender is dead? I should feel relieved, but it also frightens me. What about Natalie?"

"It's not clear, but we should know for sure where the trail leads by the time we get back from Cyprus in a few weeks. In any case, don't give up hope. As soon as we have something definitive, we'll share it. Okay?"

"Okay, I guess. As I said, this all makes me anxious. What I want to know is that Natalie is all right. I want to see her again. Anything else is unimportant. You know what I'm saying?"

"No, what *are* you saying?"

"I hope you stay focused on what's important, important to me. The other stuff, the . . . uh, historical stuff, it's just a distraction."

There it was again, Shanna thought. Marti was warding her off. There was something Marti did not want exposed to scrutiny. What was it? "I understand about what's important to you," she said, trying to be reassuring without making promises.

৪৩

At a late supper that evening, Rand stared glumly into the shadows, listening passively as Shanna shared the events of the day. "Are you all right?" she finally asked him.

"Yeah, I suppose. I just have a problem with all this paperwork for Cyprus."

"What's the problem?" Shanna could feel her anxiety rising. "Passport, birth certificate, all pretty straightforward."

"It's the proof of 'legal ability to marry' that's the rub."

"A sworn affidavit should be sufficient. We're both single, never married. That's all she wrote."

"Almost."

Shanna's heart started galloping. "Is there something you haven't told me?"

"A few things. The important stuff you already know. But maybe I'm still married."

Shanna gave him a cockeyed squint. "And when were you going to get around to telling me this? And what is maybe?"

"It's not that I was keeping it from you. I just forgot."

"Forgot that you were married?"

"Not exactly. It's . . . well, I was eighteen, totally head-over for Cynthia Halpern. We were seniors in high school. Our parents were against it—surprise, surprise. Not only were we too young, but she was Jewish."

"I see. So you have a history in this regard."

"Not really. I was so clueless in those days and so hot to get into her pants, that I just assumed she was Catholic when she insisted on waiting until marriage. Also I never thought that she might have skipped a grade and was underage. We ran away to New Hampshire. She lied about her age and used a phony ID that the town clerk didn't care about examining too closely. Very clever and resourceful girl, she was, and prudent. Before leaving she had told her best friend where we would be staying—just in case, so someone would know. When we got back to the motel after the ceremony with the justice of the peace, the state police and her parents were waiting. They got the marriage declared null and void and that was that. I never saw her again."

"So, what's the problem? Legally, you aren't now and never have been married."

"Except, how do I prove that. I don't even know what the Halperns did or how they did it or even in what state. I was devastated. And relieved that I wasn't being charged for transporting a minor across state lines. The Halperns moved away that summer. End of story."

Shanna was chuckling quietly. "So you never got to screw this Cynthia?"

"No, although we did nearly . . . ah . . . anyway . . ."

"You, Randall, are blushing."

"I was just a kid. It's like going back over teen traumas—always something there to bring out the embarrassment."

"So, what's the problem? Just go online, do some searching, and find what you need."

"I tried. No luck. Doesn't seem to be a record."

"But you can, in all honesty, make a sworn statement. To the best of your knowledge you have never been married, legally. So just do it."

"But if the paperwork isn't there and this ever came out . . . I mean."

"Do you have any idea how many instances of 'if this ever came out' are lurking in my past? Like, it's not that I went before some judge to get my name changed; I just assumed an identity. My whole life is a threadbare tapestry covering up cracks and holes in the plaster. If I worried about all that shit, I'd go crazy. I've got enough real, right-here-today shit to manage without dwelling on what-ifs of incomplete paperwork or doctored documents coming back to bite me. You know, you worry over that official and legal stuff way too much."

"I'm a play-by-the-rules boy scout at heart, even when I bend the rules."

She beamed a hundred-watt smile across the table. "You are a wonderful boy scout with me. Right now, though, we need to worry about the big stuff and let the little crap go. So, make your statement, dot the i's and cross those t's for the government of Cyprus, and let's get married. And find Natalie."

§

They soon learned that foreigners marrying in Cyprus was an industry, and for some cities, such as Larnaca, on the south coast and only an hour's flight from Israel, the marriage business had become a significant source of revenue. Technically, there was a fifteen day waiting period, but that could be reduced to three days by paying extra for expedited processing. With airfare, hotel deposits, and payments for notarized and properly authenticated documents, the costs for Shanna and Rand were mounting.

"I'm just about maxed out on my credit card," she told Rand as they sat on a bench in a shady corner of the campus. "This is turning out to be more expensive than I thought."

"Don't worry. We'll put the rest on my card. And I'll pay you back for my half as soon as I can get to the bank. Besides, it's really all from one pool."

"What do you mean?"

"Well, we're getting married. Once we're married, what's mine is yours and . . . That's how it works."

"Really?" She leaned slightly away from him on the bench. "We never talked about this, but I always assumed we'd keep our finances separate. Split the shared costs, yes, but what's yours is yours and mine is mine. I've been on my own since I was a teenager. I don't know any other way."

"Never too late to learn. I just assumed, you know, if we're married, it's one pot."

"And what else did we just assume without settling it between us?"

"I don't know, maybe lots of things. But I figure we can work it out and make it up as we go along. So far that's worked pretty well for us."

"But this is different. After we're married, the stakes are bigger. It's legal. And what about kids? And what if it doesn't work and we have to split? What if something happens to one of us?"

"Why do you have to always . . .?" His voice was still low, controlled, but the words had taken on an extra bite. "Why do you have to always think ahead five moves, and always about the worst-case scenarios?"

"Because that's how I've survived: think ahead, prepare for the worst."

"And in the process maybe miss the now or be unprepared for the best that might come along."

"There you go again, pulling out that self-help paperback

philosophy junk."

"Hey, it's real. I . . ."—he ignored the cellphone buzzing in his pocket—"I think we're going to be fine. Not because we're lucky or because of a benign universe, but because you're good and I'm good, good at what we do. We're survivors who can do what it takes. And we'll do what it takes to make the marriage work. Finances? We can leave things the way they are now, keep them separate and sort through the bills together as they come in. If later we want to change things, we can do that, details to be worked out when and if as needed. Boom. Settled." His phone buzzed again. He pulled it out and checked his messages. It's from Darlene, says we should talk." He tapped to make a call. "Do you mind? This could be important."

"And this isn't? Why do you get to say 'boom, settled'? And why are you always on-call for Darlene?"

"I'm not on-call. She's working with us, helping. And I thought we already worked out the whole Darlene thing."

"Well, that's just it. I thought we worked out the whole Darlene thing, too." Her words were smeared with a coating of sticky sarcasm.

"I can call her later, but this could be important. Thibault? Rossum? I don't know, but it's probably important." The phone vibrated in his hand as another text message came in. "It's a one-word message this time: Connecticut."

Shanna felt trapped: trapped by events and changes flying at her from every direction, trapped by all the unsettled arguments with Rand and by matters yet to be argued, and trapped by a past that would not let her move on. "Go ahead, call her." Her voice was resigned, but in her head she was already running away.

"No. I've got a gut feeling about this. I think she means talk, in person. We should head over to the restaurant before the dinnertime rush. Can we do that?"

Shanna sighed in resignation. "Sure. I'm basically done here anyway. Text her that we're on our way."

∞

The parking lot at Dahlia's was already beginning to fill up by the time they arrived. Inside, they were greeted by Nareem, who told them Darlene was in her office, waiting for them.

The kitchen was a maelstrom of well-choreographed activity, each station cranked up to speed as orders arrived from the front of the house. Shanna and Rand wove their way toward the back corner. "There you are," Darlene said, standing as they approached. "Let's take a walk out back for a minute." She led them through a double set of doors out onto a small loading dock. "Fewer ears out here," she said.

"Serious stuff, eh?" Rand said.

Darlene turned to face him. "The gun was used in a crime up in Hartford."

"What? The Luger?"

"Yes, and it's been traced to you."

"How the hell? It was never registered."

"Yeah, but it seems somebody—who knows who?—made a bunch of inquiries about that particular serial number at various sites and agencies. All the police had to do was Google that serial number and your posts and searches popped up. Didn't take a lot of detective work to recover an IP address and a computer account and then your affiliation with the university, dot dot dot."

"And how do you know this?"

"Sources. I just wanted to let you know so you wouldn't be

190

surprised when they show up at your door. But remember, I didn't tell you this and we aren't talking right now. Understood? I have too much at stake with the restaurant and all to risk getting pulled in on this."

"But what could they have? Something happened in Hartford and we're down here."

"Yeah, but they recovered prints from the gun. And I'm guessing that might include both of yours. It could take some fast talking and some change of plans to get out of this without making it an even bigger mess. If you know what I mean."

Rand nodded, and Shanna started looking around on the loading dock, checking for ways out and reassuring herself that no one else was there. She knew that running made no sense, but her escape programming was etched deep in her psyche. When it came to fight or flight, it had always been the latter for her. "What was the crime?"

"A murder. A small-timer from the Forte family. Police are thinking it was a grudge killing or an old unpaid tit-for-tat. I have my own theory."

"Which is?" Shanna said.

"Pretty obvious, to get at you, girl, through Rand or however."

"But the gun was stolen from us, from me."

"Did you ever report it stolen? Of course you didn't. As far as anything official goes, you never even had it, right? But Rand here did some web browsing and left his tracks all over the Internet. I'd advise you two to get your stories straight, whether they're true or not."

Shanna looked to Rand. He had his hand over his mouth, his eyes fixed in concentration. "I think," he said, "I should

LIOR SAMSON

take it all on myself. Stieg Rolandson is the only one around the university who knows about the gun connecting it with me. He'll tell a straight story about doing forensics for me, I'll tell about how I found it and became curious—an ex-cop thing—and, bingo, Shanna's not even involved."

"Aside from the fact that we live together," she said. "Besides, Marti Rossum also knows, and she would connect it to me."

"But there's no reason for anyone to question her. If the cops question you because we live together, you just say it was my thing, that you had nothing to do with the online research or the amateur forensics. I'll be straight about using it with my students, perfect excuse, perfectly plausible."

"And how the hell—in this scenario of yours—did the gun end up in Connecticut?"

"How the hell do we know? There were news stories about a possible break-in at the university and—"

"And then it connects to the security camera footage of Thibault, and when they go after her, she squeals on me, and . . ."

"There you go, catastrophizing again."

"It's what I'm good at."

"Well, I think we'll be all right. We'll probably know in a few days. If Darlene is right that this is an active murder investigation, they are not going to sit on their hands for long."

"It would be nice if they could wait until after we get back from Cyprus."

"I wouldn't count on it."

✌ Chapter 19

A BLACK SEDAN with out-of-state plates was parked near their house when Shanna and Rand returned to Racine Circle. Rand quickly spotted the concealed flashers in the back window of the unmarked car. "We got Connecticut company," he said in a near whisper. "Cops." He slowed and pulled into the driveway of the vacant house two doors short of the top of the circle. "Hop out your side, slip into the shadows as best you can, and we'll meet up at the East Quad in a few minutes."

"You serious? What about you?"

"I'm serious, and I'm a boy scout, remember? Always resourceful."

After Shanna slipped away, Rand turned off the engine and sat in the car for several minutes, watching closely to see whether the two in the unmarked car were watching him. He shifted into neutral and let the car roll silently back down the driveway, spinning the wheel to head it back toward the highway then letting it roll for a hundred feet before starting the engine. He kept his eyes on the rearview mirror, but there was no sign he had been noticed.

Turning onto campus through the pillar-flanked East Gate entrance, Rand took the service road that circled behind East Quad and parked at the deliveries door at the back of Shelbourne House, a bleak brick cube left over from the days of Holcomb Bible College and now under renovation to become the new International Center. He walked around to the front of the building and smiled to find Shanna leaning up against the side of the main entry steps, trying to make herself small in the shadows.

"What now?" she said, vainly attempting to suppress the shivers despite the warm evening.

"Now we head over to Weberton and get a room for the night—probably at the venerable Sal-Jack Motel—to buy time and see how serious and resourceful our Connecticut stalkers are. In the early morning we'll do a little surveillance of our own, assess the situation. Then we'll figure out our next steps."

"But we leave for Cyprus in a few days."

"Precisely. I'm thinking all we have to do is stay low and be on our way. We can deal with the Luger shit after we're back."

"And if they try to stop us leaving the country?"

"I don't think they will. They're fishing. At worst I'm wanted for questioning, and no official action has been taken yet. We are just two ordinary people heading for a much-needed holiday in the Mediterranean."

"Ordinary, huh? And some holiday!"

"Okay, working holiday, and maybe two extraordinary people. Let's go check into our luxury accommodations for the night."

"The Sal-Jack Motel? Doesn't sound much like luxury."

"Well, the room comes equipped with me."

"Okay. I'm going to need that tonight."

ക

The Sal-Jack, a single-story semicircle of simple rooms, was a hospitality fossil from bygone times that still advertised "clean rooms" and "satellite TV" in neon. It was low-rent digs whose main virtues were the row of trees and the setback from the highway that somewhat muted the noise of the overnight truck traffic.

Lying awake in the queen-size bed with Rand snoring beside her, Shanna reviewed the day much as if she were writing in a diary. It was a habit she had adopted after a painful lesson in Hartford that taught her written journals could not always be trusted to remain private. It was also the continuity check for her invented life, a way of keeping her story straight, a reminder of who she was, and a rehearsal for the next act in the continuing role she was playing in the soap opera of her life. She recited the plot line to herself as a litany. She was Shanna Grace Newsom, born in Cranefield, Connecticut, raised in Manhattan, a graduate of the now defunct Mount Cherton College in Vermont with a doctorate from the equally defunct Kennilwirth University. It was all a carefully fabricated narrative that had enabled her to leave behind another life, a life peppered with pain and past mistakes, wrong turns and wrong people. That life had been papered over. It was dead and buried beneath documents, real and fabricated, except that Jenner Thibault was now bringing it back to life.

As Shanna ticked her way through a mental recounting of recent episodes, she realized it had been more than a week since she last reviewed her day. Too much happening, she thought, too many changes and disruptions. All the more reason to hold onto ritual, the markers that maintained some illusion of staying the course.

She slowly lost the thread of her own story as she drifted asleep.

ᘒ

Before daybreak, Rand slipped away and reconnoitered at Racine Circle by parking in the visitor lot at the university and taking the shortcut path through the woods. The black sedan was still in front of their house, but now ten feet farther back with its occupants sipping coffee from the Dunk's down the road. Rand ducked back along the path, hopped in his car, and headed out to the Sal-Jack.

"Well," he told Shanna after letting himself into the room, "they are determined buggers. They're back again. Or still."

"What are we going to do? We can't hole up here until we leave. We haven't finished packing. We can't just take off for Cyprus with just the clothes on our backs."

"Sure we can, but there's no need. The guys were drinking coffee when I showed up, so they had to have left their posts for at least ten or twenty minutes to make it to Dunk's and back. Plus, they'll have to take bio breaks. Plus, they're not going to stay parked on a residential street for days on end."

"How do you know?"

"Because you don't surveil in the open like that, and if they want me for questioning, they're only going to hang tight for so long. That's how this stuff works."

"So we just wait for them to get tired and go away?"

"Pretty much. Yeah. Except, eventually one of the neighbors will complain and either the campus patrol or Taggertsville police will check them out and urge them on their way. Either way, remember, we have friends on the force."

ᘒ

Shanna and Rand concluded that a dawn raid was their best

shot at retrieving everything for the trip. That way they wouldn't need lights or risk having a flashlight spotted. Rand called Gus Creller's personal cellphone and explained they were being hassled. Gus promised to apply some pressure.

After leaving their car once more in the lot behind Shelbourne House, Rand and Shanna made their way through the dew-damp trees via the footpath to Racine Circle. The black sedan had now been joined by a gold and blue campus patrol car, and Gus Creller was leaning over the open window of the sedan, explaining that the street was not a public way but was actually private property, owned by the university. He was claiming that the neighbors had complained about a vehicle with out-of-state plates parked illegally overnight. A display of badges by the two in the car did nothing to dissuade Gus from his role as the strong arm of campus law. Shanna could not hear every word, but she caught Gus's reference to a warrant and the state police, at which point, the men in the car shook their heads, started the engine, and reluctantly pulled away.

Shanna and Rand watched until both cars disappeared back down Racine Circle before sneaking into the house through the backyard. For a frantic ten minutes, they grabbed clothes and personal items and threw them into their backpacks and a pair of suitcases. "What if we forget something," Shanna said. "I don't like winging it like this."

"They have stores in Cyprus, too, you know."

"Der. I was just—"

"Being you. I know. The one thing we can't forget is all our travel documents and the paperwork to get married."

"I'll take care of that. I have an app on my phone with a checklist."

"I bet you do. You have an app on your phone for everything." He did a quick spin around the room. "I think I have all the clothes I need. I'll make another check of the bathroom while you go through the desk with your checklist."

Rand was waiting at the back slider when Shanna showed up with a bulging soft-sided suitcase. "What are we going to do?" she said. "We can't roll this through the woods."

"Here, you take mine. It's light enough to carry, and I'll take yours."

"How you going to carry this?" She struggled to hand it over. "It's too heavy.'

"Like always, I'll use my head." He swung the suitcase up onto his head and steadied it with one hand as he used the other hand to cinch the waist strap of his backpack. "See, going native already." He grinned at her as she picked up his suitcase.

"You know, big boy, this is not much lighter than mine, and I'm not as hard-headed as you."

"Hey, if you want, I'll carry both."

"And ridicule me for being a wimp? No way." She turned his suitcase on its side and grabbed the handle. "Let's go before our visitors return. I'll let our resident boy scout do his thing and lead the way through the woods, big strong native guide that he is."

❧

At the motel, they spread out the contents of their luggage on the bed to double-check the haul in their snatch-and-grab packing ."Got everything?" Shanna asked.

"No, but I have enough. You're the one who brought everything. Now that I see it spread out, it looks like even more. Hiking shoes *and* Crocs *and* sandals *and* two pair of—"

"It"—she cut him off—"will all fit just fine in my bag. I know how to pack."

"I hope so. Let's repack and drop the keys off in the slot at the motel office. I want to get out of the area as soon as we can."

∾

From the Sal-Jack, Rand drove south and took back roads to come up on the far side of Taggertsville. He drove past Dahlia's, then doubled back and pulled in.

"We stopping for breakfast?" Shanna said. "I don't think the place is open until lunchtime."

"No, but Darlene will be here, and I'm going to see if she might be willing to lend us her car." He drove through the empty front lot and around the building to pull in beside a dumpster tucked in one corner. "We'll grab our stuff and go in through the service entrance."

Darlene put on a look of exaggerated disapproval as they entered the kitchen wheeling their luggage. "I'm sorry, we have no rooms available," she said. "Did you try the B&B down the road? Blue house with white trim."

Rand laughed. "We're not looking for a room. We're looking for a car."

"Did you try Shady Shelley's Used Cars? It's just past the B&B on the left."

"Ha ha. We were hoping to borrow a car. We want to keep mine off the road for a few days in case the jokers tailing us put out a bulletin on our license plate."

"Don't you leave for Cyprus soon?"

"That's the point, to stay low until takeoff. What do you say?"

"Well, I sure ain't lettin' you take my Camaro. Not the way

you drive. Tell you what. You can take, the Tank. Keys are in it." The Tank was her vintage Honda Odyssey sometimes used to run errands to and from farmers' markets. With its patchwork paint job of gray and rust-red primer resulting from too many partially repaired fender benders, it resembled an army van with a bad camo job.

"Sure we couldn't take the Camaro?" Rand put on his best puppy-dog face. "No? Okay, it's a deal. While we're overseas the van'll be in the long term lot at the airport. Keys and parking ticket in the usual place if you need to retrieve it."

"Good, settled. Now, would you like some coffee? Tea?"

"Thought you'd never ask," they said in unison.

℘

Although it was not yet the summer travel peak, Charlotte Douglas Airport roiled with people. As Shanna collected her shoes from the belt at the security checkpoint, she glanced over to where Rand was getting a pat down at the metal detector two lanes over. It had been a tense three days of a broken field run dodging unseen pursuers, paying cash for everything, and spending each night at a different cheap motel. Shanna feigned interest in the departure board as she waited for Rand to clear security. "What was that all about?" she said as he approached.

"Ah, nothing. The pin in my leg set off the metal detector. I don't fly that often, so I forget."

"Pin in your leg?"

"Yeah, jumping off a retaining wall while chasing a perp. The bastard shot me, too. Didn't need to. I wasn't going any farther after that landing."

"What happened? Did you get him?"

"No, but my partner did. Darlene stuck the landing off

the wall and ran him to ground, tackled him. She was a lot more agile in those days."

"So I heard, and not just running." She smirked.

"Do you ever let go of things? It was once, one time. That's all. We were hardly more than kids, still in boot camp."

Shanna looked chastened. "I know. But she's still in your life."

"And lucky for us she is. She feeds us, she snoops for us, she lends us her car, and she pays for us to go abroad."

"What?"

"How do you think I can keep paying cash for everything. She slipped me a wad of big bills at the restaurant. Said she thought we'd need it and that it was a mortgage payment. Which she doesn't owe me, by the way, since all I did was co-sign, as I have told you a dozen times. It was her money that bought the restaurant."

"I'm sorry. I guess I'm really feeling unsettled and inse-cure of late. Brings out the petty part of me."

As they approached the fork where Concourse D and E branched off, Rand nodded. "There it is, the plane."

"What? Ours?"

"No, the Wright brothers' rig, look." He pointed up to a replica of the famous plane suspended overhead. "I hadn't realized it was so small."

"Don't be silly. That's a half-scale model."

"Hey, I'm the techie, and I don't think so."

"And I'm the quantitative historian. The Wright Flyer had a forty-foot wingspan, and that up there can't be more than twenty. Half-scale."

"Okay, my numbers nerd, what's our gate number and departure time?"

"We're scheduled at 6:40 for London Heathrow. The gate is D—"

"Shh!" Rand held up his hand. "What was that?"

"One of those paging passenger what's-his-face announcements. Something about . . . there it is again."

Over the PA came, "Paging arriving passenger Warren Tonely. Warren Tonely, please pick up the nearest white courtesy phone for a message."

"Shit. That's for me. It's a code from Darlene, always the punster. There's a warrant out for me."

"What do we do?"

"Go to the gate and hope the word hasn't gotten to the airport people. Just stay cool and act normal."

"That's my starring role, acting normal. What about you?"

He shook his head and gestured for her to hustle.

At the gate, the wait to board seemed excruciatingly long. They were finally inching along in the line backed up along the jetway when Rand spoke quietly into her ear, "Don't look, but two uniforms just showed up in the gate area and are approaching the gate agent."

"What do we do?"

"Keep inching forward and don't look. If I get detained, you go ahead anyway."

"No way. I'm not going without you. Besides, they're eventually going to connect me as well to the Luger."

"Eventually, maybe, but maybe not. Just do it. I'll be all right. I can talk my way out of almost anything."

Then the page came. "Is passenger Randall McMurphy in the boarding area? Randall McMurphy, please see the gate agent at the service counter."

They were already at the door to the plane, and Shanna

showed the flight attendant her boarding pass. When she turned to check on Rand, he was gone. She started to back up, but the crush of boarding passengers behind her made it hard. She let the line move her along the aisle to her seat in the rear cabin.

Shanna lifted her bulging backpack into the overhead bin and slipped into the window seat, trying to stay calm. Passengers streamed by until a family blocked the aisle as their three preteen kids argued over who got which seat in the center block of five across. Shanna watched up the aisle, expecting at any minute to see someone in a TSA or airport police uniform approaching.

What would she do if she ended up in Cyprus alone? Rand would want her to continue with their pursuit of Natalie, but obviously their other plans were out the window. Time to start strategizing, she thought. She was running scenarios in her head when the dreaded announcement came. "Boarding complete. Flight attendants arm doors and crosscheck."

She was on her own, once more in the oddly familiar territory of parachuting alone into the unknown. She closed her eyes and was busy redrawing plans for a solo op when she heard a voice.

"Excuse me, is this seat taken?" She opened her eyes and looked up to find Rand standing over her and grinning. Shanna, agape, said nothing. "Well, is it all right? May I sit here?" he continued.

"Ah, sure. I . . . what the hell?"

He stowed his backpack and sat down. "I told you I could talk my way out of anything."

"What did you do? What did you tell them?"

"I convinced them they had the wrong guy. I started by

telling them they had the wrong guy and asked to see the warrant, which I knew they wouldn't have, but the bulletin had them looking for Sean Murphy, which is what I go by in all my online accounts. Plus, they had me at your address, which they must have gotten from our friend in Connecticut. So I showed them my passport and driver's license. Randall Sean McMurphy, with the old address, my place in Taggertsville. Close but no cigar, boys, I told them. I started schmoozing, taking my time swapping old cop stories with them about mistaken identity and the one that got away. Good luck finding the guy you're looking for, I told them, and we parted good friends. At least until they figure out they were suckered. If they figure it out. I was not impressed by the intellectual prowess of either of them. Hell, they're ex-Staties on airport duty. What can I say? That's a cushy posting for guys killing time until retirement. So, we are off to Cyprus, my love."

‰ Chapter 20

THE HINGE COMPLAINED as Marti Rossum opened the door to the disused little bedroom at the end of the hall, now demoted to storage room. There were more bedrooms in the house than she and Natalie had ever needed, even when they had guests or Natalie had one of her infrequent but always over-subscribed sleepovers. Natalie called the little bedroom their family black hole. Things went in but never came out.

Some impulse, perhaps triggered by all the current inquiries into the personal past, impelled Marti to once again look through some of her father's effects. In the far corner was his desk, the antique mahogany that she remembered from her childhood, with its mysterious odd-sized drawers and the locked cabinet in one pedestal. Marti remembered the day when she was in first grade that she hurried home to retrieve the skeleton key from the drawer where she had seen her father stash it. And she remembered the shock of disappointment when she discovered that the cabinet was empty. That, she came to learn, was signature Abel Rossum. His secrets were locked away behind words, which themselves were few. And when a door was opened, nothing was learned.

Now Marti crossed the room to the desk, next to which were stacked several bankers-boxes worth of papers and an ancient analog oscilloscope that she had kept because she remembered being mesmerized by the light-drawn Celtic knots of the Lissajous patterns her father had once shown her. When he died, she had been told the obsolete instrument was worthless, but she wondered whether by now it might be regarded as a genuine antique and actually have accumulated some value.

Although a collector of art, Abel Rossum had never been much of a collector in any other way. The house, his clothes, the oscilloscope and other tools, and the few boxes of personal papers were the only things beyond the art that he had left behind. That and an investment portfolio much larger than expected. After his wife died and Marti had moved out, he had lived in his progressively emptying house surrounded by his still growing collection of paintings. At the time of his death, Marti had sold off all the furniture except the desk and made a quick scan of his papers. Consistent with his elision of the past, there was little that told the story of a man who was so well-known and so mysterious.

She lifted the lid from the top box, labeled with marker "Patents, Tech, etc." in her own careful lettering. She started riffling through the folders then stopped herself. She had done this before the move. What would be the point now; she already knew the gist of what was there, though she had never read them carefully. She looked around, spotted a drab stepstool, and pulled it over to sit on as she began her systematic perusal, opening every folder, binder and document, and skim-reading every page. There were copies of technical reports to clients, patent applications, and letters of recommendation and commendation spanning decades. One folder marked "Correspondence" was empty. Mixed in with his own work were a few printouts of patents and technical articles by others, some annotated in his cramped handwriting. One folder contained copies of U.S. and German patents dating from the Forties and Fifties, mostly having to do with guidance and control systems, although she wasn't always sure about the ones in German.

She almost missed the scraps of yellowed paper at the back of the folder. Smaller than playing cards, they were covered with tiny, almost microscopic lettering. She stood to bring the top one closer to the overhead light, squinted, and brought it to her face. They were Hebrew letters, miniscule and meticulously scribed. Marti cradled the small stack of paper in her open hands as if it were a sacred object and carried it downstairs to her home office where she turned on her task light and retrieved a magnifying glass from the top left-hand drawer.

The scraps looked as if they had been torn, carefully and neatly, from packing paper of varying weight. The writing completely filled both sides, with occasional lines crowded in vertically along the edges, as if added later. Her review of Hebrew for her bat mitzvah years earlier had been enough for her to complete her part of the Torah reading she had shared with Natalie, but the text in front of her defied her attempts to find any recognizable word. If it was Hebrew, it did not seem to be a copy of any sacred text she knew. She wondered if it might be Yiddish.

Some of the sheets bore backgrounds of letters and numbers at odd angles in faded purple ink, as if from a stamp pad. One of them appeared to be a date, the first part cut off: "ärz 1944." German? Perhaps *März*, a date sometime in March of 1944.

As to the tiny text, with her limited knowledge of Hebrew and none of Yiddish, Marti would need help.

℘

Nikahywot Solomon was another recent hire in the slowly diversifying faculty at Holcomb. Like Asaf Tingley, Dean of the School of History and Human Sciences, who helped recruit her, she enabled the university's human resources people to tick more than one diversity box. Solomon was an Israeli-American, Black and female, descendant of the Beta Israel, the Ethiopian Jews who had emigrated to Israel. She was also a gifted teacher who had lived in four countries and was fluent in seven languages, including Hebrew and Yiddish, the latter thanks to the Ashkenazi heritage on her father's side. She had the ebony complexion and tall slender build of her mother's side and the wavy hair and rounded face of her father. Marti Rossum was not the only one who found her appearance striking.

"Well, I must say, Marti, you have given me a puzzle worthy of my family namesake, the wise king of the Bible."

"So, you weren't able to translate it?"

"I didn't say that. It was a challenge. As you already surmised, although it is written using the Hebrew alphabet, it is not Hebrew, save for a single phrase near the end. And it is not Yiddish, although a few Yiddish words creep in here and there. That was my first clue, that maybe, like Yiddish, it is really another language expressed in—or one might say transliterated into—the Hebrew alphabet, much as English speakers may transliterate Hebrew into the Latin alphabet, such as in words like 'Torah' or 'mitzvah'."

"Were you able to read it, then?"

"Yes, as can you if you know the Hebrew alphabet and

understand the *niqqud*, the vowel marks. It's English. And the reason for this mode of writing is in the first lines." She turned to her computer screen and started reading aloud.

"I write this way because, if they find it, they will expect it from a Jew—Hebrew or perhaps Yiddish—but they will not be able to read it. I have not the time to work out a true cypher, so this is my cypher. I hurry because it is cold, the light is faint, and I have only these scraps torn from shipping material. If you are reading this, you are not only multilingual but both bright and persistent."

"Who is it? Who wrote this?"

Nika ignored her and continued. "I am Able Rothman. I work in a factory in a cave, a manmade tunnel deep underground. I do not know where it is. Somewhere in Germany, near Nordhausen or Peenemünde, I have heard. We make parts for terrible weapons. The story I have heard is that these are giant bombs that fly themselves to their targets, but I do not know if that is true. I do not expect to live long enough to know the truth. We work for 16 hours each day, at the production tables in the cavern under the overhead lights and the watchful eyes of the guards. It is a death sentence, a frenzy carried out slowly but no less inevitable. We are many thousands down here, but of the hundreds first brought here with me from the other camp, only a few dozen of us are still alive. Because I am good with my hands and smarter than some of those here, I have been 'promoted' to lead a team, which means I get an extra few ounces of bread a day. I share this bread, but am still resented for having been set apart."

Marti listened, open-mouthed. "This is . . . was written by my father, his diary from the Holocaust. He never spoke of any of this. Is there more?"

"Yes, several thousand words. I'll give you a printout so you can read it on your own, in private. It's rather personal. And quite surprising."

"How so?"

"It seems he survived in part because he was befriended by a Nazi, a member of the SS, who said he was from Canada, a Canadian engineer who worked in Germany, a Nazi sympathizer who joined the Waffen SS when the war started. But you will read all that on your own."

₮

Alone at home, in a house that seemed to keep growing ever larger and more empty, Marti finished reading the transcript for the first time. Its few thousand words added up to more than all the things her father had said over the years when he was alive. On the last pages, Abel Rothman told of the junior officer, quoted but never named, who said, "It is soon over, the war, and this I promise: Abel Rothman will return to America. That I swear."

Marti read again the closing lines of the brief journal. "So, I am determined to hang on, to cheat death and the Nazis, to live until I can get out of here with the help of the Canadian. He gave me a date and a time when he will summon me, and I await 'more eager than the watchmen await the dawn.'" The translation was followed by a note from Nika Solomon. "This last phrase was actually written in Hebrew (my liberal translation above). You may recognize it, from Psalm 130." Beneath, she had copied out the Hebrew:

מִשֹּׁמְרִים לַבֹּקֶר שֹׁמְרִים לַבֹּקֶר

Marti reached for the desk phone and dialed Shanna Newsom's cellphone. There was no answer. She let it ring through to voicemail. "Shanna, it's Marti. I have made an amazing discovery about my father that I want to share with you. Please call me back when you get a chance."

She put down the handset and scrolled back to the beginning of the document, reading it yet again, slowly, the tears dribbling down her cheeks as she let herself cry for her father for only the second time in her life.

༰ Chapter 21

THE HEAT AND HUMIDITY of Cyprus, almost identical to what they had left behind in Charlotte, blasted Rand and Shanna as they finally exited through the multistoried glass-fronted arches of Larnaca International Airport. Larnaca owed its modern airport and role as an international hub to the partitioning of the island in 1974 that left the old Nicosia International Airport an isolated derelict in the no-man's land of the United Nations' demilitarized buffer zone separating the Greek and Turkish-occupied sectors. For many visitors, the divided capital city of Nicosia was the central destination, but Larnaca on the southeast coast was the port of entry.

With their delayed arrival on the British Airways flight from London, the unhurried processing by indifferent customs and immigration personnel, and a long taxi ride to their hotel, it was the end of the day and nearly time for dinner when Shanna and Rand finally checked in.

After over-tipping the porter, Rand leaned against the door as Shanna paced. "What do you think we should do now that we're finally here?" he asked.

"Not be quite so casual with our money, maybe. We have to make that cash last."

"Don't worry so much. It'll last, I'll keep track. But what do you want to do?"

"Walk," Shanna said. "Too many hours of sitting and waiting and waiting and sitting. My backside is exhausted."

"Okay, let's head down toward the beach, take our shoes off, and walk in the sand until we're hungry."

"Did Darlene recommend a destination for dinner?"

"She said the seafood restaurants along the waterfront were pretty much interchangeable, but her sources did give names of a few less touristy places with more authentic local dishes. Let me grab the list from my backpack."

ଛ

The palm-lined Foinikoudes beach promenade was a featured attraction of a city with not a great deal to offer tourists looking for more than a beach holiday. As it was shoulder season and already late in the day, the beach was uncrowded, and only a fraction of the umbrella-topped sites along the broad expanse of sand were occupied. Shanna and Rand held their shoes and socks in their hands as they strolled along the edge of the water.

"The sea smells good," Shanna said, "especially after a long day of aircraft air. It's starting to make me hungry."

"Me too. Keep your eye out for a sign for a little café called Epic. It's supposed to be up near the end of this stretch, maybe a few hundred yards farther, set back from the promenade. It was first on Darlene's list, recommended by someone who knew someone who . . . You know, the usual food-and-wine grapevine."

"Funny how those chains work—in academia, hospitality, law enforcement—it's so often all about the unofficial channels, isn't it."

"Yeah, we're primates. We trust people who are trusted by people we trust. Oh, there it is, I think,"—he pointed—"just beyond that hotel and up from the promenade."

The entrance to Epic, squeezed in at the end of a narrow walkway between a hotel and a nightclub, looked too small for much of a restaurant. Shanna was dubious, but Rand told her to trust Darlene's recommendations. At the entrance, they were greeted in English by a tall, black-haired woman. "Welcome to Epic," she said with only the slightest Greek accent. "Are you here for the wine tasting or looking for dinner?"

"We better go for the dinner." Shanna looked toward Rand for agreement. "A wine tasting on an empty stomach might be too much for us right now."

"Do you like wine? Because, if you do, we have some very special selections tonight, all local. I can ask Micah if he can arrange a food-wine pairing, a series of small plates with the wines from the tasting. Would you be interested?"

"Yes, I think so. And who's Micah?"

"Our chef and sommelier . . . and my husband. He's also from America."

"It's already so obvious to you where we're from?"

"Well, we do get a lot of practice here, spotting the English and the French and the Germans . . . you know. I try to make everyone feel welcome."

"So, you're married to an American?"

"Yes, he's from Boston."

"Really?" Rand's face lit up. "I'm from Boston."

"Wonderful. I've never been to America, but Micah trained in Boston. That's where he learned to cook. I'm sure he'll want to meet you. I'll let him know you're here so he can find a break to say hello. Would you like me to show you to your table now?"

The Epic turned out to be larger than it looked, narrow but deep and with additional seating in the cellar below. When offered, Shanna chose the cellar, which gave them a quiet table for two in a brick-lined room with arched ceilings and rack upon rack of wines along the walls.

They were just finishing their third small-plate—*sheftalia*, a grilled lamb sausage served here with a minted Asian pear sauce and paired with an inky-dark old-vine red from a nearby winery—when a Black man with his hair in cornrows and wearing a chef's jacket approached. "Hi, I'm Micah Jonathon. You already met my wife, Ariadne. Welcome to our restaurant. I understand you two are from Boston."

"He is, originally, but I'm from . . . well, a lot of places," Shanna said.

Rand stood and offered his hand. "Hi, I'm Rand McMurphy. I grew up in Boston."

"Well, how 'bout that. I actually grew up in Worcester, but I studied at the Somerville Culinary Institute and apprenticed in Boston."

"Hang on. You went to the SCI? You wouldn't happen to know a Darlene Shirley, would you? She actually taught there for a while."

"Darlene? Of course I know her. I actually worked for her for several years before I ended up here."

"No kidding. She's a good friend of ours. Wait a minute, did you by any chance once have a restaurant in Nicosia?"

"Yeah, but we lost our lease, so Ariadne and her father bought this place in Larnaca. Now she's my boss. 'Course that's nothin' new." He winked.

"Wow, this is amazing, because Darlene has been trying to get in touch with you but couldn't track you down."

"Maybe because the restaurant is in my father-in-law's name. Ariadne persuaded him that it would be a good investment and a nice wedding present. It also allowed us to keep a lower profile when our former landlords threatened to go after us."

"You lost the lease?"

"Well, it was a perfect storm of misunderstandings about how business is done around here. We were actually doing pretty well, finally starting to do a little better than break even, when everything went south. I actually thought we should name the new restaurant 'Epic Fail' but"—he started to laugh—"but Ariadne persuaded me to shorten it. So, here we are. What do you think?"

"I think . . . we both think it's wonderful. And this last dish, the little sausages, fabulous. And that wine was just the perfect match. Deep, savory, but with a hint of sweet fruit. It was absolutely amazing."

"Well, I can tell you're an aficionado. The *sheftalia* is my adaptation of an authentic island specialty. I leave out the pork and compliment it with the sweet-sour pear sauce. And I'm glad you like the wine. It's from a boutique winery called Oinos Dafni run by a couple of Frenchmen. I'll let them know that they scored a hit with you."

"You do that."

"And I'll get back in touch with Darlene. Do you happen to know what she wanted from me?"

Shanna leaned forward. "Actually, it has to do with why we're here in Cyprus. We're trying to track down some people, Americans."

"Well, maybe I can help. The American ex-pat community on Cyprus is bigger than you might expect, but the grapevine and the smoke signals can cover a lot of territory. Who are you interested in?"

"Natalie Rossum and Preston Fender to start. Oh, yes, and a guy named Deverell. I don't think we ever got his first name."

"I had a line cook once named Devereaux, and there is an art dealer named D'aureville I heard of back in Nicosia."

"No, this was Deverell."

"Then no. No bells ringing. I don't recognize any of those names, but I can do some asking around for you. Are you in town for long?"

"Long enough to get married. And see what we can learn about those people."

"Getting married! Wow, congratulations." He shook their hands in succession. "Ah, here comes your next course, a palate-clearing salad of *halloumi*, a local goat cheese, and mixed greens topped with a citron vinaigrette. The pairing is a grassy, punchy sauvignon blanc."

"I see you don't flinch at pairing wine with the salad course."

"I don't flinch. Darlene Shirley taught me well. Wait until you taste my pairing with the dessert course." He flashed a fluorescent smile. "Well, I have to get back to my kitchen. Enjoy the rest of your meal."

Two more courses left Shanna and Rand ready to waddle home, contented and looking forward to a good night's sleep. After they asked for the check, Ariadne showed up. "Here's your receipt," she said.

Rand looked down at the strip of register printout. It was marked paid. "Wait, this isn't right."

"Of course it is. You're friends of Micah's mentor. You

know that's Greek, mentor, from the Odyssey. So, you're our friends, too, and we both hope you come in again."

"Can I ask you about something, about Cypriot culture? Would friends be insulted if a friend left a, uh, gratuity?"

She laughed, a hearty open-mouth laughed. "Micah might be offended, but his boss wouldn't. He's the artiste; she's the one who pays the bills. But, don't feel it's necessary. Just do come back."

After she left, Rand took a hundred Euro note from his wallet, folded it carefully, and slipped it partially under his coffee saucer.

ॐ

Shanna and Rand spent the next morning getting lost on the streets of Larnaca only to discover that the Town Hall where they need to file their application to be married was only a matter of blocks from their hotel. They stood nervously while a clerk checked their identification, then slowly and meticulously examined all their documentation and scowled as she read through each one and double checked the attached apostille, the authentication required for international acceptance of foreign documents. "You will need two witnesses to come with you in three days' time. Here's your appointment. Thank you."

That was it. They walked out into the blinding sunlight holding hands. "It's real," Shanna said. "We're really going to get married."

"Almost. Three days. All we have to do is get two witnesses. I had forgotten about that."

"I know who. Our new friends, Ariadne and Micah. We'll go there for lunch and ask them."

"But they have a restaurant to run."

"It's a short walk and the ceremony is quick—ten or fifteen minutes according to the website. I think they'll say yes."

Epic was not yet open when they arrived, but they got the attention of a waiter setting tables who let them in after they explained that they knew Ariadne and Micah. "You're early, we open in an hour," Ariadne announced as she made her way to the front.

"I know," Shanna said, "but we wanted to ask if you and Micah would be willing to be our witnesses when we get married in three days. It shouldn't take long."

"And," Rand added quickly, "We'd like to book our wedding dinner here at Epic, if that's possible. We can invite all our friends here in Larnaca, have a big party. Is that something you could do?"

Shanna leaned away. "All our friends? Who do we know here in Larnaca besides Ariadne and Micah?"

"Well, a friend of theirs is a friend of ours." He grinned at her and then beamed at Ariadne. "What do you say? Party time?" He opened his hands in invitation.

Ariadne shook her head side-to-side like a slow-motion bobble head. "You Americans can be so . . . so impulsive. Micah asked me to marry him two days after we met." She sucked in air. "I'll have to check with Micah to see if we can do it on short notice, but . . . Well, he is American and can be so impulsive, so the answer is probably yes." She closed her eyes in concentration. "I think maybe twenty or twenty-five is a good number. More and it gets too chaotic and too hard on Micah. We want him to have some fun too, right?"

"Right!"

❧ Chapter 22

THE DAYS OF PLAYING tourist in Larnaca followed by nights of good food, good wine, and dancing had a certain comfortable sameness but passed quickly. The morning of the ceremony, Rand donned a sports jacket and Shanna dressed in her elegant new crushable crepe travel dress, and they walked toward the Town Hall where Ariadne and Micah were to meet them. When their witnesses finally showed up only a few minutes before the appointment, Rand tried to hurry them inside.

"Relax, this is Cyprus," Micah said. "I've learned that things happen here when they happen."

Inside, they followed the multilingual signs to the room for marriage ceremonies. At the door they were greeted by a man with a pasted on smile and a bored look in his eyes. Rand told him their names and that they were there to get married. His smile broadened as if he were amused. "May I see your identifications, please. Thank you, I'll be right back."

The man returned moments later shaking his head sadly. "I am so sorry, but there is a problem with your passport Mr. McMurphy." He handed the passports back.

Shanna could feel the panic rising. Was Interpol now on their trail? Would they have to run? Was there anywhere to run? She could see Rand working his shoulders as he tried to psych himself into his cool-cop persona.

"Problem? What sort of a problem?" Rand said, his voice full of practiced innocence seasoned with authority. "The clerk the other day checked everything and said everything was fine." It was said as if it were fact, incontrovertible, cloture on any further debate.

"Yes, that may have been true at the time, but things have changed."

"Like what?"

"Your passport is no longer valid."

Shanna watched as Rand struggled not to overreact. "What are you talking about?" he said. "Look, here, I can show you and you can check. This is a perfectly valid United States of America passport."

"But it is no longer valid for you to get married in Cyprus."

"What are you talking about?"

"It is the law. The passport of a foreign citizen must be still valid for at least six months following the marriage or you cannot be married here. I'm sorry, but that is the law."

"But the woman, the clerk, she said everything was in order."

"It was, as far as she was concerned. She looked at the calendar and the passport and saw that the expiration date was more than six months ahead, but now it is less than six months and we cannot perform the ceremony."

Rand looked down at his passport, then up at the man. "You are telling me that because it is now one day short of six months, we can't get married."

"No, I am only telling you that you cannot get married in

Cyprus, not today, and not on that passport. You can always come back and reapply after you renew your passport. We would be happy to be of service again."

"Of service? Again? For one fucking day, you're going to tell us to fuck off?"

"Sir, there is no reason to raise your voice. I am only telling you the regulations. There is nothing I can do. Perhaps at the American Embassy in Nicosia you can get a new passport. I do not know; it is an American matter. Now I must ask you to leave so that we can help the next couple."

In the plaza in front of the Town Hall, Rand paced and cursed under his breath as Micah tried to calm him down. "Dude, it's just the system. It's not the end. You can probably swing up to Nicosia and get a new passport. How long can it take?"

"As I've heard, in an emergency, like if you lose your passport or it's stolen, it still takes two to three weeks. We're not here that long. And now we have this whole party thing, and we're going to have to cancel, and pay you and . . ." Shanna was doing her best not to cry. She knew that if the tears started, she would be unable to stop them and might fall apart completely.

Ariadne put her arm around Shanna's shoulder. "Who says the party is canceled. You two are still going to get married, right? So it's an engagement party, a pre-wedding party. It's still a party, and you will love the food and the wine, and you will love all your new friends." She looked over at Micah who was inching away. "And now, alas, we must get back to the restaurant and prepare for the lunch crowd and then finish the preparations for the big party, a celebration for our two new friends, Shanna and Rand, who are getting married. Sometime soon."

℞

The afternoon was spent stuck in their small hotel room making phone calls, checking websites, querying discussion groups hoping to find an answer, some shortcut around the bureaucracy, either of the United States or of Cyprus. As the hours piled on, tension and disappointment rose in synch. By five o'clock, with offices closing down, they had confirmed that there was no way they would be able to get married on this trip. Rand slumped on the edge of the bed. "I'm sorry, Shan. I thought I had everything taken care of," he said. "I even checked that six-month thing, but . . ."

""It's not your fault"—she stroked his hand—"and it's not the end of the world. Let's take Ariadne's advice and enjoy the party tonight celebrating that we're getting married. And we will, we will."

℞

When they showed up fashionably late at Epic, the restaurant was already wall-to-wall with people. A short man with brown hair in gelled spikes turned toward them. "Welcome to the party. I'm Giovanni, from Sicilia. I escaped one baking island to land on another."

"Hi, I'm Rand and this is Shanna. We're—"

"Oh, you're the happy couple. Congratulations!" He hugged each of them with great enthusiasm. "The drinks are up on the right. Serve yourself, open bar. The food is a little farther along, same rules. And the band is at the back, no rules. Here, let me introduce you to some more people."

It was the beginning of a long chain of introductions, continental-style cheek kisses, and more hugs, as they were passed from one friend to another. When Calista from "around here" noticed they still had no drinks in their hands, she grabbed a bottle of Ouzo from the table along the wall, expertly poured two glasses from a height of a foot and a half, and handed them over. "*Ya mas!*" she shouted above the noise of the crowd as the three of them raised their glasses. "To the bride and groom, or soon to be!" Suddenly faces turned toward them from all around with shouts of. "To the bride and groom!" and "*Prosit!*" and more "*Ya mas!*"

Calista took Shanna's hand and tugged her forward, inching edgewise between partygoers. "Come on, Ariadne is here somewhere. She'll want to see you. Micah is still in the kitchen but promises he'll show soon, and I'm *not* tending bar tonight." She put her head close to Shanna's. "Your husband, he is very cute. And tall. You might have to keep an eye on him. Cypriot girls like tall men, especially foreigners." She winked and laughed. "Oh, there's Ariadne." She pushed through a knot of people. "Ari, Ari, look who's here."

Ariadne threw up her arms. "Oh, Shanna, look at you, the beautiful bride-to-be, with your hair in flowers and all. Come, come, I want to introduce you to some special friends. Where is Rand?"

"I think I lost him on the way back here." She looked around. "A big crowd tonight. This looks like a lot more than twenty or twenty-five people."

"Well, you know, what you call 'plus ones' and the word gets around and . . . Don't worry, there is plenty of food and all. It will be fine. Oh, here's your guy, surrounded by admiring young women."

Shanna turned to look. Rand smiled and poked out his tongue at her over the heads of several people, all women.

"Don't worry," Ariadne said. "They do that with any new

225

male face. Besides, I am sure you can trust him, although it might be good to get that ring for real as soon as you can." She poked at Shanna.

Shanna could feel herself blushing as Rand finally pushed through. He grabbed her and pulled her into a passionate kiss that brought cheers from those around them. "Sorry, I was waylaid by those three," he said. "Turns out they're interested in becoming police officers, but it is still hard to do that here, so they say. They were pumping me for advice, you know."

"Yeah, Ariadne was telling me about that, about their interest in law enforcement. Especially when it comes in such a tall, handsome package."

Before Rand could respond, Ariadne had grabbed him. "Come, please, there is someone I want you to meet. This is Alphonse Allemand, one of the two crazy Frenchmen making waves in the wine world here. Oinos Dafni made the wine you admired so much on your first night here."

"*Bonsoir, enchanté*," Alphonse said, taking a little bow toward Shanna, then Rand. "I am so happy that you liked our wine. We are trying some new things that some of the other winemakers . . . Well, some of them ridicule us, but then we notice they try to do the same thing. Except we are ever so much better."

"You're French," Rand said, "but you speak English without an accent."

"French-Canadian, actually, from Quebec. So in Paris they think I speak with an accent, but I know that they are the ones with the accent. And your English is very good . . . for an American." He raised his eyebrows and smirked in jest.

"Fair enough," Rand said. "I've slowly learned that I'm hopeless when it comes to languages, English included."

"And what do you do?"

"I'm a professor, sociology and criminal justice. Well, adjunct professor, which means I work harder than Shanna here, who's the real thing and gets paid a lot more."

"Oh, I know all about that. My husband and I are both escapees from academe. Now we grow grapes and make wine, neither of which play departmental politics with us. It's a good life. Ah, the band has started playing again, and I think they are expecting you two to dance, so I will let you go." He backed away into the crowd.

It was quite late before Micah finally showed from the kitchen. Ariadne teased him about being too shy and neglecting their guests. "And you call all this food 'neglecting' our guests?"

"Well, you certainly have been neglecting me," she said.

"Okay, let's fix that. But first a toast from the host for the guests of honor." He started tapping a spoon rhythmically on the edge of a punch bowl, increasing the vigor until the room finally went silent. "Everyone, please get a glass in your hand and raise it with me in a toast to our new friends, Shanna and Rand. May they find what they are looking for and find happiness and long life together. And may they eventually actually get married! *Ya mas!*" The room erupted in laughter and cries of "*Ya mas!*"

There were more toasts, including one ouzo-fueled discourse that began, "To our guests and their happiness" and moved on to "justice and equity" before "tribes and neighbors" and finally being cut off by someone else with a loud cry of "To long life and short speeches. *Ya mas!*"

It was well past midnight and the party was still going strong when Shanna and Rand made their excuses and slipped away. A cool breeze, crisp with the smell of the sea, revived them as they walked slowly along the beach toward their hotel.

Shanna put her hand to her forehead. "I haven't partied like that since, I don't know, since my college days in New York. Fun, huh?"

"Yeah, a lot of nice people, interesting people. Did you meet Pedro, the computer programmer from Portugal? Very funny guy, went on and on about designing apps."

"No, I missed him. Did you meet the couple from Israel, Yael and somebody. They had come here originally to get married, like we did, stayed on for an extended holiday, and now are wondering whether they might make it permanent."

"No, I missed them. As you said, so many people there. And I kept hoping to talk again with that guy from the winery who said his husband had once been a professor."

"Well, we still have time in Cyprus, maybe we can visit the winery. Once we're sober again, maybe in a week or so, we can get back to looking for Natalie, like maybe just before we head home. I am looking forward to seeing Nicosia . . . and to getting out of Larnaca."

❧ Chapter 23

THE DARK-TANNED MAN waiting as Nareem approached the podium at Dahlia's restaurant had a round, boyishly handsome face framed by a close-trimmed beard and curly hair. "The name is Lavigne," he said. "I have a booking for eight o'clock. I'm afraid my flight from Europe arrived late and the drive down here took rather longer than I remember. I hope that isn't a problem."

"Not at all, sir." Nareem ran a finger down the first page of the reservations book. "There it is. Please follow me. Your table is waiting."

"Excellent. And could you tell the chef that, when she has a moment, I bring regards for her from Cyprus."

Lavigne was just starting on his appetizer when Darlene came out from the kitchen. "The maître de told me that you have a message from Cyprus? Do we know each other?"

"We do know *of* each other, yes, although I don't believe we've ever met. I'm Anatole Lavigne, co-owner of a winery in Cyprus, Oinos Dafni. We supply wines to, among others, a boutique restaurant in Larnaca called Epic."

Darlene's eyes narrowed. "Look, if you're here to pitch your wines, you'll have to come back in the morning, before we open. Either Tiana Graves, our wine steward, or I can talk with you then. As you can see, we're rather busy at this hour."

"I'm not here to sell wines. You see, Epic is run by this lovely young couple, and the chef suggested I look you up when I arrive. I must say, he is rather good, very creative with his reinterpretations of local classics and a veritable genius in his wine pairings. He says he owes much to his mentor and former boss, who taught him—as he put it—not to flinch in the kitchen."

"Ohmygod, Cyprus. You're talking about Micah, right? Micah Jonathan?"

"Yes, I am. He rather worships you but was too shy to reach out after you stopped talking with him."

"Well, he disappeared and I couldn't track him down and . . ."

"Yes, he knows all that now."

"But you didn't come all the way here just to tell me this."

"No, I also came here to sample the cuisine of his mentor and teacher, who obviously inspired and taught him well. But the urgency, the reason for my sudden overseas travel, is because of a perverse team effort to find people who may not want to be found, which I understand you are a part of. Not so?"

"Uh, well, you already think you know it all, so who am I to rain on your parade?"

"Ah, the Americanisms. I have missed them. Although they are tossed off occasionally among the ex-pats around Larnaca. In any case, rain never stopped the local Gay Pride Parade, so why would it stop me now? But I am here to try and stop the pursuit by your team, which, regrettably, may be rather close to their objective, maybe closer than they re-alize."

"They are not my team. I'm just a contributor, and I'm

hardly in a position to stop the so-called pursuit"—she made finger quotes—"even if I wanted to. Besides, I would need a good reason to stop. If I could."

"Is it enough reason to not ruin or maybe destroy the lives of half a dozen people?"

"Maybe, but I'm not the one you need to convince. The 'team' as you call it, is really working on behalf of someone else. That's who you need to be talking with."

"You're right, of course, and a visit is already on my itinerary. As you said, I wouldn't have come so far just to deliver Micah's regards or to sample your cooking, legendary though it may be. There's a great deal at stake."

"Then why don't you spell it out for me. I'm going to get Vanessa to take over in the kitchen and keep us supplied with wine and small plates for the rest of the evening while you give me a spelling lesson. The food and drink are on the house."

"How could I refuse?"

Marti didn't recognize the man standing outside her office when she arrived in the morning. "Are you waiting to see me?" she said.

He nodded and smiled. "If you have the time. Or I can come back later."

"No, sure." She keyed open the door. "Come on in. I'm afraid my office is more chaotic than usual. I'm frantically trying to finish up a book manuscript to get it off to my editor before my sabbatical runs out. My filing system has by this point in the process degenerated into a piling system."

He nodded again with a close-mouthed smile that accented the sun-deepened wrinkles around his eyes. Shifting a reference book from a side chair to a precarious perch on the corner of her desk, he sat, stretching out his long legs. Still nodding, still smiling, he said, "I know what that's like."

"You do? Are you here, I mean at the university?"

"No, not any more. But I still have a book manuscript that whimpers at me now and then from a cupboard, where it shares quarters with my own piling system, long boxed up and ignored but too proud to whimper."

Marti laughed. "I believe I have heard those voices myself, only mine are more like *cris de cœur* than whimpers. So, before I respond to those cries, what can I do for you? Or is this just a courtesy visit of some kind."

"I'm impressed, by the way, by your French. *Tres bien*. You toss it off without an accent."

"My mother was French, although I never thought of myself as good with languages. My daughter is a different story, she was always—"

He didn't wait for her to finish. "You don't recognize me, do you? I didn't think you would. Time takes its toll, but it can also pay dividends. In my case, the years of working the vineyards have erased most of my limp, although not the scar on my left thigh. It was rather a rush repair job by a student nurse working with what she could pick up at the CVS. Thanks to her, I walked away with both the scar and the bullet as souvenirs. Of course, I was fortunate to have her help and doubly lucky because the shooter was somewhat unskilled. I think she was aiming rather higher."

Marti tightened her grip on the edge of the desk where her hands rested. "What are you talking about? You can't . . . this can't be." She glanced first toward the phone on her desk, then toward the filing cabinet to her right.

"Before you call in the cavalry," he said, "or make another attempt at hitting the bullseye—what would it be, your third or fourth shot?—maybe you should hear me out."

"But you're dead. You died in Paris."

"Apparently not."

"Then give me one reason why I shouldn't fix that, or at least see you sent off to jail for what might remain of your pathetic life."

"Reason? You love your daughter, you're still looking for her, and you want to know that she is all right. There, that's three for the price of one. I can extend the list if you want."

"Then what are you looking for, Fender? Tell me that before I call the police and have you arrested for kidnapping, felony sexual assault, and a thick catalogue of sins and high crimes."

"It's not Fender, it's Lavigne. My father, Emile Lavigne, was French, my mother, Karin Fender, was American. I have dual citizenship. My American passport is under my mother's name, my French under my father's. So, these days I am Anatole Lavigne with permanent residency in Cyprus."

He paused as if trying to remember something. "Oh yes, and what am I looking for? Actually, I'm not looking for anything, but I happen to know that you are, that you're searching for something, for someone. That's why I'm here, because I learned that you sent two people chasing after me. Well, not me so much as your daughter. I just happened to be within the target range. And I can reassure you that she is all right, that she is doing well."

Marti stood up behind her desk and leaned toward him. "What have you done with her?" she said, spitting out each word.

"Nothing. It's not at all the way you think. I can tell you the whole complicated story if you have the time and are willing to listen, but the bottom line is simple. Your daughter is happily married, settled in a new life, doing work she loves."

"Where is she? And why hasn't she gotten in touch with me?"

"She has her reasons. I can't tell you where she is, but she has gotten in touch with you. She sent me. Or at least she let me know it was all right, the time was right, or maybe it was necessary."

"Why would she send you, you pervert, you fucking predator, you . . ."

He held up his hand to silence her. "I'm no pervert and definitely not a predator. But I am a homosexual."

"You're gay?"

"Proud and out, which is not always easy in a place like Cyprus, still a very orthodox island, very Greek—at least where I live—and somewhat homophobic. Which is ironic considering the history of pederasty in ancient Greece. But that is neither here nor there. Alphonse persuaded me to drop the pretentious Preston and start using my first name again. So, we became Anatole and Alphonse—don't you just love that, like characters in some LGBTQ book for young children—anyway, we got legally married when we were in France and have slowly become accepted locally as a couple, especially in culinary circles and among wine lovers around Larnaca. Oinos Dafni, our winery, makes some really distinctive fine table wine, which even has something to do with my dropping in on you, but that is another really, really long story."

"But you and Natalie . . ."

"Me and Natalie? There is no me and Natalie. I helped her get where she was going. I certainly love her, but not that way. And yes, Alphonse was my student for a time, but not when we got involved. We met at a conference in Montreal and fell in love before he decided to move down here."

Marti was still standing, leaning on the desk. Slowly shaking her head, she lowered herself back into the chair. "I am utterly . . ."

"Indeed you are, and I can empathize. It must be very disorienting. Do you want me to enlighten you?"

Marti sat, mouth open, stunned. "Yes. I think so."

"Okay," he looked at his watch. "You're sure you're ready for this?"

"No, maybe not, but we're not always ready for what we need."

"Well put. Okay, so your daughter first came to me because she wanted help learning French and German. Something to do with her roots, her grandparents. She was not satisfied with simple rough translations of some letters and papers she had found secreted along with a certain object that seems to have become the MacGuffin of our interthreaded stories; she wanted to follow where it all led. We hit it off. She has this gift for words and language, as you know, and when she started pulling off multilingual wordplay during our conversations, I was smitten. That was part of the spark that ignited things between Alphonse and me, too. Frankly, with Natalie on the scene, he was beginning to wonder how far he could trust me. He kept popping in on Natalie and me just in time to catch us doubled over in fits of laughter or hugging and wiping tears from our eyes. But he had nothing to worry about. I knew there had been rumors about me being bi, but let me tell you, when it comes to the bedroom, I'm a Kinsey 6—know what I mean?—but, yes, emotionally, Natalie and I clicked."

He squinted and looked off as if listening to distant voices. "She was not happy, as you must have known, and really needed someone to talk with about all that was troubling her. So we did—much of it in German and French—building her fluency as we got to know each other and as she began to know herself better.

"All this was happening as the shit began to hit the fan at the university over rumors about me, about transgressions with students. In this case, there was a basis in reality because Alphonse and I were sleeping together, and by this time he was a grad student at Holcomb, but everything else was rumors and bullshit, bits of nothing amplified in the echo chamber that is a college campus.

"However, it was becoming apparent that the universe was telling the two of us it might be time to leave academia while we still could exit on our own terms and pursue our dreams of a Mediterranean lifestyle. At the same time, things between you and Natalie were building to a head, with everything coalescing into that one night, the one the three of us came to call our own personal 'night of the shooting stars.' You already know a little of the prologue; let me tell you the rest of the story."

He closed his eyes. "I can still picture Natalie storming into my place at the top of Racine Circle. You remember it? She was livid, in the midst of a funk and a tantrum that would have done credit to a three-year-old."

⍩ Chapter 24

NATALIE SLAMMED THE front door behind her, stomped across the room, threw her backpack on the floor, and sat on the couch, arms crossed, face molded into a fierce scowl.

"No hello for your beloved tutor and confidant?" Preston said, as he entered from the kitchen. "Do I dare say you're uncharacteristically early for our session."

"Hello. Fucking hello. There. Happy now? Do you want to know what that fucking bitch is threatening to do? She thinks we're having an affair—can you believe it?—and she wants to bring charges against you." She looked up and pointed. "And don't you start laughing, either. I know it's funny, but it's also not funny. Shit, you know what I mean."

"I do, even though your vocabulary this evening seems to have been reduced to a pale fraction of its usual polysyllabic dazzle."

Natalie stood up. "I'm sorry. I just . . . I need a hug."

"Of course you do." Preston opened his arms and swept her in.

Alphonse Allemand picked that moment to enter the front door. "I do hope I'm not interrupting anything," he said, full knowing that this was their regular time for tutoring. "I mean, don't let me stop you," he added as he passed the two of them on his way to the kitchen. His nostrils flared as he exhaled sharply.

Preston turned from Natalie and followed Alphonse into the kitchen. "Don't get all bent, my dear. Natalie is having a hard day, and she's worried about us. Her mum seems to think I'm fooling around with her pretty young daughter and is threatening to report me. Now, isn't that *le plus ridicule?*"

Alphonse spread his hands. *"Vraiment?"*

"Yes, really, my dearest Alpha, you know you are the one, my singular sensation. Besides—no offense, Natalie, nothing personal, but you just do not have the right anatomy to turn me on. So your mother is barking up the wrong side of the tree, and my somewhat insecure true love here has nothing to be jealous of over you—or anybody else, for that matter."

Alphonse's lower lip began to quiver. "I . . . I don't know what to say."

"Try, 'I love you and want to spend the rest of my life with you making love and fine wine under the Mediterranean sun.' That should do just fine." Preston held out his arms. "Come here, my Alpha." They both understood the nickname as both affectionate and ironic, since it had always been clear that Preston was the alpha male of the pair. The two men embraced, but their long kiss was interrupted by a crash and clatter coming from the back yard.

"You two stay here," Preston said. "Let me check it out." He opened the sliding door in time to see a woman picking herself up from where she had tripped over a collection of gardening tools dumped from the cart she had upended. It was Martine Rossum, and she was carrying a pistol.

"Preston Fender!" she shouted. "You deserve this."

"What are you talking about?"

"You and Natalie. No jury is going to convict me for protecting my daughter." She pointed the Luger at him and fired, but her shot went wild. Preston turned and tried to get back into the house. She fired again. He stumbled with the blow to his left leg. She followed his fall but her third shot was low. On the way down, his head struck the edge of the jamb, and when he hit the floor, he lay there, not moving.

Martine Rossum stood in the middle of the garden, staring at the body straddling the threshold, blood spreading on the decking. She looked down at the gun in her hand as if seeing it for the first time, an alien thing. She dropped it, turned, and ran into the trees behind the house.

Alphonse and Natalie were at his side when Preston opened his eyes. Natalie was already using a pair of kitchen shears to cut away Preston's pant leg to get at the wound high on his left thigh. "I think I've been shot," he said, as he came to, "maybe twice." He put his hand to his head.

Natalie looked up from where she was checking the wound. "No, doesn't look like it. You hit your head on the way down. You do have a bullet lodged in your thigh, and judging by the bleeding, it did some real damage but didn't hit an artery. I don't see an exit wound so the bullet is still in there."

Alphonse scowled. "Do you know what you are doing?"

"I'm a nursing student."

"Well, then let's call an ambulance and get him to a hospital."

"No!" It was a barked command from Natalie.

"But Preston is . . ."

"That was my mother who pulled the trigger. You want

them to put my mother in prison? No, I can take care of this myself, but I'll need some things." She rattled off a list of supplies.

"We have some of that, but only the little Band-Aids."

"Then make yourself useful and run to the drugstore for the rest. But first help me get him on the kitchen table where I can work on him. And bring me that bottle of rubbing alcohol and the box of tissues and your razor blades."

"Oh my, this is intense. I don't know . . ."

"Just do it. And the sewing kit, if you can find it."

৪৩

By the time Alphonse returned from the drug store with the large gauze pads and bandages and antibiotic ointment, Natalie was already starting to close the wound with neat stitches tied off in surgeon's knots. "You got it out?" Alphonse asked anxiously.

"Yeah, no thanks to your lover here, who would not lie still and not stop moaning. It's a good thing you both like to cook. I couldn't go deep enough with the damn razor blade without making a real mess, but your kitchen knives are all wicked sharp and those little tongs came in handy."

"Wow, that's pretty . . ."—he swayed slightly and turned his head to the side—"pretty impressive, but now can we take him to the emergency room?"

"What part of 'no' did you not understand. Gunshot wounds have to be reported to the police. So, no! Just help me bandage him up and get him into the bedroom."

Preston tried to roll over and sit up. "You keep talking about me as if I wasn't here. And who anointed you Queen Natalie of the Nile? Man, you do have a bossy streak."

"It comes with the job title, even when you're still a student nurse. And you, my annoying patient, need to rest. I really don't know about those stitches, so we're going to carry you and you're going to call in sick—home with the flu or something—for the rest of the week. We'll see how you're doing after the weekend. In the meanwhile, I have some maternal tracks to cover over."

Alphonse was scowling again. "I thought you and your mother, like, you hated each other."

"I hate what she did to me and to herself to get where she is, and I absolutely have to get away from her, at least for a while, but I still love her and I don't want to see her life ruined by this."

"But what about Preston?"

"He's good with all this. As soon as he is up to it, he's going to move in with you while we plan the next phase of our getaway."

"Our getaway?"

"Yeah, he and I talked it over while you were gone. By the way, just how slow do you drive? The CVS in the strip mall is just down the road."

"Oh, I didn't know that. I drove down to Taggertsville, speeding all the way."

"Now I understand the stories."

"Stories?"

"Yeah, the ones Preston tells about—"

Preston cut her off with a loud groan of pain. "None of my stories, not now. Just get me into bed and bring me a drink, a stiff one."

੪⊃

Before it became completely dark, Natalie scoured the back-yard, retrieved the Luger, and tried to make sure there was

241

no evidence that her mother had been there. Inside, she wiped down the Luger to make sure there were no prints on it. From her backpack, she pulled a vintage cookie tin and held it above the Luger. "I thought so, just big enough." She dumped the contents of the tin onto the table: a stack of letters, photos, and papers bound with a rubber band. "You guys ever bake with parchment paper?" Alphonse nodded. "Good. I'm going to need some. And I'm going to duck over to campus and raid the chem cabinet in the art department. They're more lax about inventory than either chemistry or the school of nursing. I just hope I remember enough chemistry and about preserving metal objects."

"What is this all about?"

"The gun. I don't know much about guns, but I'm pretty sure this is German and it has a story. I need it to disappear now, but I also want to be able to learn its story, which, in some way I still don't understand, is part of my story, my family's story."

It took the rest of the week for the three of them to work out their elaborate departure plan and put all the pieces in place. Natalie prepared her special wrapping paper and buried the gun in the garden at a spot she figured she could return to. She and Preston got tickets for Paris out of New York the following week. Alphonse, who was not yet the focus of campus attention, would wait until the end of the term to leave for Europe, then meet up with them in Cyprus.

✌ Chapter 25

Anatole smiled at Martine in her office. "Ever been to Paris?"

"Once, for a tattoo arts conference."

"Oh, yes, that's right, your academic specialty. Natalie showed me her tattoo, the one she got with you. Alphonse and I also have matching tattoos, but they're . . . it doesn't matter. Anyway, Paris. So you probably know what a special city it is, a city of lights, a city of love. And Natalie fell in love and realized she wanted to start over, a new beginning, so we got married."

"Wait a minute. You said you were gay."

"I did and I am. But I married Natalie in France. It was a sham, a scam so she would have a new name and could get a new passport through the embassy there. Everything took time, and in the meantime, she and this guy and . . . well, it's Paris, winter turns to spring, and after the two of them returned from Germany, that was it. But we had to cover our tracks. We needed a way to make sure the trail ended there, even after you sent that inept private eye in pursuit. He was not terribly bright, but he was so damned persistent. That's when we concluded that not only did Natalie need a new name, but she needed to become a widow."

"And how did you manage that?"

"It was an elaborate scheme that took many months to set up and follow through. Based on an actual case that we heard about, we had Alphonse bring a trumped up lawsuit against me, a suit for damages. When it went to court, Natalie appeared in my stead and explained that her husband, her much older husband, had died recently of heart failure. The judge, annoyed with having to deal with the matter, threw out the case because—official reason, written into the judge's decision—the respondent, A. Preston Fender, was deceased. There it was, a legal decision, published. Thereafter, Preston Fender was legally dead as far as France and the world was concerned. So, Anatole Lavigne, a citizen of France with a valid French passport, leaves for Cyprus with the plaintiff in the case, Alphonse Allemand. Trail broken. Preston Fender is dead, long live Anatole Lavigne, now de-Fender. Uh, sorry about that. Punny habit."

"And Natalie?"

"On her new passport, she is Mrs. Fender, N. M. Fender, who slowly makes her way to Cyprus by way of Germany, where she and the real love of her life first do some personal and professional digging."

"So, she is in Cyprus?"

"No. I guess I can say that, because the sleuths you sicced on her figured it out on their own and are likely to confirm it any day now. She later left Cyprus for Israel."

"Israel? Natalie lives in Israel?"

"I . . . I can't say."

"But you have to. After what you did."

"What I did? You now know what I did, and it was not what you thought at all, was it?"

Marti studied her hands. "No, it wasn't," she said quietly.

"And she tried to protect me, you both did."

"Yes, as you tried to protect her. And now you know what happened in Paris. The rest is history, as they say."

"But you still haven't told me the rest of the history about Natalie."

"Nor can I—not that I know all that much—but I made a promise to someone I came to love dearly. I wish I could say more, but that is it. She will have to tell you herself, when she is ready. And I believe she will."

"And when might that be?"

"Maybe sooner than either of us expect, maybe sooner than is safe or healthy, especially since that trio of amateur detectives keeps pushing on the case. I was hoping that they might be persuaded to let it go. Is there any chance that you could help in that?"

"Is it true, what you said, that Natalie will tell me?"

"I said what I believe, and I do know Natalie, almost as well as I know my Alphonse. She will reach out to you at some point, I am quite sure. When it is safe."

"Is she in danger?"

"I really can't say any more. But do please ask your colleagues to back off and let this one go. Would you do that?"

"I can send them a message, but that doesn't mean it will make a difference. They seem to be ignoring my texts."

"Well, they have been rather busy. And they have had some setbacks of their own to swallow. But give it a try. Please."

⬧ Chapter 26

THE TEXT MESSAGE from Marti arrived their second day in Nicosia, just after their in-person search of the marriage records. Rand tucked the phone back into his pocket. "She wants us to call it off again. She says to just enjoy the rest of our vacation."

"But we now know what happened next. The guess about a marriage in Cyprus was right. Tal Fender married Yagil Sigal, an Israeli. Now we have another name to follow up on. We're closing in."

"But maybe that's not such a good idea. Marti's text is long and sounds pretty determined. Something must have happened. She was the one who kept insisting that this was all about finding her daughter, and now that we may be able to do that, suddenly she changes her mind."

"She didn't say why?"

"No, just that she thought it might be too risky."

"What is the risk?"

"How should I know, but as long as we're here in Nicosia, we might as well see what else we can find out. Micah did mention an art dealer in Nicosia. It wasn't Deverell, but maybe this guy might know something. Who knows?"

Shanna scowled at her phone. "It was like Dora something. Ah, D'aureville. Google shows a Charles D'aureville,

Objets d'Art, on the Turkish side of Nicosia."

"Great, we've been wanting to visit the Turkish quarter, and now we have an excuse."

❧

As they entered the Turkish-controlled half of the divided city by way of the busy Ledra Street Crossing, the change in their surroundings was abrupt. Church spires gave way to the minarets of mosques. The streets, even those obviously catering to tourists, were subtly more drab. The multinational fast food chains that were abundant to the point of nearly crowding out local fare on the other side, were all but absent here. It almost seemed that people lowered their voices once through the checkpoint.

"Do you realize," Rand said, "the border agents hardly glanced at anyone's identification, and the Turkish border guard didn't even stamp our passports. We are now no longer in Europe, but there's no official trail. How interesting. I'm betting there are groups and certain kinds of people who make regular use of that, uh, informality."

"You're probably right. And keep your wallet and passport well tucked."

"Aren't you being a bit racist, or at least making assumptions based on ethnic stereotypes."

"No, I'm reading the guidebook entry on my phone."

"Which probably gives us away as clueless tourists, wouldn't you say? And where do we go next on our wild goose chase?"

"Google Maps makes it three streets up, left, then right, and then what looks like a short way up on the right. Not far."

Charles D'aureville, Objets d'Art turned out to be a small

storefront with iron grating over its windows and a painted sign above the door in French, Turkish, and Arabic. A smaller sign beside the door in English read, "Charles D'aureville, dealer in modern and ancient works of art. Paintings a specialty. Buy, sell." Paragraphs in German and French followed. Evidently, the main appeal of the store was not to the locals.

Rand opened the heavy door and entered the quiet gloom of the store. Sunlight streaming through the windows created a barred pattern on the scene and highlighted dancing dust motes in the air. The room smelled of wood and old lacquer. Small sculptures sat on several low tables, and the walls were nearly covered floor to ceiling with oil paintings, large and small, mostly showing modern technique and subject matter. Next to a doorway at the back, a rack held an assortment of art prints and photographic works in plastic slip cases. The man entering through the doorway greeted them in German, but immediately switched to English.

"Hello. You'll have to be forgiving me. We don't get many Americans, not this time of year this season, and most of our regulars are Germans, from Germany." The man seemed ill at ease, as if, oddly, he was not used to speaking with customers, and his English seemed guided by an awkward syntax.. "So, how can I help you maybe?"

"Are you Mr. D'aureville?"

"Yes, that is true, I am D'aureville. Are you here for any special reason, for anything in particular?"

"Not really, just curious. A friend down in Larnaca mentioned your place."

"Oh, really? That's interesting. Could it have been a Monsieur Lavigne?"

"No. I don't think I know a Mister Lavigne."

"Of course not. So, how might I help you. If you are looking for Cypriot works, work by local artists, we have quite a
few, but also some older items from mainland Europe:
France, Germany, Italy mostly. What you see here is only
what we put out to attract the eye, if you will. More of our
collection is in the rooms downstairs where it is protected
from the heat and the sunlight. As it should be. But we have
to keep some paintings up here, of course, or people will
think we're out of business." He coughed. "Which we aren't,
of course, as you can see self-evidently with your own eyes."

"Yes, of course." Shanna scowled at the man, trying to
place what so nagged at her about his odd manner of talking. "You wouldn't happen to know a Mr. Deverell, would
you? C. T. Deverell."

D'aureville looked like a deer in the headlights. "It's
D'aureville, Charles D'aureville." He spoke his name in the
French manner, with guttural Rs and with his first name
pronounced 'sharl'. "It's French," he said. "I'm French. Now,
can I show you some paintings?"

"How about those in the basement," Rand asked.

"No, I don't think you would be interested in those."

"And why is that, Mr. D'aureville?"

"Well, many of them are rather rare, for collectors of particular taste and means, if you know what I mean."

Rand took a step forward. "And what if we are such collectors," he said, using his best voice of authority.

D'aureville laughed. "Oh, I hardly think so. First of all, you
are Americans and second of all . . ." he scanned them up
and down as if checking their clothes.

"If not Americans, then who might be your best customers? I mean for the works downstairs."

"Well, I couldn't say, but . . ."

"But who?"

"Well, Germans maybe, uh . . ."

Rand scowled. "Not Irish? I'm half Irish."

"Well, I suppose if . . ." Suddenly D'aureville's face lit up and he crossed over to the wall and touched a switch. An array of small overhead spotlights highlighted the paintings hung there. "This one, of a mother and child, is by a talented young woman—a mother herself—who lives here in Lefkoşa, in Turkish Nicosia. I could let you have it for a hundred Euros."

Rand studied the painting. "I like the saturated colors and the exuberant brush work, but I don't think so."

"But it's a twenty-first century Madonna and child, very Irish appeal. I could give you a discount, because it's Friday and I shall have to close soon. Let's say eighty Euros, and I'll even pack it for shipping for you."

"No, thank you."

"Seventy then, but that leaves me with nothing after I pay the artist."

Shanna could tell Rand was having fun with the man but she was also getting impatient. "Come on, darling. We've seen enough. And we need to talk before you buy any more paintings. Okay?"

Rand pretended to be put off by her intrusion. With subdued annoyance, he said, "Okay. I suppose we can always come back." He followed her toward the front door. As they exited, Rand turned and called out, "Thank you, Mr. Deverell."

"You're welcome," came the response just before the door

closed. Rand pulled Shanna to the side and around the corner, putting his finger to his lips. As they waited, the man stuck his head out of the shop and looked up and down the street. After the door closed again, Rand said, "I think we found the missing Mr. Deverell, and I don't think he is a completely honest businessman."

"I don't think he is either. And he speaks as poorly as he writes reports." She poked him in the ribs. "I could tell you were really getting a charge out of dishing it to the poor man."

"Advanced interrogation technique. There's more than one way to trip up a suspect."

"Well, you had me almost choking to keep from laughing. So what do we do next? I think we should let Darlene in on our progress."

"Right, let's go back to our hotel here, do a little online research on one Charles D'aureville, then have a chat with Darlene after she gets up but before she's off to work. And what about reporting in to Marti, too?"

"I don't know, maybe not yet, maybe after we check in with Darlene. Let's take another route walking back to the checkpoint, one that makes it easier to see if we're being followed."

"My, you're really getting into this, Shan."

"Just the surveillance awareness protocol I picked up at Langley."

Rand chuckled. "You are so full of it, you know that? Surveillance awareness? Langley? Bullshit."

By the time they were through the Ledra Street Crossing, they were both certain they had been followed, but not by Deverell.

ಏ Chapter 27

THROUGH A GAP in the hotel window curtain, Rand kept peeking out to surveil the pedestrians on the street below, watching for any movement or gesture that might be a tell. "I wish there was somebody to turn to, to consult with. Times like this I almost wish I was back on the force, with a chief of detectives above me."

"You know, I never had that," Shanna said. "I was always pretty much on my own, in charge whether officially or not."

"Still are, I can attest." That earned him a squinting glare from Shanna. "But what about Dean Tingerly? He's your boss and seems to have been a pretty good mentor since you arrived at Holcomb."

"I meant, like, well . . . No, you're right, I have had people above me, but not people I could really turn to, as you're talking about, not when things were messed up. I mean, are we going to ask Afsa Tingerly what to do next?"

"No, but we can use the resources at hand. Do you recall who put us onto Monsieur D'aureville in the first place?"

"I think it was Micah."

"Then let's ask him what he knows and how he knows it before we hear from Darlene. I texted her to call when she wakes up, said we had picked up the trail on Natalie and had located Deverell."

"Micah will be busy at the restaurant, but I can text him to call when he gets a break." She was thumb typing on her phone when Rand's phone buzzed on the nightstand beside the bed.

He turned it over. "It's from Darlene. She says, 'Me too. Too busy for call. Talk when you get back."

"Well that helps a lot." Her phone buzzed and she answered on speakerphone. "Hello?"

"It's Micah, I was on break. I don't know this D'aureville cat. I just remember Anatole from Oinos Dafni mentioning him once. Why don't you swing by the winery when you're back in Larnaca and talk to him about it before you leave."

"Okay, thanks."

"And don't leave without coming to Epic again. Ya hear? We all want to see you."

"We hear. See you soon." Shanna set the phone down and sat for a minute with her hands in her lap. "I guess we're on our own."

"Yeah, and I'm getting this creeping feeling about Nicosia, like there are now eyes on us."

"Me too. Micah said his source was the guy at Oinos Dafni. Maybe we should check into it.

"So, let's check out early and go tour a winery. What do you say?"

"I say it sounds like a plan, Rand."

He grinned at her. "But first we have to drop off the key, Lee."

Shanna threw a pillow at him before going to the closet to fetch her suitcase to begin packing up.

„

With Rand in the passenger seat as navigator, they managed

to get lost on the drive down to Oinos Dafni, but the un-planned detour allowed them to confirm that the dust-gray Range Rover they kept spotting was actually following them. As Shanna doubled back on an unpaved road that had reached a dead end, they passed the Rover. Through the dust cloud kicked up from the road, they saw the driver and two passengers, one of whom looked a lot like it might be D'aureville.

Rand glanced back over his shoulder as the driver of the Rover negotiated an awkward three-point turn on the narrow road. "You don't happen to know the fine for speeding around here, do you?"

Shanna shook her head as she stepped on the accelerator. "Nope, but we might find out. Frankly, maybe attracting the attention of the local gendarmes might not be such a bad idea."

"I've got a better idea. Get back to the main highway as fast as you can, but head north, back toward Nicosia, then immediately reverse direction."

"On a divided highway? You forget there were barriers, not a median strip, and it's quite a ways to the next inter-change."

"Well, we could pull the same thing on the secondary road. The B1's not divided."

"Too slow, too much traffic. Look, I have this figured out." She sped up. "The B1 and A1 are right next to each other along here. I seem to remember a little crossover or some-thing of the sort that should be coming up really quickly."

The Range Rover was back on their tail several cars back when Shanna suddenly made the right turn onto the B1 heading north. She floored it as she pulled into the far left lane, cutting off a high-top delivery van to also put it between them and their pursuers. The sharp left of the short crossover to the A1 came up faster than she expected. Shanna skidded around the turn, hit the brakes, and pulled to a stop on the left shoulder of the connector, putting a dense grove of trees between them and the B1. She kept her eyes locked on the rearview mirror until she spotted the Rover speeding on past the turnoff to the connector. The tires spun as she pulled out and accelerated toward the A1, matching the speed of the southbound traffic and slipping seamlessly in between a blue sedan and a van.

"There, that's how you do it!" she said.

"I'm impressed. And you did all that driving on the left. You have many hidden talents."

"Watch and learn, Grasshopper."

In less than a quarter hour, with still no Range Rover in the mirror, they took the correct exit. Before long they were turning into the front gate at Oinos Dafni. The winery, perched on gentle slopes that steered the cooling night sea breezes through row on row of grape vines, was an artful blend of the new and the old. Several of the original buildings had been lovingly restored. In front of a rustic stone-faced cottage that was marked as the tasting room, painted chairs and mosaic inlaid round tables decked a covered porch. Just beyond were the two-story shingled main house, a barn, and a small guest house. Farther upslope arose a thoroughly modern structure with multicolored clerestory windows. It looked like it housed offices as well as winemaking facilities. Shanna pulled up into the small empty parking lot in front of the tasting room and released her grip on the steering wheel. "I had no idea that being a tourist could be so . . . so, uh, exciting?"

"You loved it, admit it."

"I did, but I don't think I'd do it again. Still, the driving was . . . wow!"

"When we get back I'll have to introduce you to some of the highway patrol maneuvers. There's this one called PIT, pursuit intervention technique, that, well . . ." He stopped himself when he noticed Shanna's disapproving sidelong glance. "Ah, right. Let's check out some wine and see what we can find out about Mr. D'aureville. Or Deverell."

The tasting room was empty, but there was a bell on the polished wood counter with instructions in several languages to ring for service. Shanna tapped it twice. As they waited, they explored the room, which carried racks of wines, a stand with souvenir postcards, and a wall-sized mural illustrating both the history of the original vineyard and its modern revival.

Behind them, a voice announced, "Welcome to Oinos Dafni. I'm Alphonse and this is . . . . Oh, yes, hello again. You're the couple from the party at Micah and Ariadne's, aren't you."

"Yes, hello." Shanna put down the postcard she was examining. "We thought it might be fun to visit your winery."

"I'm sorry Anatole isn't here, too, so you could meet him, but he had to fly to America." He reached beneath the counter and pulled out two wine glasses. "Would you like to taste some wines? We always recommend working from lightweight to heavyweight, starting with white and working up to our powerhouse reds."

"That sounds wonderful, but we're also here on a mission. Can we ask about some things while we're sipping?"

Alphonse flipped his hand at them. "Of course you can, don't be silly. Besides I already know some of what you're going to ask about. Here,"—he ducked down behind the counter, opened the door of a small cooler, and lifted a bottle onto the counter—"let's start with our Malvasia Bianca, a light and flowery sipping wine, perfect for a hot afternoon like this." He poured two half glasses and recorked the bottle. "We are the only ones on Cyprus growing this varietal, which elsewhere is often finished somewhat on the sweet side. Ours is much drier, a perfect aperitif on its own or the accompaniment to light appetizers."

As Shanna took a tentative sip, Rand swirled his glass and held it to his nose. "Yes, flowery," he said. "Is that a hint of lavender I detect?"

Shanna took another sip. "Very nice, very nice. But you said you already know what we are here to ask about."

"I do, which is why my impetuous husband flew to America to visit a particular university familiar to all of us."

"Are you talking about Holcomb? He went to Holcomb?"

"Indeed. I wish we could have gone together—so many memories, most, but not all, sweet ones—but someone has to keep the business going. Besides he is the right man for the job, owing to his special, ah, relationship with a particular professor there."

"Now, you really have us going. Specifics, please."

"Certainly." He ducked behind the counter again. "This is our sauvignon blanc, which you might have tasted at the restaurant, but this specific wine is our reserve bottling, which benefited from a gentle barrel aging in French oak to add an extra layer of roundness on the palate, enhanced further by blending in a small amount of our chardonnay. If you have the patience to wait for it, the parade of flavors will delight you."

"You're having fun with us, aren't you?"

"Why not? Life should be fun."

"Agreed, but our questions are somewhat urgent. We may have some rather nasty looking men pursuing us."

"Yes, they do look rather nasty, don't they. I assume you are talking about D'aureville's men. They are all glower and growl, just local boys with nothing better to do than to pretend they are tough guys for a few extra Euros. I don't know why D'aureville keeps them around. When the reckoning comes—and it will, I can assure you—they will skitter away in a wink, leaving him to face his fate alone."

"All right, now you really have us intrigued. How do you know all this?"

"We know D'aureville—or Deverell, as he styled himself then—from Paris, after the professor sent him to track down her daughter and her daughter's putative abductor, otherwise known at the time as Prof. A. Preston Fender, but now come into his own as my beloved, Anatole Lavigne. But that's a digression. You want to know about Deverell, which may not be his real name either, but he did once have a passport and driver's license attesting to the case, so who are we to question?" He reached beneath the counter for a third glass before filling all three. "If you like a white with something to say, this is the wine for you. One of my favorites. Well, one among the many." He lifted his glass to toast, then waited for them to raise theirs. "*Santé*." He took a sip and bubbled it in his mouth.

"About Deverell?"

Alphonse closed his eyes as if entering a state of religious ecstasy. "You have to wait for it to appreciate the layers as they unfold on the tongue." He took another sip. "How delicious: the anticipation, the elaboration, and the finish. Like good sex. Or a good story."

"Let me guess," Shanna said. "You were a modern lit major or something."

"Philosophy, polluted by a minor in literary criticism. Someday, I want to turn all this"—he turned full circle with both hands pointing—"into a novel of depth and character to match the wines and the weather and the people."

"No short story, I imagine. What about Deverell?"

He sighed deeply and took another drink of the reserve sauvignon blanc. "Americans, always so in a hurry to get to the point. Okay, Deverell is a thief, but a blundering one. When Natalie's paintings disappeared, we suspected him immediately, but he was already headed for the border."

"Natalie's paintings?"

"Yes, the ones she took from home and smuggled to Paris. Clever girl made it look like somebody else stole them, but I'm pretty sure her mother figured out who the thief was, although the local police, being true to that spurious species, never did solve the case."

Rand straightened his shoulders. "Not all police—"

"Yes, I know, I know," he said with patient annoyance. "You were in law enforcement and maybe still are, in a way, but I am talking about a phenomenon about which we can have a long debate now or save it for later so we can get on with the story for which you two are so eager to reach the *dénouement*." He stooped behind the counter once more and retrieved a tall stylish bottle of deep pink liquid. From his pocket he took a waiter's corkscrew and proceeded to cut the capsule and uncork the wine in a ballet of flashy handiwork almost too fast to follow. He grinned at them as he filled three fresh glasses.

"And this," he said, "is what you get when you take a fist-pumping over-ripe red, give it minimal skin contact, and leave in a *soupçon* of residual sugar. Behold, our rosé noir! *Santé!*"

Shanna and Rand echoed with "*Santé!*" and each took a generous swallow. "I admit," Rand said, "I'm usually not much of a fan of rosés, but this . . . this is something else. Lipsmacking, rich."

"Rich, like our faux art dealer was when he first arrived in Cyprus. Not so much now, which is why we think the dreaded overdue invoice will be arriving before too long. But he was already quite well off when we caught up with him after he had sold the first painting. Of course, being a bumbling and inept thief, he still had no idea the true value of the paintings. He was also lucky. The first French dealer he approached was every bit as shady but less bumbling. That dealer was also, like all too many of certain old-guard French, deeply anti-Semitic and immediately recognized the painting for what it was. He was generous with Deverell, in part because he was hoping there might be more to come, but Deverell was paid less than half what the painting was worth and a small fraction of what it sold for the next time around."

"Are you saying that these paintings, the ones Natalie smuggled out of the country, were Nazi looted art."

"No, I am not. There is no need to say it. Even Natalie as a teenager had already figured out the truth in plain sight."

"Then why did she smuggle them to Europe?"

"Youthful idealism. She had this fantasy sans plan that somehow she would be able to track down the rightful owners and return the art. Restoring Nazi art is a specialized and highly demanding enterprise, and on her own she had almost no chance of succeeding while at the same time possibly putting herself and her mother at no inconsiderable risk." He took another drink, this time a generous swallow. "Good, no?"

"Good, yes."

"Yes, and as to Natalie, her pilgrimage to the putative homeland with her then new boyfriend was derailed by the loss of the paintings even before the two of them could depart for Germany."

"But there were two paintings left. Didn't you say that Deverell had sold one?"

"I did, and there were. We let Deverell get away with them. It was a quid pro quo. He dropped the pursuit in exchange for a substantial pension. We all four got to disappear and make our chosen new beginnings in exchange for letting go of the paintings, which were never ours in the first place, not even her mother's nor her grandfather's, certainly not the Nazi's who stole them from the Jews. We made the deal without Natalie knowing who had taken the paintings. She was too much of an idealist, a purist, to let the paintings be sold at a profit in exchange for silence. All she knew was that the paintings were gone." He raised the bottle and tipped it toward Shanna and Rand. "More?"

"I better slow down," Shanna said. "I have to drive. But you can go ahead, Rand."

"And I will." He held out his glass for a refill. "But tell me, Alphonse, what kept you from turning Deverell in or him exposing you?"

"It's a stalemate, a Mexican standoff, double handcuffs. So, we wait. Sooner or later someone else will expose Deverell. Or merely finish him off. Through deception and ineptitude, he has accumulated a growing list of dissatisfied customers, and I don't mean the tourists who now and then stumble into his amusing little shop. Between those unprincipled dealers who would traffic in Nazi stolen art and the principled groups that are working to shut them down and return the art, he is outflanked. His days are numbered." He made a show of finishing the last drops of pink fluid in his glass before restoring the bottle to the cooler beneath the counter. "And now we continue the journey toward the darker corners of our wine cellar." He reached to the shelf behind him for a bottle whose contents were only a shade darker than the rosé they had just sampled.

"This," he said as he uncorked it, "is our lightest red. It is a blend, mostly Pinot Noir enhanced by the addition of some varietals with a longer local history. One would not call them indigenous, but they have been grown here for millennia. Our blend becomes the perfect accompaniment to lighter fare and,"—he suddenly stopped himself—"oh, please, please forgive me. We have done this all wrong. I should have laid out an assortment of breads and crisps to clear the palate between wines, along with some cheeses. I am so, so sorry, I was so caught up in the storytelling and the *camaraderie* that I forgot who I am. I am"—he pulled himself stiffly erect—"Alphonse Allemand, co-proprietor of Oinos Dafni, at your service. And, despite the French name, I am not German nor even French but *Québécois*."

"And you are also clearly becoming rather happy to be at

our service," Rand noted. "Glass after glass."

"Ah, we are singing the chorus of the same tune, I see." He reached out and placed his hand on Rand's shoulder, eliciting a grin and a deep, repeated nod from Rand. Shanna could see that both men were well on their way to an alcohol-stoked new friendship. It seems, she thought, beer goggles work across nationalities and even across sexual orientation. Or was there more to Rand that she had not yet sorted out? She stepped back from the counter to watch as the next round of tasting played out.

By the time Alphonse announced the *pièce de résistance*, both men were weaving and hovering on the edge of actually bursting into song. "This," Alphonse announced, "is our special reserve bottling of the wine we call *Deux Fois Noir*, twice black. It is a devilishly daring combination of a raisiny Cabernet Franc with an inky black Alicante Bouchet, both fermented *sur lis* before spending twelve months in a mixture of American and French oak and then being blended and cellared for an additional three years *en bouteille* before being released in a limited edition. Prepare yourself for an experience. I will decant this bottle and let it breathe while I get Mariliza to put out a late lunch for us. Nothing fancy. Some meats, cheeses, dolmas, just something to eat while we face the hurricane force of the twice black. That way we can keep talking."

By the time the three of them made their way to the table on the front porch, a middle-aged woman with a patterned kerchief over her nut-brown hair was already setting out a platter of Cypriot treats. Alphonse went over to her, kissed her cheek, and said something in Greek that led to a playful hand slap from the woman.

"Mariliza is the other love of my life and more dependable than the first one. Anatole is intelligent and generous, but one cannot count on him to finish what he began or to honor a commitment by the clock." He gestured for Shanna and Rand to be seated, then reached for the decanter that Mariliza had just ceremoniously carried out to the porch. "And now, prepare to meet the twice-black night itself." He slowly poured three glasses being careful not to disturb the bit of sediment just settling out in the decanter. They raised their glasses, toasted in unison, and then each approached the wine in their own way. At the first sip, Rand jerked his head backwards as if he had taken a sucker punch, Alphonse's face went slack as he savored the first blast at the front of the palate, and Shanna smiled and nodded. Rand said, "Oh, wow, too much, over the top." Alphonse said, "Transcendent, every sip a religious experience." Shanna laughed at the two men and said, "This is really good, really, really good."

Late lunch, including a second platter from Mariliza, stretched out until the approach of dinner time. Fueled by the winery's finest and catalyzed by its resident philosopher, the energetic discourse ranged over the nature of reality, the reality of good and evil, and the beauty and indifference of the natural world.

"And we finish," Alphonse announced at last, "with a bow to the past. Here at Oinos Dafni we specialize in table wines of thoroughly modern pedigree and interpretation, but the island was more known in the past for a different style of wine, Commandaria, a sweet amber-hued dessert wine. Ours is made in the traditional manner entirely from the local varietals Mavro and Xynisteri, with none of our usual experimental flourishes. I hope you like it. And then Greek coffee and perhaps a short retreat, maybe even a nap before a late light supper."

Shanna looked skeptical. "Thank you, but I think not. We have already imposed too much on your hospitality. We really need to go."

"Perhaps you should listen to the vote of your partner before finalizing the decision." Alphonse nodded toward Rand across the table, whose head was tipped back and who had started to snore.

☙

The crowing of an asthmatic rooster awakened Shanna. Bright morning sun streamed across the poster bed in which she had been sleeping. She had vague memories of the evening and some of the discussions centering around privacy and the right to self-definition. She rolled away from the sunlight to find a depression in the bedding where she expected to find Rand.

Once dressed, she made her way from the guest house to the largest building, where she could hear talking and laughing. As she entered through the open sliding doors, Rand turned toward her and waved. "This is interesting, you should join in. Alphonse was telling me about making sparkling wine, and we got into a discussion of what is cheating, what allowed, and whether it is right that wine made through *méthode champenoise*, the traditional method developed in Champagne, France, cannot, within the European Union, be labeled *méthode champenoise* if it was made elsewhere. From there we got into a heated discussion of personal labels and who is allowed to use them and when and how."

"Let me guess, this is the whole gender identity thing that

has been stirring up campus."

"Yes, more or less. Can anyone just decide they are female and call themselves that, or are there limits and prerequisites? Can we even discuss such issues without being attacked as transphobic? And then we moved from the sociopolitical and psychological to the personal. What allows any person to take on a new identity? For instance, what allows A. Preston Fender to call himself Anatole Lavigne?"

"A passport?" Shanna said.

"So, if a passport declares it so, then it must be true. Is that how it works?"

"For some purposes, yes. Where is this going, Rand?"

"Wherever it leads. We're just talking. And what about a profession? Not just anyone can declare themselves a doctor without a lengthy—and expensive—process, but you become a poet by writing poetry, a novelist by writing novels, a professor by—"

"A thief by stealing."

"Exactly."

"You're still a little drunk, aren't you."

"Hung over, perhaps, but pleasantly so."

"I've never had a pleasant hangover, so you're way ahead of me. But I am neither tipsy nor hungover, and I think it is time for us to express our deepest gratitude and be on the road to Larnaca."

Alphonse, who had been following their exchange with interest and amusement, spoke up. "They are looking for you in Larnaca, and my sources say this time the boys from Nicosia have armed themselves."

"You have sources?"

"One needs people who know things in order to remain

unknown to others."

"And what are you recommending?"

"That you enjoy my hospitality until I go to the airport to pick up Anatole, with you undiscovered in the back of my truck. We work a little change of itinerary in your flights, and you are up, up, and away, still intact."

Shanna held her hands to the sides of her head. "Too much, too fast. Rand and I are going to need a little time to talk and take all this in." She gave Rand a pleading look overlaid with some disapproval. "So, shall we? A morning stroll?" Her tone of voice said this was a command, not a question.

Outside, as they made their way along the fence line, Shanna snapped at him without turning toward him. "What was that all about in there?"

"We were just talking, you know, hashing over ideas and principles. Like last night."

"Not like last night. This may be ideas and principles for you, but this is my life. You were on the edge of taking one step farther than you have any right to do."

"I just figured, you know, they understand. They've been scrupulous in protecting Natalie, or whoever she is now. And its personal for them, too. I thought it would be all right if . . ."

"Well, don't think like that. It's my story to tell or not, not yours. And I am saying no one can have my story."

"But it's hard. Don't you ever wish you could just blurt it out and have it over with, move on?"

"Of course I do, but I can't. It has to be enough for me that you know I was once somebody else, and it has to be enough for you that I trust you and no one else."

"There is no such thing as an airtight cover story, you

know. That I learned in my stint as an undercover cop. Sooner or later, you make a slip or somebody sees through or maybe even just makes lucky guesses. My guess is that Anatole and Alphonse have already made some of those."

"Well, let them keep guessing, lucky or not. You are not going to confirm their suspicions. Is that clear?" Her last words were razor-sharp commands.

He stopped and put his hands on the top rail of the fence and looked out over the sea below in the distance. "One of the things that did me in as a cop was the strain of constant vigilance, that, while you are on duty, you are always in the role, always in costume even if you're not in uniform. I don't know."

"Well, you better figure it out, because that's what it takes if you want to stay with me. You're off duty in that sense only when we are alone, just the two of us. The rest of the time you wear the mask and weigh your words." He started to say something, but Shanna shook her head. "Maybe you can understand, then, what it's been like for me. Starting over with a blank slate is a beginning, but it's a beginning that never ends. You're always beginning, and there's no going back, no reprieve."

He turned toward her. "I think I know that, and I understand the toll you've paid to become Shanna Newsom—are still paying—but maybe you can understand what it means to an old boy scout who covered over his own misdeeds but still looks for absolution, even as a lapsed Catholic."

She made the sign of the cross in the air like a priest blessing a congregant. "I absolve you."

"Don't joke like that. It's blasphemous, not funny."

"I'm sorry." She held up her hand in the Vulcan sign of

greeting from Star Trek and started reciting in Hebrew.

"What's that?"

"Another priestly blessing, older, in fact the oldest known biblical text.'"

"What does it mean?"

"Oh, you probably know the lines, since the Christians also use them in translation in their services. 'May the Lord bless you and keep you. May the Lord make his face shine upon you,' dot tot dot."

"Yes of course, the Benediction."

"So, there you are, no blasphemy, although I am not male and it is unclear whether I descend from the priestly class who are the ones who are supposed to offer the blessing. Strictly speaking. Anyway, you have been blessed."

"I have been. To know you and your patience and your love and generosity, it's all a blessing. I sometimes forget that and take it all for granted. It may not be easy, but it's worth it. I'm sorry. Forgive me?"

"Already said and done. I'm sorry, too." She ran her fingers up the hairs on the back of his neck. "Now, what are we going to do about getting home safely."

"We're going to go back up to the house and sit down with Alphonse to work out the details. I trust him. Let's pool our experiences and get it right."

As they approached the main house, they noticed their car was gone. In the same parking spot was now a dust-gray Range Rover, and on the porch of the tasting room, Alphonse was talking with two men.

"So much for trust," Shanna whispered.

ಇ Chapter 28

THE PATH BY THE FENCE afforded Rand and Shanna little cover, but they had not yet been spotted by the three men talking outside the tasting room. Rand tugged her hand and the two of them flattened themselves on the ground. They were too far to hear what was being said, but the men seemed to be talking amicably. When the visitors finally turned and headed back toward their Range Rover, Shanna tried to make herself even skinnier. She dared not look up until she heard the engine start. She caught a glance as the car headed back down the long driveway to the road. She was about to get up when the driver slammed on the brakes, threw the Rover in reverse, and backed up into the parking lot again, squealing to a stop. The passenger, a mule of a man with an old face and the body of a young wrestler, hopped out, and looked around.

Shanna tensed her muscles, getting ready to shoot up and sprint away.

After a sharp command from the driver, the man trotted back toward the tasting room and disappeared inside. In the meanwhile, the driver lit a cigarette and drummed on the steering wheel in impatience. Finally, the passenger came out of the tasting room and jogged toward the car carrying a three-bottle cardboard wine caddy. As the driver shook his head in dismay, he said something in a language that might have been Greek but was gobbledygook to Shanna. He put the car into gear and sped back down the driveway for the second time, kicking up dust before turning onto the road. The Rover accelerated away and quickly disappeared around a curve.

"Do we risk questioning Alphonse or just head out of here?" Shanna whispered.

"On foot? Our car's gone. What can we do?"

Shanna was about to answer when she spotted Alphonse coming out of the building, heading straight for them. "I put them off your trail," he said. "They should be on their way toward Paphos now. You can come out."

"Where's our car? What happened to it?"

"It's in the barn, with the tractor and other equipment. I put it out of sight as soon as I got the call from Euandros up in Nicosia. He keeps his eyes open and his mouth shut. A good man, and as fruity as the orchards he tends."

"You have your own network of queers?"

"*Naturellement*, we are a minority community, and we must look out for each other. Our status before the law is much improved in recent years, but the experience on the ground is still mixed, and the police have been known to look the other way when violence threatens. Socially, the LGBTQ scene is evolving. Nicosia is especially popular; Friday is unofficial LGBTQ party night—on the Greek side, of course, in places like the Ithaki bar—but there are many other friendly places, like Mackenzie Beach in Larnaca, which you may have seen. In any case, I was forewarned."

"Thank you for acting so quickly and decisively. It's probably a good idea to keep our rental car under wraps until we're ready to leave."

"I was also acting in self-interest. If I were perceived by D'aureville to be an active threat, it might destabilize the stalemate that grants us immunity. Come,"—he gestured toward the main house—"let's not stay together in the open longer than necessary. We have details to work out, like how to deal with your car and how to get you safely to the airport, to say nothing about what is on the menu for your last night in Cyprus."

As they walked toward the main house, Shanna's face clouded over. "We won't get to see Ariadne and Micah before we go if we leave directly for the airport from here."

"Nonsense," Alphonse said. "Today is their day off. They are friends. We can invite them up for dinner tonight. In fact, their presence will make the perfect excuse for the place to be all lit up. Any excuse for a party, I always say."

&

After several hours of discussion working out every detail of the departure the next day and changing their flight reservations through an app, Alphonse excused himself. "I have a vineyard to tend, people to supervise, a kitchen staff to get prepared, and, most important of all, a wine list to finalize. We will make your last night in Cyprus most pleasant and memorable, that I promise."

&

The celebration was as promised, a complete blowout that, though it was a weekday, lasted into the small hours of the morning. Ariadne and Micah brought their bartender, Calista, with them as well as their Sicilian friend Giovanni. The evening was spent around the outdoor barbecue, featuring a series of skewers laden with marinated meats and sausage

specialties supplied by Mariliza and her husband and a series of stories supplied by everyone.

As always, Shanna felt at a disadvantage when it came to
swapping stories because it exposed what she regarded as
the paucity of good stories from her life since becoming an
academic and it meant having to edit or censor vignettes
from her life before. When everyone started sharing stories
of their youth, Shanna recycled the story of her window-box
garden in Manhattan and offered up a redacted version of
Eli, her first love, relocating the besotted older boy from
Manhattan to the campus of Mount Cherton College in Vermont. Such revisions and rewrites made her anxious, and
she always later regretted having started each narrative, because each one had then to be committed to memory, added
to her constructed history, and recited in order to avoid a
future slip-up that might betray the discontinuities and
blank pages of her life story.

The group from Larnaca left early, but she and Rand and
Alphonse stayed around the fire after Mariliza and her husband retired for the night. Now alone, the three of them
made one last review of the plans for the next day before Alphonse weaved his way inside and Rand and Shanna staggered back to the guest house.

Shanna and Rand slept in until long after daybreak and
spent the day tagging along with Alphonse as he checked the
status of several plantings and then supervised the bottling
of a cabernet franc that had over-wintered in oak. After a
late midday meal, Shanna excused herself to take a nap. It
seemed that she had only just slipped into dreaming sleep
when the knock came on the guestroom door. "It is Alphonse, you must get dressed quickly so we can depart in

time. I will be waiting at the van in the barn; everything is ready."

Shanna looked over to discover that Rand had slipped in beside her. She shook him awake and the two of them pulled on their shoes, closed up their luggage, and carried it out and around to the waiting van. Alphonse held the door at the back open for them. "Your bags go in the crate there. You two, over to the side on the mat. I will pull the tarpaulin over you and put the lid back on the crate. It should not be too uncomfortable. It is not a long ride to the airport, but a bit bumpy on the route we will be taking this afternoon. It is a day early for your departure, which means even if people have knowledge of your itinerary, you will not be expected, not now and not by this route, one which gives me many opportunities to assure we have not been followed."

As Alphonse reached for the edge of the tarpaulin to pull it into place, Rand asked, "Have you done this sort of thing before? I mean, you almost seem to know little bits of tradecraft."

"That is amusing, and also with a sand-grain of truth. Before entering graduate school at Holcomb, I worked for a while as an analyst for the *Service Canadien du Renseignement de Sécurité*, Canada's intelligence service. I was merely reading papers and translating documents and writing reports, but I am a generalist, so I also learned a lot just by watching and listening and drawing out some of my older colleagues. There, enough conversation for now."

He covered them up and closed and latched the rear doors.

At the airport, he pulled into a close-in parking space and climbed between the seats into the back. "Okay, we are here.

I will help retrieve your bags, and then you will exit from the front. It might look odd and attract attention if you climbed out the back. Then we go together to arrivals first to meet Anatole, whose flight arrives before yours. Then we will shift to departures for your flight and say our farewells there."

As they walked from the van toward the terminal, Shanna felt a shiver that she realized did not come from the breeze on her back that blew warm and humid.

∽

When Anatole emerged after clearing customs, he scanned the waiting crowd and flashed a smile toward Alphonse. His face took on a puzzled look as he spotted Rand and Shanna. The two men approached each other through the crowd, their smiles growing as they neared. They embraced and kissed, then stood looking into each other's eyes. Finally, Alphonse took a step back. "I suppose you're wondering," he said. "Let me introduce you to our new friends, Shanna Newsom and Rand McMurphy, professors from Holcomb University in the States."

"Well, how interesting, an unexpected pleasure. Of course I know about you even though we've never met, but I wasn't expecting to run into you at the airport. I assume you two know Martine Rossum, then."

"She is the reason we are here. And now, as it happens, we are on our way back home to Holcomb."

"Is that so? How curious. And my love,"—he turned to Alphonse—"from you not a word of warning as to this criss-crossing of journeys."

"A matter of prudence. It was a last-minute change of plans. To throw a couple of not-too-bright henchmen of one not-too-bright art dealer off the scent."

"Are those boys giving you all trouble now?"

"It seems those boys may actually have some new money and muscle behind them. The last time they showed their homely faces they were armed with shiny new handguns tucked into their belts."

"And I assume that, too, is related to our new friends here."

"It is, but it is hardly their fault. They are merely the search party sent by Martine to look for her daughter."

"Of course. I knew that, which is why we sent me back to Holcomb to talk with Martine. I just didn't expect that you and they would . . ."

"Well, they managed to bump into the lost Mr. Deverell along the trail. Everything will be revealed in time, but now we need to get them over to departures to pick up their new tickets and boarding passes so they can leave the island before those threadbare thugs realize they missed the opportunity to do whatever dirty deed they imagined." He turned to Shanna and Rand. "You have your passports? Now let's all move. We don't want you missing your flight. Just follow Anatole, he knows this airport like the back of my hand."

༄

Shanna and Rand were past security and on the way to their gate when they heard shouts and a ruckus in the distance behind them. Shanna started to turn but Rand took her arm and steered her toward their gate. "Whatever it is, there's nothing useful we can do. Besides, it probably has nothing to do with us. Our job is to get on that plane and leave Cyprus."

They hurried to the gate, but as it turned out, boarding was delayed and then their plane sat on the tarmac for a long stretch waiting for clearance for takeoff. It was not until they had cleared the runway that Shanna took a deep breath, let it out, and started to relax. She closed her eyes and listened to the multilingual hubbub around her blanketed by the roar and whine of the engines straining for altitude.

❧ Chapter 29

WHEN SHANNA AND RAND exited from customs and immigration at Charlotte International the following day, Darlene was waiting. "Hey, strangers," she called out as she approached. "Let go of your wheelies long enough for a big welcome hug." She spread her arms and bear-hugged each in turn. "My oh my, you two really do know how to stir things up. What a mess you left behind in Cyprus."

Shanna frowned, confused. "I guess. You mean with that D'aureville guy, with Deverell?"

"No. You don't know? Haven't you heard the news?"

"We've been flying for what seems like forever, squeezed in and sweating in the back of the Airbus, and trying to catch a little sitting-up sleep along the way. News? What news?"

"Come on, let's get you poor things home. I'll catch you up about everything on the drive. You need help with your luggage?"

"Naw, I think we're fine. Lead the way."

Rand brought up the rear as they snaked through the crowd of arriving passengers and eager greeters. "At least bring us up-to-date now on that news about Cyprus," he said.

"Sure," Darlene said, as she kept playing point man. "Terrorists attacked the airport in Larnaca yesterday. I thought it happened before you left. I had my fingers crossed that you weren't going to be delayed or might not get out."

"Terrorists?"

"Yeah, two gunmen tried to breach the secure area of the airport. They opened fire, airport police returned fire, and both gunmen were killed. One woman working the security checkpoint and two passengers were wounded in the cross-fire, but last I heard they were treated at a hospital and all three were out of danger."

"Did they say anything about the attackers, who they were, what was their agenda?"

"Yeah, the Cypriot government is playing coy but hinting they were Turks, part of some obscure underground group with fantasies of taking over the entire island and putting it under Turkish rule. Turkish-controlled North Cyprus claims that the attack was made by disaffected Greek Cypriots who want to pull out of the European Union. Nobody knows for sure, and the gunmen are obviously not available for questioning."

"I think we know who they were," Shanna said, glancing toward Rand who returned a knowing look. "Which means we had a narrow escape. If they were D'aureville's men, it was a close call, much closer than we realized at the time."

"But why would D'aureville try to take you out? Doesn't he understand that none of us are after him? You were only trying to get a lead on Natalie."

"Obviously, which means there's more going on there than we were aware of. D'aureville and his associates must be involved in something bigger that they think is under threat."

Darlene's smile was now completely gone. "I have some

guesses, and they all have to do with Nazi stolen art. When Lavigne, the former Professor Fender, dropped in on me, he explained how Deverell originally set himself up with the proceeds from the sale of three paintings, and for a while he did all right as D'aureville, parlaying it into what he hoped would be self-sustaining semi-retirement. But things have not been going as well for him lately. Maybe he has something cooking, something that he worries you two might spoil."

The three of them looked at each other with simultaneous flashes of recognition. "You two thinking what I'm thinking?" Shanna said. "I'm thinking of Marti Rossum and the artwork in her home. And I'll bet D'aureville is thinking he can dip into the same well again. Some or all of those paintings must have the same provenance. That could explain all the trips to Germany by Marti's father as well as that, according to her, the collection was often changing while she was growing up. And the unexpectedly large estate."

"But he was Jewish. What was a Jew doing dealing in Nazi plunder? And what about Marti? If Natalie knew and tried to return some of the paintings, the ones D'aureville intercepted, Marti must have known, too. That doesn't make sense either."

"And now, she may be in danger."

"Or involved. Maybe she has already made some kind of deal with D'aureville."

They reached the parking area and Darlene looked around, scowling. "The van should be right here." She pressed the button on her key fob, triggering a chirp and flashing tail lights one row over. "I don't know what's in the works with this D'aureville character. What I do know is that it's time we had a blunt conversation with Professor Rossum."

"Can we get something to eat first?" Rand pleaded. "I'm starved."

"I'll take you back to the restaurant. We can nibble while we do some more internet research and plan our next move. Given the events in Larnaca, I think we need to make that move sooner rather than later."

ಬಿ

Dahlia's was a madhouse, so Darlene set them up in a small private dining room in the annex. "It'll be quieter here with more room to spread out. I'll get some food on the way and grab my laptop so we can all work the Internet. Okay? I'll be right back."

While Darlene was fetching food and her computer, Shanna pulled the laptop from her backpack, straightened out the Wi-Fi connection, and picked up where she last left off with her online research. From the marriage record in Cyprus, they had Natalie's married name. For the second time, she had taken her husband's surname, creating another branch in the trail of names. Shanna started looking for anything on Tal Sigal.

Darlene arrived with her laptop in one hand and a platter of appetizers balanced on her other hand. "Everybody else is busy, so I just threw things on a platter. At least they're still warm. Should be good. Where's Rand?"

"In the men's room."

"I see you're already at it, girl. Any luck?"

"No. Tal Sigal returns to Israel a married woman again—this time no sham, we assume—and then vanishes once more. How can this keep happening?"

"What about the new husband? What was his name?"

"Yagil."

"Are you kidding? Yagil Sigal? What kind of a name is that?"

"Hebrew. It means he probably comes from a family of kohens, the priestly class. I don't know about his given name." She typed into a search box. "Ah, here it is. His parents had a hopeful future for him. The name means 'he will rejoice.' Now let's see if we will rejoice." She started fresh searches and was still typing and clicking away when Rand arrived.

"How's it going, Shan?"

"Better. I lost the trail on Tal Sigal, but I have something on her husband. I have a news article about a, quote, hush-hush high-tech startup, unquote, called AnaQueue getting a major defense contract. One of the founders is named as Yag Sigal, formerly with an intelligence unit while serving in the military."

"So, maybe he's still a spook or at least involved in the tech side of spycraft. Let me see if I can get anything on him from that angle."

"And how do you propose to do that?"

"I have my ways." He stuffed a chilli-cheese canape in his mouth and closed his eyes.

Darlene set up her laptop on the other end of the table. "While you guys are chasing spooks, I'm going to make another jaunt down the shady-art rabbit track. And help yourself to the goodies. There's plenty more. These are leftovers from an engagement party. Seems everybody was too busy patronizing the open bar to make much inroads into the buffet."

The silence over the next hour was interrupted by occasional cursing at computer screens and wordless expressions of pleasure over the food. It was finally broken by Shanna shouting "Bingo! Got you."

"Who? What?"

"I found a picture, a grab shot at a defense-contractor trade show in Germany that shows Yag Sigal of AnaQueue Technologies with Rahel Turnasov from the Israeli Consulate in Munich."

"So?"

"So, look at the face; it's Natalie Rossum, I'm certain. I'm just not sure what to make of it."

"I know what to make of it," Rand said. "There's only one way Natalie or Tal could be working at the consulate under a false name. She's a spook. And connect the dots working back on the timeline. When Natalie and Yag met in Paris, he would have still been in the military. We know he was with an intelligence unit. He must have recruited her or arranged for it."

"This is hairier than we thought. We may have stirred up a nest of criminal art dealers and now we are about to step into a nest of spies."

"We already have. If they're Israelis, then they already know. It's possible that within minutes of when you started doing online searches for Natalie Rossum, they were alerted, and the moment we showed up in Nicosia and requested the marriage record they would have gone on high alert. I'll wager that even now . . ." He put a finger to his lips.

Shanna scowled as he wrote out a note on a cocktail napkin and held it up at an awkward angle. It read "Computers off. Now!" He carried it to the end of the table and flashed it at Darlene. She started to protest but he shook his head forcefully.

He waited until all three computers were fully shut down and closed before he held up his phone and pointed to it. He powered it down completely, then nodded toward their phones resting on the table. Once those, too, were powered off, he let out a sigh. "Even all that is not an absolute guarantee, but we're probably okay talking now."

Shanna was looking at him as if he were crazy, but Darlene was smiling. "He's right, girl. If those Israeli dudes want to, they can turn your phone or your computer into a 24/7 listening device. When I got briefed about spy technology, back in the day, they even told us to take the battery out of our phones to be absolutely certain they weren't being used to track us or spy on us. Except these days, who can take a battery out of their phone without tools and a workbench?"

"But I thought that was all, like, paranoid hype."

"It might have been back then, but trust me girl, those kind of operators—and that includes our people—have come a long way. Maybe the restaurant has even been bugged. I mean, that Lavigne dude was here twice. I didn't watch him every second."

Shanna was making mental lists and putting asterisks after names. "I actually don't think we have to worry about Anatole or Alphonse. They're on the other side."

"Which side is that, girl?" Darlene said. "You got your art heisters, your buyer network, your Israeli spooks, maybe Interpol. Seems to me there's a lot of sides."

Nareem burst into the room without knocking. "We just got a call, a bomb threat. How do we handle this?"

"By the book. Start by notifying the police."

"Already did."

"Good. Did the caller give specifics?"

"He said we had twenty minutes to get everybody out and away from the building."

"Short timeline, sounds like a serious threat." Rand turned to Darlene. "I'd start evacuating. And I need to make a call." He picked up his cellphone and put his finger to the scanner on the back. "Oh, shit, I turned it off."

Darlene was already at the door, speaking quietly to Nareem. "Let's do this as smoothly and orderly as we can. First, alert the back of the house and pass the word to the staff in front. We apologize to the customers and reassure everyone. Don't use the word bomb. Say there has been a warning of a possible threat. Start moving everybody toward the exits, no hurry, no panic, but moving. Now."

Rand and Shan were waiting for their phones to boot up and closing their computers. "I gotta go and handle this," Darlene told them as she left.

"All right," Rand said. "I've got three bars. Let's get out of here. We'll take the computers but leave the luggage."

"This is some weird-ass shit, wouldn't you say? And the timing. That's outright freaky. We turn off our phones and a bomb threat gets called in."

"They're not going to find anything."

"You can't know that for certain."

"Yes I can. Take a look at this." He turned his phone to show her. His news feed carried a headline: "Israeli Security Startup AnaQueue Calls for Talks."

෨ Chapter 30

THE BOMB SQUAD showed up, swept the restaurant for explosive devices, and declared it clean, but the evening was over. While customers milled at the far edge of the lot, Darlene had her staff distributing vouchers for free dinners and drinks and reassuring everyone that Dahlia's would be open the next day. "This is going to cost us," she said to Rand. "It may take some time to recover."

"Not if the right story comes out, like maybe that investigators tracked it as a prank call et cetera."

"Nice fantasy, but we don't know what if anything they'll find."

"Yes we do. I think they'll find whatever story makes the most sense for us."

"How can you say that?"

"Look at this." He showed her the phone.

"Does that mean what it looks like it means?"

"Yes, our phones—at least mine—have been hacked into and pwned, as they say."

"And how do we talk with the hackers?"

"I think all we have to do is wait. They'll call us."

Darlene was back inside supervising when Rand's phone trilled. He glanced at it. A secure communications app was flashing at him. He tapped to accept and put the phone to his ear. The female voice was blunt and specific. "Don't turn off your phone. Put Newsom on." Rand took the phone from his ear and looked at it before handing it to Shanna. "It's for you."

Shanna took the phone from him with a puzzled look. "Yes?" she said.

"Good, we got your attention. Your boyfriend is the only one of you with the EndlyComFree app installed, so that's why all this sideshow."

"Who is this?"

"Later. For now, just know that you can best protect your interests by stepping to the sidelines."

"My interests?"

"You, Rand McMurphy, my . . . uh, Martine Rossum. Among others."

"You staged the bomb scare."

"Well, it was rather impulsive, but we needed you to get back online, and that seemed likely to succeed. Tell McMurphy that paranoia doesn't always pay. Keep the lines of communication open. We need more time to make this work out all around."

"You're not being very clear."

"Clear as I can at this moment. Just wait and watch."

"And if I don't?"

There was a long pause. "I understand that your . . . your fiancé is being sought for questioning. How would that go down?"

Shanna suppressed a shiver, then focused her thoughts. "And you, how's your art history hobby progressing? Of course, I don't want to go into details over the phone, especially using a pseudo-secure app, but I suppose they, your people upstairs, know all the sordid details of your family history."

"You are in water so deep you cannot even see the surface above." The woman's voice deepened. "There's a lot more at stake than you realize."

"Back at you."

"What?"

"What you said. A lot more at stake than you realize."

"Are you threatening *me*? You have no idea, you . . ."

Shanna had a sudden flash of insight. "No, no threat, just playing the game, letting you know I know how, that I understand about the haunting past and about starting over. Now let's back off and talk." She glanced up to see Rand staring wide-eyed. She had been so absorbed by the exchange that she had forgotten he was there. "Girl talk," she said. "Gives us a few minutes to finish this up." She walked away from him and continued to talk.

It was several minutes before she returned and handed Rand his phone. "Hoist by your own petard, eh?" His clueless frown made her laugh. "Your clandestine proclivities," she said. "You downloaded a popular end-to-end secure communications app and thereby ensured your insecurity. EndlyComFree is made by KrypterLocs, a subsidiary of AnaQueue Technologies. It's got a back door."

"So who were you talking to?"

"Mostly they were talking to me. Very enlightening. We have more in common than I would have suspected."

"You're not going to tell me more?"

"Later, maybe. Need to know basis. Now let's wrap up here, head home, and enjoy a vacation before summer classes start."

"We just used up what scant vacation we had."

"But we're home a day early. We have more than twenty-four hours to recuperate."

"I don't know about you, but I could spend the next twenty-four in bed. I am so sleep deprived."

"I was thinking along similar lines, but I was not thinking of sleep. Funny, I'm not even tired. More like jazzed."

&

On the drive back to Racine Circle, Shanna wondered what she should tell Rand and where might be a safe place. If Rand turned his phone off, the listeners would know. She wondered if the techniques she'd read about—turning up the radio, running a vacuum cleaner, turning on the shower—really worked to drown out voices. It creeped her out to think how much of their life had been spied on. Someday she would have to find out from Rand how long the app had been on his phone.

They were coming up on the drug store down the road from the university entrance when Shanna had an idea. "Pull in up here. I gotta pick up a prescription that's waiting for me."

In the store, Shanna bought two pre-paid cellphones and a bottle of generic ibuprofen. In the car, she handed one of the phones to Rand, who accepted it with a knowing smile.

It was late the next day when Shanna was running the Speen's Hill trail, that she heard the ringtone on her new phone. She slowed down and pulled the phone from her waist pouch. "I take it you're somewhere private and away from your secure app."

"I am. In fact, I can see you from where I am on the top of the hill. We both have the same excuse now. You said the conversation last night was on a need to know basis. I need to know."

"Not yet. I'll just tell you that Tal and I made a connection, that we have far more in common than either of us might have thought—our jobs, our hobbies, our need to break from and paper over our pasts—and I now understand where she is coming from and what she is trying to accomplish."

"If not now, when are you going to tell me?"

"Based on Tal's constraints and what she has to put together, maybe by the end of the summer. Can you sit on your hands that long?"

"That's asking a lot."

"I know." Shanna sat down on a boulder beside the trail. "But if this blows up instead of plays out, a lot of people are going to be hurt. Maybe some of them will end up dead."

"If it's that dangerous, all the more reason to let me in on it."

"You know when you talk about something being a cop-to-cop thing? Or a guy thing? Well, this is a little like that, only this is a woman-to-woman thing that only two people who have rubbed out big chunks of their past in order to begin again would understand."

"I started over, too."

"You did, so you can be sympathetic, but it's a difference of scale. You didn't have to forget your origins or invent a new past."

"I think I'm beginning to understand, although I really don't get exactly how your life story—stories—relates to this whole . . . this whole thing."

"It doesn't, but there are other people whose life stories are in peril unless they're allowed to sort this out without us kicking the door down. It's only a few months. And it's only about the Natalie case. You can still work with your cold-case network on the Thibault case. And we can have a slowed-down summer to refuel some, get reacquainted, spend more time making love. What do you say? Can my boy scout bull-dog let go for once, let go and let things just be what they are? It might do you good."

"Now you're beginning to sound like another supermar-ket self-help book."

"Really? I wonder where I got that from."

There was a long silence on the phone. "Okay. I'll just have to trust you. Completely. Hey, listen, I'm going to finish my run with an extra lap. You wanna catch up with me? We've not been trail running together in ages."

"Sounds good. I'm on my way up."

She waited until Rand had hung up. "I got me a good one, a keeper," she said to the boulder at the side of the trail. "I better get up there and keep close."

⨯ Chapter 31

LOST IN THOUGHT, Marti strolled across the campus toward Righteous Hall, the once elegant centerpiece of Holcomb Bible College and now the less elegant administration building of Holcomb University. The manuscript for her book was finally in the hands of the editors, and she had survived the chaos of the start of a new academic year. It was now nearing the Jewish High Holidays, and the cooling autumn breezes were picking up. Marti cinched her sweater coat tighter. Behind her, just audible amidst the rustle and whistle of the wind, a woman's quiet voice grew closer, reciting or reading something, something that began to sound familiar.

> "Along the spiral path we lead, we plead for clarity:
> renewal, a seed, the offer of redemption that heeds
>   the Head
> of each new year—
> if only we can summon true intention, resuming self-
>   invention
>   that we be rewritten here
>   once more into The Book.
> Another turn, another day, we look into another
>   chance,
>   another rightful choosing,
>   until that one and single end.

Until that then, until that loosing,
  we advance:
Always beginning."

Stunned, Marti turned. The woman following her looked up from the booklet she was reading and smiled. Marti started to cry. "That . . . that's mine. I wrote that poem for Rosh Hashanah years ago. How I struggled over those final lines. How . . ."

"I know, mom. But please don't say any more or make a scene. I'm not supposed to be here. Just keep walking and ignore me. There's a bench ahead, just past the turnoff for the amphitheater, set back a little too far from the path. Wait for me there. I'll be along in a bit."

"But . . ."

"Just wait for me there."

Marti took the next fork toward the amphitheater. She had been this way many times before and never noticed a bench. But there it was, almost invisible from the walkway unless you were looking for it, the seatback marked with a bronze donor-recognition plaque. She went over to it, sat down, and closed her eyes, thinking about voices and poetry and tattoos. When she opened her eyes, Natalie was beside her, on the other end of the bench, wearing a padded vest over a long-sleeved blouse that covered her tattoo. She was reading a nursing textbook. Without turning or looking up, Natalie started talking in that same quiet voice.

"I don't have a lot of time, so just let me talk. I will try to make arrangements to see you again, but it may not be for some time, not until after the baby is born."

"The baby?" Marti turned in surprise.

"Stay cool, mom. I don't want it to look like we're talking.

Close your eyes as if you were napping or meditating or something. It will help you just listen." There was a pause and the faintest sound of pages turning. "Yag and I are expecting our first in the spring. We've waited a long time for this. Our work . . . well, it's demanding and it had to take priority. I can't say exactly what it is, but you will probably make some good guesses, just like your friends did after Cyprus. But you must not try to confirm those guesses or track me down. I hope you understand. We'll all meet, but not yet, not until I retire." There was more page turning.

"In a few weeks, a man will contact you about tattoo art, about the work of a French artist named Jaques Maudin. You will tell him that you know the artist and can arrange a meeting. Then you will tell him a time to meet, actually some night when you will not be home, when no one else will be there, and when you will be certain the alarm will be disabled. You will not return until the next day, and you will not notice any changes. If you understand, just say mmm."

"But . . ."

"Do you understand?"

"Mmm."

"Good. I'm sure you've figured out this is about the paintings, as you must have guessed many years ago, even though you always pretended to know nothing. I've come to understand that you thought your studied ignorance was necessary, that the price of knowing was too high. As to your father, I am still trying to wrap my head around what he did and what that means for you. And for me. As to the art, it's taken me a long time to set it all up working on the side, but I've arranged for the paintings to be passed anonymously to an agency that will, with elaborate discretion, attempt to return them to the heirs of their rightful owners."

"I always wanted to do that, but I didn't know how without . . ."

"Shhh, please. I know that now. It seems fitting that this happens now, as the High Holidays approach, a time of *teshuvah*, of return, of repentance. So I return and apologize. I hope you will forgive me for being so hateful and distrusting when I was younger, but your denials, all the deceptions, and then your father's papers, and finally you arriving with the Luger. It was all too much." There was a short stifled cry. "I have to go now. I'll leave the textbook on the bench. You'll find the chapter on treating gunshot wounds most interesting. It's rather thorough. Wait a few minutes after you hear me leave. And remember, I love you. *L'shannah tovah*. For a good year. Next year in Jerusalem."

ജ Chapter 32

SHANNA WAS NOT expecting Marti to be waiting outside her office when she arrived in the morning. "Well, a surprise. A pleasant one. Do come in. What's the occasion?"

"*L'shana tovah v'metukah.* I wanted to come wish you a good and sweet new year."

"And to you. It's been . . . a while."

"A while, a time of turmoil and truth." She crossed the room and sat down in front of the desk while Shanna hung her coat. "I read that somewhere." She set a blue wrapped package down on the desk. "Here, I brought you something. It is, appropriate to this season of repentance and new beginnings, a token of apology, a way of asking forgiveness. I am sorry for being so difficult and for drawing you into my struggles with facing my past."

"What is there to forgive? It's past."

"Then consider this an early Hanukkah gift or a late birthday present or whatever. It is also a way to thank you so much for giving me back my daughter."

"What are you thanking me for? We ended up being blocked, warded off, dead-ended. I'm the one who is sorry, sorry that we were unable to finish the investigation."

"Oh, you finished it, all right, and I am pretty sure we both know something about just how and by whom you were warned away."

Shanna sat, waiting for the next words from Marti or the next from her own inspiration. "Perhaps," she said.

"I suppose that has to be the way it is between us, the way it is in this world of redacted history. Perhaps. At least for now. I am still struggling, still trying to own up to my failures as a parent, as a person. I was afraid, afraid to look too closely, and out of my fear I failed my daughter. And others." She pushed the package across the desk. "So, this is for you, for you and Rand. Thank you. Thank you both."

"I . . . I don't know what to say. What is this?"

"It will speak for itself. And now, I have classes to teach. It feels strange to be back in the classroom again, hoping to inspire a new generation."

"It always feels strange to me, too, and yet I also always have this sense that this is where I belong, with students, fostering new beginnings that will lead . . . who knows where? It's a story without resolution. We know only these beginnings, not where it leads or how it ends."

Marti tapped the package on the desk. "This might help sort some of that out. I hope you find it interesting. I hope you, too, can learn from it." She left without saying more.

Shanna sat for a minute before unwrapping the package. Inside was a thick college textbook with an interdepartmental envelope on top. She opened the envelope to find several pages of folded stationery and a High Holidays tribute booklet from a synagogue in Minnesota. She unfolded the stationery and read the neat handwriting:

"Dear Shanna, my friend and colleague,

Thank you for returning my daughter to me. I am forever

in your debt. She has returned and will again; we have spoken and will again. She has, without intention, reawakened the artist in me, which has nothing to do with tattoos or any of the visual arts, unless you go back to hieroglyphics. She reminded me that I once wrote poetry, that I was once a poet —if I can assume that mantel.

I recall speaking of this early excursion into art and the teacher who told her students never to write a story about a rock rolling downhill. I rebelled—my whole life was then tumbling downward, beyond my control—and she applauded my rebellion. I found a copy of that early effort in some forgotten files and decided to share it with you, not for its euphony or brilliance but because it is about the deceptively simple things that defy analysis and deny our simplistic assumptions. It is juvenilia, from my days of college innocence, so be generous in your reading.

The second item here included is more to the point and even more personal. It was published in a saddle-stitched booklet printed by my synagogue of the day. You can keep it; I have other copies.

The textbook is self-explanatory, but only if you start reading on page 193 about gunshot wounds. After you're finished, please return it.

Marti

Shanna turned to the next page of the letter to find a poem with an unlikely title.

"Plot: Rock Rolling Downhill."
Dislodged in mischief and out of boredom,
a once-settled stone, a small boulder,
begins its downhill roll, plunging into

its unseen fate already marked,
from the starting gate
a race toward a future dark
but known,
its trajectory predictable.
The witnesses, like us, believe they can project its
    story,
        but this conclusion
        is arrogant illusion.
The unplanned path has no solution.
The math's abstract and incomplete,
    the stone, concrete.
No perfect sphere,
    this mineral aggregate,
        misshapen, oblate, hollowed and hilled.
It reaches a gully unwilled and bobs and careers,
    bounces and veers,
        kissing other rocks along the way.
Stone chips fly.
Striker and struck are both reshaped with each
    collision:
        deflected, diverted,
        detoured without decision,
launching other pebbles becoming tumbling rebels
unled along unfollowed histories;
each final resting space, location and circumstance
determined only by chance, mysteries
until that moment of stasis restored.
Above, the watchers stand, no longer bored.

Shanna glanced at her watch. She wanted to keep reading,
but it was nearly time for her lecture. Reluctantly, she

slipped the material back into the envelope and laid it atop the textbook.

બ્ર

Shanna had struggled to get free of the swarm of anxious students worried about the upcoming first quiz in her quantitative methods course. As she entered her office, the material on her desk drew her like a magnet. She set aside the envelope and opened the book, a glossy 700-page bound college text: *Emergency Medicine: An Introduction for Nurses.*

She checked the table of contents and opened to the chapter on gunshot wounds. The pages appeared to be properly bound in, but they were not about nursing or gunshot wounds. The recto page resembled a redacted government report, with black bars obscuring some of the text. She recognized the face in the photograph at the top of the page. It was an identification photo of the young Abel Rothman, but the caption below read: Leon Beauchamps Huber, (b. 1919, Burlington, Vermont; d. 1989, St. Paul, Minnesota).

Flipping ahead, she realized the section was hundreds of pages long. She started reading the report.

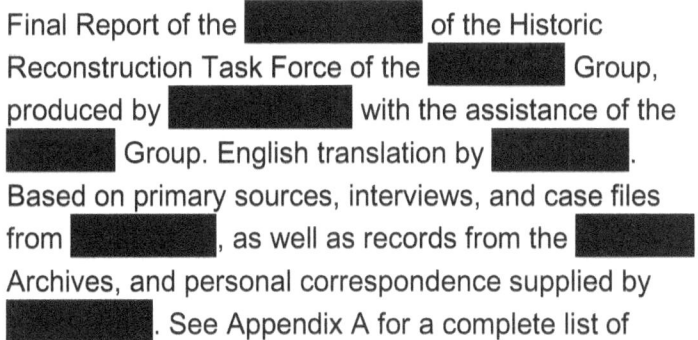

Final Report of the ▮▮▮▮▮▮▮▮ of the Historic Reconstruction Task Force of the ▮▮▮▮▮▮ Group, produced by ▮▮▮▮▮▮▮▮ with the assistance of the ▮▮▮▮▮▮ Group. English translation by ▮▮▮▮▮▮. Based on primary sources, interviews, and case files from ▮▮▮▮▮▮, as well as records from the ▮▮▮▮▮▮ Archives, and personal correspondence supplied by ▮▮▮▮▮▮. See Appendix A for a complete list of sources and source material.

Leon Beauchamps Huber (hereinafter BH) was born in 1919 to Helene Beauchamps, a French Canadian, and Otto Huber, an American of German descent, in Burlington, Vermont. He was raised in a bilingual household speaking French and English and studied German in high school at his father's urging. Although not politically active, his parents were openly critical of America and American culture and often regarded Europe, but especially France and Germany, as exemplifying superior, more sophisticated societies.

BH showed an early aptitude for mathematics and science. Encouraged by his parents, both of them teachers, he completed high school at sixteen and ap- plied to and gained admission to McGill University in Montreal, Canada, where he excelled academically.

While at university, he made friends with a number of international students from Europe, among them ███ ███, who went on to become known for his pioneering work on ███████. At the age of 19, BH traveled to France where he met ██████, a German engineer working at the time for Krupp on munitions develop- ment. Sparked by a shared hatred for communists and disgust for the declining "New World," BH and ██████ struck up a friendship. ██████ persuaded BH to come with him back to Germany, where BH became enam- ored with the National Socialist agenda. With the help of the influential ██████, BH was able to obtain a work permit, probably based on falsified documents, and began working alongside ██████, first at Krupp and later at a unit of Siemens.

Initially regarded with suspicion, BH gradually earned the trust of the Germans, eventually joining the Nazi party, again possibly aided by forged papers. He volunteered for the Waffen SS, where he quickly impressed his superiors with his zeal and intelligence. Owing to his fluency in French, he was assigned for a time in occupied France but eventually was recalled to join a special unit of the Waffen SS, where he eventually rose to the rank of *SS-Unterscharführer*.

❧ Chapter 33

SHANNA LET THE BOOK drop onto the kitchen table, and Rand looked up from slicing onions when he heard the thud. "Looks like you've been doing some heavy reading," he said. "New history text?"

"You might say that. Sorry I'm home so late, but I got caught up in reading. It's been a long and enlightening day. Much to talk about. How about you?"

"Same. I got some really surprising news. Give me another half an hour and I'll have dinner on the table and we can fill each other in."

"Sounds great. I'm going sneak in a quick shower with hopes that the sommelier has a nice glass of wine waiting when I come back."

"I'll see if I can find the guy."

❧

Rand was plating the dinner when Shanna returned. "Perfect timing. Your glass is poured and the kabobs with aji panca are on the way. So, tell me what your headline story of the day is?"

"Well, I have two front-page stories. The first is rather long and the second is much shorter but has to wait until the end," she said. "Maybe you should go first."

"Okay. Actually, I have two stories, too. First story. I

dropped by the newly christened Exact Sciences Building today to check in on Stieg Rolandson—don't you love the way the bean-counters and branding people keep retitling things, as if that was actual progress?—but he wasn't there. His old lab has been taken over by this Pakistani wunderkind who doesn't look old enough to vote but has an endowed chair and a shitload of fancy new equipment from a big grant he brought with him. 'Pakistani wunderkind.' Is that invidious mixing of ethnic references or some kind of slur? Beats me. But apparently everyone knows the story of Stieg's departure. We must have missed the memo, or maybe we were overseas. At least it went viral in the now reconstituted School of Exact, Mathematical, and Computational Sciences. SEMCS. Students, clever creatures that they are, pronounce it 'semi-kiss.' Not sure whether that's better or worse than calling our school 'shush' when we're not around."

"And? Is this going someplace?"

"University of Wisconsin or Michigan or someplace in the Midwest. Get too far inland and my mental map blurs. Anyway, that's where Prof. and Mrs. Rolandson landed."

"Mrs. Rolandson? He was married?"

"Yes, to his former student, apparently for some time. The Holcomb faculty ethics people were unable to reach consensus on whether or not to bring him up on charges or call for his resignation or dismiss him. In the meantime, they of the land of snow and ice made him an offer, rendering it all moot in view of the fact that no action was taken here and the student, the former Sandi Besslar, married to him and by this point very pregnant, was certainly not complaining."

"You sound as if you approve."

"Hardly, but I am disinclined to judge, in as much as I am

myself in a relationship of uncertain designation with a fellow faculty member under whom I was formerly a student and—"

"It's not the same."

"Of course not, except that it, too, is comparably complicated, or at least ambiguous. Real life. So it goes."

Shanna was unsure about how to respond. Part of her wanted to protest on principle, but part of her was too busy spiraling down all the alternative perspectives and possible arguments and counter-arguments. Finally, she just said, "Maybe."

"Exactly. In any case, she got hired as a research assistant in an unaffiliated lab and is expecting any day now. I wish them well, although I just can't see it. Time will tell."

"Time always tells, except when it has to be goaded by tenacious people who will not let go."

"That, my Shanna love, is a lead sentence if ever I heard one. Which means it's your turn."

"Not yet. What's your other news."

"Closer to home. I finally got word back from the people in the IceColdSolutions network."

"They worked out who killed Jess Thibault?"

"No, but in the process they ended up helping the police catch the perp in the shooting with the Luger, a hired gun named Dom Vecchio, and guess who hired him."

"Jenn Thibault?"

"The same and only. Could take a long time to go to trial, and with two like Thibault and Vecchio and their mob lawyers, there could be a lot of plea bargaining and playing Prisoner's Dilemma, but our persistent miss Thibault is sitting where she's not going to be harassing you for the foreseeable future. It's not a final resolution by any means, but it does buy time, maybe a lot of it. Now, finally, what's your story?"

"It's in the book." She pointed to the nursing textbook now resting on the stand by the door.

"You read that whole thing?"

"Only the good parts, the ones about gunshot wounds."

Rand's face was plastered with puzzlement. "Is this about the Luger or the shooting or . . .?"

"All of the above. And none. If you have and take the time, you will find that there are over a hundred pages starting on page 193 that will reveal all."

"Okay, you got me. I'll beg. Please, please tell me what this is all about and give me the benefit of an executive summary. Or a plot précis."

"I have no experience with executive summaries, and I *detest* plot synopses. However, I can tell you what it's all about, but not until you pour me another glass of wine. What is this? It's really quite nice."

"It's one of the bottles we brought back from Cyprus, that Alphonse slipped into our luggage. I didn't have a Malbec on hand, so I thought this might be the right wine to go with the spicy Peruvian-style kabobs."

"You thought right. Where was I?"

"Page one, paragraph one, if I remember."

"Page 193, actually. That's where the dossier has been bound into the textbook as if it belonged."

"What?"

"Here, I'll show you." She popped up from the table, grabbed the textbook, and plunked it down in front of Rand. "See for yourself."

Rand flipped through the book until he found the page.

"This is not part of a nursing text."

"Der."

"And this man here looks vaguely familiar, like I've seen other photos of him, but I can't . . . Wait a minute. This looks a little like that old photo you showed me of Marti Rossum's father."

"It should. But read the caption."

Rand stared at the page, unblinking. His eyes narrowed as he turned to Shanna. "So, I take it this is somehow about Abel Rossum. Or Rothman."

"Or Leon Beauchamps Huber."

"Who are we talking about?"

"Yes, that's what I said."

"But I . . ." The light of recognition finally shone from his face. "Are you telling me that Rothman or Rossum was actually someone else?"

"Rothman was always Rothman. The same can't be said for Able Rossum."

"What happened? What is this all about?"

"It's about what people are willing to do to survive and the awful choices made along the road to survival." Her face took on a grim look and her jaw quivered.

Rand took her hands in his. "Tell me. Tell me the story, what you learned today."

"The story begins with a young man from Vermont named Leon Huber who studied engineering in Canada and went to France for a summer then moved on to Germany as the curtain was rising on World War Two. Rather than leave the country when he still could, he stayed on. After he joined the Nazi party, he enlisted in the Waffen SS."

"Wait. An American serving in the German military? How

is that possible?"

"Well, paramilitary. The Waffen SS was the armed branch of the Nazi party and was known to have recruited and conscripted foreigners from both occupied and other countries. Huber, bright and ambitious, distinguished himself quite quickly and even rose to reach the rank of *SS-Unterscharführer*, a non-commissioned officer roughly equivalent to a sergeant. That was about as high as he could go without formal officer training, which wasn't going to happen in his case. When given the opportunity to join a group assigned to the German rocket program, he leapt at the opportunity. In the end, it was not what he had hoped. His assignment involved overseeing a production line producing rocket parts at Mittelwerk, the bombproof underground tunnel complex the Nazis constructed as a secure manufacturing facility using slave labor.

"Huber ended up disappointed. His fantasy was that he would actually get to do some engineering or design work, but he was a glorified guard watching over a production line. Always curious, Huber began to study the parts being made and to ask questions about the engineering and manufacturing. Eventually, his inquisitiveness began to raise suspicions, but these were soon allayed after he used what he had learned to propose several small improvements in workflow and how units were assembled. At the same time, he started thinking about engineering improvements to the products themselves, but, owing to his low-level position and the fact that he was a foreigner, he was never able to gain the attention of the real engineers and scientists on the project.

"Before coming to Peenemünde and the Mittelwerk complex, Huber had also been involved with an opportunistic

group of low-level SS officers that were siphoning off paintings and drawings from the artwork being seized and collected by the Nazis. The group stayed below the radar by
sticking with smaller pieces and avoiding works from the
most prominent or best-known artists. Huber was lucky to
have moved on to Mittelwerk because the heist group was
exposed and punished shortly after he left. The ringleader
was executed after a summary court martial, and most of
the others ended up being sent to the Russian front. None
survived the war."

"I'm beginning to see where this is going."

"Don't get ahead of the story. Okay? So Huber is guarding
and goading prison laborers in these underground factories
where they worked sixteen hour days under absolutely in-
human conditions. One day he overhears a prisoner whis-
pering in French. Talking while on the line was strictly forbidden, and Huber approaches the man with his Luger
drawn and confronts him. 'Silence, Jewish pig-dog!' he says
in German and strikes the man with his pistol. In French he
adds, 'What do you think you are doing? Do you want to die
here, in this pit, right now?' The man answers him quietly.
'You speak French, but you speak it with an American accent.' Leon puts his pistol to the man's head and says, continuing in French, 'So do you.' The man, assuming he is
about to be shot, says simply, 'That's because I am an American. My name is Abel Rothman.' Leon pulls him aside and
makes a show of disciplining him while continuing to con-
verse intermittently in French."

She paused for breath and speared another kabob. "This is
great, this version. My compliments to the chef."

"Compliments acknowledged. Now, back to the war. How

did Rothman, another American, end up as a prisoner working on a Nazi production line?"

"Rothman, who had traveled to France during a summer break, hooked up with a German girl, who persuaded him to travel to Germany with her. She was, no surprise, Jewish but was also a communist activist. Through a chain of minor disasters, Rothman is robbed, loses his passport, gets caught in a sweep, and tossed in jail—all the while protesting his innocence and insisting he is American. He won't let it go and ends up pissing off his jailers, who beat him severely, leaving him concussed and unconscious on the floor of the cell. When he wakes up, he is in a boxcar on a train to the first of a whole series of camps, eventually landing at the Mittelbau-Dora camp along with some 15,000 other prisoners supporting the Mittelwerk operation.

"After meeting Rothman, Huber, sensing some as yet unclear opportunity and intrigued by the prospect of continued conversations with an American Francophone, takes Rothman under his wing and installs him as an overseer for the immediate group of prisoners on one section of the line, giving him extra rations and some small privileges."

"It is by now late in the war and by this time, although few dare give voice to their concerns, many in Germany are beginning to doubt that the country can emerge the victor. Huber is beginning to wonder about his own fate if Germany loses and is invaded. He already suspects that some of the German scientists and engineers will strike bargains with the Americans, but he is not one of them. He is an American and a traitor who took up arms against his homeland. The Germans will fare better than the American, he concludes. In one particularly candid exchange, Rothman says to Huber that, if only he can survive until the Americans come, he will be all right. The Americans will save the Jews.

"At this point, Huber begins to hatch his plan to take on Rothman's identity, to become the victim to be freed by the Americans rather than the traitor to be shot or imprisoned himself. He continues to probe Rothman about his background, his family, his youth, and about his life as a Jew.

"He comes to realize that timing will be everything. Rothman must be kept alive, otherwise the always meticulous Nazi bookkeeping will show the man as having died at the facility. At the same time, Huber can't assume the identity of a Jewish prisoner until after liberation. He takes on the role of protector, passing on bits of his own rations and telling tales and making promises to bolster Huber's spirits.

"Although there is no record, it can be assumed that Rothman, the real Abel Rothman, died in the chaotic evacuation of the Mittelbau camps in April of 1945 as the Americans were advancing. In all, an estimated 8,000 Mittelbau prisoners were killed during transport and forced marches to Bergen-Belsen and other camps.

"Huber could not himself simply mingle among the few prisoners who were not evacuated from the Mittelbau camps since he was known to be an SS officer and would be outed or even killed by them. It is not known exactly how he made it to France, but it is suspected that he traveled under false papers, possibly with more than one identity, eventually to become part of a group of Jews liberated there. Somewhere along the journey to France, he tattooed his arm with the prisoner number of Rothman, which could, in principle, be checked against the camp records. That's how it is that Lena Schlüssel, the German historian I contacted, could verify from the number I supplied her that Abel Rothman had indeed been a prisoner in the camps, more than one, but there was no record of his death.

"Huber did not want to remain in France but rather to return to America with his new identity. While in France, he met and courted Marie Halévy. It is not thought that she was in on the deception, but it is possible she was guilty of being willfully ignorant of the truth. Marti told me her parents never seemed to be emotionally close or romantic with each other, so it is possible that Halévy saw marriage to Rothman primarily as a way to get to America.

"Once in America, Rothman began to present himself as an American Jew caught up in the Holocaust, a self-taught engineering genius who had learned through his forced labor on the German rocket programs. He picked up on his interrupted education at the University of Minnesota, switching majors to engineering in order to put the official stamp on what he had already learned at McGill and gleaned at Mittelwerk. And he changed names again to add another layer of obfuscation in the way of anyone trying to follow his trail."

"But what about the paintings?"

"Only Huber survived from the original gang, remember, and the Nazis never found where the paintings had been cached to await the end of the war. Once settled in his new life in America, Huber, that is, Rossum devised excuses for trips to Germany, first to verify that the stolen art was still hidden, and later to begin smuggling it to America by drips and drabs. In the process, he made trades and sales that, along with the compounded interest of passing time, increased the value of the collection considerably.

"The report confirms that in the later years of his life, the pace of sales had picked up some, and he was beginning to attract some attention from the international networks interested in Nazi stolen art. That may be why he stopped traveling to Germany. In all, though, very little of his estate had come from outright sales. Essentially, he had laundered his income through shrewd investments, mostly in defense technology stocks."

"What is going to happen to the paintings now?"

"The report refers to a plan to quietly and discreetly return them to the rightful heirs. 'Details outlined in Appendix B' it said, but the appendices are not included with this copy."

Rand was shaking his head. "So, Marti's father, Abel Rossum was a living lie. He was willing to do anything to survive, to escape his past. Is Marti complicit? Did she know the truth about her father and the provenance of the paintings?"

"No and yes. I believe she suspected more and more as she got older, but she chose not to know. She never sold any of the art herself, which I imagine she feels gives her some moral cover. On the other hand, when her daughter started putting the pieces together, she refused to consider what was coming to light and even tried to stop her daughter from pursuing the truth, perhaps to protect them both."

"And now? What's the daughter's story? Is there an epilogue to this novel you just outlined?"

"There is, but the manuscript is still a work in progress. Marti has spoken with her daughter—that much I now know—and we have already guessed that Natalie, well Tal, works for Mossad or one of the Israeli clandestine services. I don't know if we are ever going to learn much more. Maybe,

maybe not. It's a beginning, but beginnings are always full of uncertainty."

"And the Luger?"

"It was Huber's, issued by the Waffen SS and stashed by him somewhere for retrieval after the war. Presumably he, as Abel Rossum, smuggled it into the country at some point, perhaps with some parts or engineering prototypes for his work. Marti discovered it only after he died. It had been hidden in a tool cabinet in his basement workshop."

"Wow, what a story. Hard to top that."

"Maybe, maybe not. You haven't asked me about my other news."

"Oh, right, you did say you had two things to share. So, what's your other news."

"It can wait. You know something almost ironic? Sandi Bresslar is expecting. And, from what I understand, Marti is now in line to become a grandmother."

"How is that ironic?"

Shanna got up from the table and went around to kiss his neck and then whisper in his ear. "Beginnings. What do you think about a return trip to Cyprus to finish what we started? Are you ready for another beginning?"

"Always. With you. So, what is this about?"

"You are infuriating and wonderful, wonderful and . . . Guess who else is pregnant."

☙☙☙

Be sure to read Shanna Newsom's exciting origin story, **Always Me** (Gesher Press, 2020), available from Amazon and other booksellers.

❧ Appendix

Always Beginning: Reflections on Life After a New Year
Martine Rossum, Rosh Hashanah, 5767

Life after, awaking from a dream into the dream, the
   drama of You,
     calling out to You
     after falling out with You.
Are You still there? Or are You here?
Are things as they seem to You?
Or are You as things seem to me?

I know this place, this loom of woven thought,
   cobweb draped, the room You once escaped
   before I even noted You were sought.
A store for tomes unbought, an antiquarian preserve
   of memoirs and vignettes,
     triumphs and regrets,
     arcana of the self
     successively arrayed but unarranged.
On one low shelf, there rests the book I penned,
   the paper, parchment-like with age, yet half each
   page remains unprinted still.

I know too well how it begins but nothing of the end.

On its half-title page, I strain to read a two-line title
    halved:
    on one line, Life;
    on one line, After.
After what, I ask myself. After that, I answer.

The book is signed, a dedicated brief:
    To Me,
        I hope you find anticipated peace.
    From Me, forever yours.
This slim collection, a juried selection,
    the only extant copy of a first edition—
What is its worth, this soul-bearing history?
What would it bring if sold, what if abandoned to the
    earth?
A mystery.

Already text is blurred and ink is smudged
    from readings yet unheard,
    unviewed but not unjudged,
    marked up by marginalia and riddled with
    redaction,
    as if the reader—or the writer—
    still struggled to sort out the story's action.

True.

But truth evolves.
Some beginnings are lost, others revised at some cost
    until unrecognized,

forgotten but memorized as told and retold to the
end.

Then.

Do we rise awake or fall for Time asleep?
Are we tossed like refuse bulldozed
    into stinking heaps,
    transfer-station limbos,
    before becoming landfills
    piled to the sky?
Are we more? Is there more?
And why?

From the first place I read first words:
    In the beginning, it states.
The folio is numbered third, but here bound first, a
    quirk,
    as is a custom of the trade, even in self-published
    work.

Who remembers their beginning stage, earliest years:
    the screams, the scramble,
    laughing terror, sudden tears,
    discovery, recovery,
    the climb to be at cause,
    to rise and walk without a tumble?
    Up the stairs?
To where?

Recalled or not, beginnings still survive, arrive,
    starting over and again:

reiteration, reprise without repeat,
always beginning, another beginning for as long as
we feel
we reach to be real, to be alive.

Beginnings. Plural.
But in the end. Singular.

The end: a singularity.
Along the spiral path we lead, we plead for clarity:
    renewal, a seed, the offer of redemption that heeds
    the Head
    of each new year—
    if only we can summon true intention, resuming
    self-invention
    that we be rewritten here
    once more into The Book.

Another turn, another day, we look into another
    chance,
    another rightful choosing,
    until that one and single end.
Until that then, until that loosing,
    we advance:
Always beginning.

ঙ Acknowledgements

Shanna Grace Newsom is a complicated character, and it was always my hope that her story of love and mystery, whose genesis began in *Always Me*, would continue. Whereas the first draft of that novel was delivered in a crush of creation, the sequel was slow to grow from the germ of an idea. I was finally prodded into persistence by an unexpected and enthusiastic email from a friend and colleague who said that *Always Me* was my best work and urged me to keep writing.

I did. The slow struggle to find shape and fill in the form of this novel stretched out far longer than I anticipated. Through false starts and detours, rewrites and rearrangements, my ever-true partner, Lucy, would take a break from her own research and writing to help me clamber over and around the barriers that blocked the way forward. I cannot say enough in appreciation. As always, her intelligent suggestions, incisive critiques, and unqualified support have helped make this novel a far better story.

Once again I find myself in debt to my daughter Tovah for her input on the development and refinement of the book cover. With her eye for design, she pushes me to go the extra distance to get it right.

Whenever I find myself out of my depth in specialized areas, I turn to subject matter experts to help me get the details right. Vintage arms dealer and expert Brad Simpson answered detailed questions regarding the Luger P08 pistol. For information about the metal cookie tin, I am indebted to Dr. Birgit Nachtwey, art historian at Bahlsen GmbH & Co. KG, and to Kerstin Deike, who coordinated communication with Bahlsen. For their efforts to answer various other obscure questions, I also thank David Goff and Dr. David Hamilton, teachers of French and chemistry, respectively, at the Pingree School in Hamilton, Massachusetts.

Reader Bonnie Levy generously offered comments and suggestions on an advance review copy. I cannot thank enough fellow author Mary Patterson Thornburg, who helped shape the previous novel and once more took time from her own writing to read and give generous feedback on the manuscript. It is a better story for her contribution.

The final polishing pass was completed by my faithful and always effective copyeditor, Janet Lemnah, who finds and fixes the flaws that all the rest of us have missed. Thank you, Janet, for working your red-pencil wizardry to make this a better book.

ℰℯ About the Author

LIOR SAMSON is the pen name of a former university professor who has won awards for both fiction and non-fiction writing as well as for his innovative work in industrial design. He has more than two dozen published books, including fifteen novels and two collections of short fiction. As a consultant and teacher, he has traveled the world, lived in Australia and Portugal, and served on the faculties of two international universities.

He resides in Massachusetts with his family, where he cooks creative fusion cuisine and composes serious choral music. He is a freelance journalist and photographer and one-man technical support team for the three students in his life.

The readers who write with questions, kudos, and criticism are vital parts of the dialogue he seeks to spark through his writing. He enjoys hearing from readers and appreciates those who take the time to post reviews on Amazon and elsewhere. Reach him by email at: lior@liorsamson.com

www.ingramcontent.com/pod-product-compliance
Lightning Source LLC
Chambersburg PA
CBHW030642260626
47157CB00007B/2446